BETRAYED BY MAGIC

A NEW ADULT FANTASY NOVEL

JASMINE WALT

Alan's bookstall
17, Wellington rd rhyl LL18 1AY
Tel 07881 407637
Email chappy28uk@gmail.com

DYNAMO PRESS

Cover illustration by Judah Dobin

Cover typography by Rebecca Frank

Edited by Mary Burnett

AUTHOR'S NOTE

Dear Reader,

If this is the first book you've picked up in the Baine Chronicles series, I've included a glossary in the back of the book to help illuminate the backstory. If you've already read the rest of the series, this glossary will help reacquaint you to the people, places and things introduced to you in earlier books.

You can either read the glossary first to familiarize or re-familiarize yourself with Sunaya's world, or you can plunge into the story and refer to it as needed. The guide is in alphabetical order, and characters are listed last name first. To the new reader, welcome to the Baine Chronicles! And to those of you who have read the first book, welcome back and thank you! Your support allows me to continue doing what I love most – writing.

Best,
Jasmine

*W*arm hands gliding up my sides awoke me from a sound sleep. They were big hands, strong and sure and confident, but their touch was gentle, teasing even as they roused me from my slumber. Mumbling a little into the pillow, I tried to roll over, but a heavy weight settled atop my body, preventing the motion.

"Good morning, *a ghrá*," Iannis murmured roughly in my ear. I smiled at the foreign endearment he sometimes used when we were in private. His hands trailed higher, sliding beneath my torso to cup my breasts, and I sucked in a tiny, sharp breath as his thumbs flicked over my nipples.

"Morning," I said, arching my back as he pressed kisses along the tops of my shoulders. The answering rock of his hips into mine sent a thrill through me—he was hot, hard, and hungry, as he was every morning. Heat spiraled through my body as he stroked and kissed, teased and played, and I clenched the sheets, resisting the urge to buck him off so that I could move things along faster.

Giving someone your back when you were on the ground— or in this case, on a magnificent, four-poster king-sized bed with satin sheets—was pretty much the worst thing you could do. It was an extremely tough position to get out of, even if you were stronger than the other person. I would have never assumed such a position with a casual lover, never mind an enemy.

But Iannis wasn't my enemy, though I'd considered him as such when we'd first met.

He was my friend. My lover. My future mate.

When he finally turned me over, finally slid himself inside me and joined us as one, the gasp of pleasure that sang through the air came from both of us. Sometimes, we played rough, rocking the heavy bedframe as we tangled ourselves up in each other, pulling hair and nipping at sensitive spots on damp skin. But this morning, we went slowly, drawing as much pleasure and enjoyment from each other as we possibly could. I lost myself in shimmering violet eyes, threaded my fingers through dark, cherry-wood hair, and savored each kiss from his full, wickedly talented lips.

"I'm not sure I'm ever going to get used to this," I murmured afterward, my head nestling against his hard chest as I curled into his arms. Closing my eyes, I greedily inhaled his scent—a combination of sandalwood and magic that never failed to fill me with warmth.

"Good." He stroked my hair with one hand, gently squeezed my ass with the other. "I certainly wouldn't want you to get bored."

I lifted my head to look him in the eye. "I'm more afraid that *you'd* get tired of *me*," I said, and my chest tightened a little at the admission. I knew Iannis loved me—he'd more than proved that —but he was centuries old, and part Tua, a long-lived, practically immortal race of beings. I couldn't help but worry that to him, what we had would turn into the blink of an eye in his long life, to be swept away as he turned toward something, or some- one, new.

His eyes darkened as he read the thoughts flitting through my head—I wasn't great at hiding my emotions. To him, I was probably an open book. "I could never get enough of you," he assured me, lifting his hand so he could stroke my cheek. He kissed me, then added, "And there's no chance of us growing complacent, not with your talent for getting into trouble."

"Hey!" I smacked at his chest, a grin tugging at my lips, and he laughed. "If that's the case, then I'll make sure to go out of my way to find trouble. You'll never know a moment's peace."

"Is that not what you do already?"

Growling, I started tickling his ribs. In the next second, we were tangled up in the sheets again, rolling around on the mattress and howling with laughter. Who knew that the great and powerful Lord Iannis had such a basic weakness? And that I, of all people, would get close enough to actually exploit it? The stern, forbidding expression he wore in public was gone as he slid on top of me—his cheeks were glowing, his eyes sparkling. His white, even teeth flashed as he gave me one of the widest grins I'd ever seen from him.

"I have you now," he growled playfully, leaning in to nip at my collarbone. A spark of heat lit inside me, and I arched against him.

A bell rang, interrupting what would have been our second round, and I grumbled a little. But my stomach grumbled louder, signaling it wanted breakfast, so I held back further protests as Iannis rolled off me and reached for the blue robe hanging on a hook by the bed.

"Wait here while I let him in," he warned, disappearing into the living room of his suite.

"Yeah, yeah, I know the drill." Sighing, I sat up and ran my hands through my mess of curls. My eyes wandered around the bedroom as I listened to Iannis open the door to the server. It was twice the size of my own bedroom, with a high ceiling, extensive wooden paneling, and a custom, matching wooden four-poster bed. Unlike the blue and gold that dominated his sitting area, study, and office, his bedroom was done in dark greens and browns—masculine but earthy colors. Potted plants sat in the corners, a partitioned wall with a fireplace separated a small sitting area from the bed, and double doors off to the side led out to a private balcony that could be viewed through a large picture window.

On the opposite side of the bedroom, next to the sitting area, the wooden paneling cleverly disguised a door that opened onto a secret passage connecting my new bedroom suite—conveniently located in the west wing—to Iannis's. Even though I retired to my own rooms at the end of each day, I always woke up in his.

Hopping off the bed, I snagged a white robe hanging on the wall and shrugged it on, then sauntered out into the living room. The server was gone, and I eyed the cart he'd left next to Iannis's dining table, piled high with eggs, potatoes, sausage, bagels, and other breakfast foods.

"Don't you think he knows he's feeding more than one person every time he comes up here?" I asked as I sat down across from Iannis. I picked up the fancy ceramic plate from the table and began heaping food onto it. "I highly doubt you were eating all of this for breakfast on your own."

"Of course he knows," Iannis said mildly as he buttered his bagel. "The palace staff will have guessed my ulterior motive behind moving you to the west wing as well." He smirked a little, then took a bite of his bagel. "But appearances must still be kept up. We are not married yet, Sunaya, and we cannot publicly flaunt convention."

"Right." I pressed my lips together, then picked up my fork and stabbed at a potato. "Why do engagements have to take so long, anyway?"

Iannis arched a brow at me over his cup of coffee. "I thought you were happy with the idea of a long engagement."

I scowled. "I was, because I didn't think it would be good to rush into the whole marriage thing." Truthfully, I needed more time to get used to the idea. Marriage was forever, a huge commitment even when I didn't consider Iannis's lifespan, which would likely be significantly longer than the three hundred or so years I could hope for. "But even though we're engaged, we *still* have to skulk around. It's starting to grate on me." Secrecy and discretion in relationships wasn't really something I was used to as a shifter.

Iannis's expression tightened, and he set down his coffee cup. "I don't know what more you would have me do, Sunaya. I am still the Chief Mage, and I am supposed to set a good example. I must follow the rules, at least in public."

"I know." I softened my voice as a pang of guilt hit me—I was being unfair. "It's just... frustrating."

Iannis nodded. "Why don't we eat?" he suggested, picking up his fork and knife. "We can talk after you've gotten some food into you."

I did as he suggested, digging into the mountain of food I'd piled onto my plate. Even pacing myself, I still polished off my food before Iannis, and was well into my third helping by the time he reached for more. Shifters relied on super-fast metabolisms for our healing powers and strength, so we required much more fuel than the average person.

"Feeling better?" Iannis asked, a hint of amusement in his tone as I leaned back in my chair with a sigh.

"Much." I patted my belly, then allowed myself a few moments to savor the sensation of being full before I sat up again. "Now tell me why mages have to have long engagements."

"Traditionally, a marriage between mages isn't just the joining of two lives, but an alliance between families. There are agreements to be negotiated, contracts to be drawn up, reviewed, and signed. That process should not be hurried, to avoid later complications. But more importantly, the engagement period is meant to ensure that mages do not rashly enter into an eternal, unbreakable commitment. A full year's betrothal gives time for either family, not to mention the bride or groom, to change their minds. The contracts are legally and magically binding only when the marriage ceremony is complete and the marriage is consummated. Until then, they can be cancelled even if both sides have already signed and agreed."

"Huh." I pursed my lips together as I thought about that. "But why does this apply to us? You and I aren't involving our families."

"Not if we can help it," Iannis said, frowning. "My father has already passed, and my mother is content to let me make my own decision. However, if *your* father gets wind of our betrothal, he could impede our union. I would prefer to have the ceremony over and done with to avoid such a possibility, but alas, we cannot."

"Well, that's just lovely," I said, sarcasm thick in my voice. "And yet, despite the fact that we're engaged and my father could appear on the scene at any moment, you still don't want to tell me who he is."

"It is better that you not know," Iannis said firmly. "It could lead to all kinds of complications, and only cause you needless pain. If anyone should contact you claiming a relationship of any kind, you must play dumb and demand proof, then contact me immediately. We cannot take chances with this."

"Yes, sir." I saluted, and Iannis frowned at me. But before he could say any more, the phone sitting on the side table next to the couch rang.

I cocked an ear to listen as Iannis took the call. It was Dira, the Guild receptionist, relaying an urgent message from the

Minister to call him as soon as possible. Well, that was the end of breakfast, then. There would be no more discussion about my father when Iannis's mind was on Federation business. Resigned, I rose from the chair and headed toward the bedroom.

"Wait," Iannis called as he hung up the phone.

"What—" I began, but he cut me off, pressing me into the wall as he kissed me deeply. Ever since he'd revealed to me that he had super speed, he used it to surprise me at every opportunity. His dark, exotic flavor filled my mouth, overlaid faintly by expensive coffee, and hunger ignited in my lower abdomen, eclipsing my anger.

"I love you," he murmured softly, his warm breath tickling my face as he ran his fingers through my hair.

"And I love you," I said, the words leaving my lips in a resigned sigh. No matter our arguments or disagreements, I did love him, and I wouldn't withhold that just because I was angry.

"Good." He kissed my forehead, and then he was gone, leaving his robe behind in a gust of wind as he shot through the bedroom and into the shower.

I snatched the robe out of the air, pressing it to my face so I could inhale his scent. And then I left, allowing the blue silk to flutter to the ground as I went in search of answers.

.

2

I took the secret passageway back to my suite, which was only three rooms away from Iannis's. The bedroom wasn't much different from the one I'd had back in the east wing—in fact, Iannis had moved all the same furnishings into it since I'd liked them so much—but I now had my own private bath, and a sitting room I could use to entertain guests if I ever had any.

I tugged off my robe and dumped it into the laundry hamper that the Palace staff emptied every day, then sauntered into the marble-tiled bathroom and took a long shower. I stood beneath the hot spray and closed my eyes, allowing myself time to think about my conversation with Iannis.

Truthfully, I was conflicted about the whole engagement thing. I hadn't wanted to rush into marriage, but I also hadn't wanted to skulk around, hiding our intimate relationship as if what we were doing was dirty and wrong. The sheer joy and pleasure I'd experienced over the past few days felt more than right—it was perfect, and I wanted it to last forever.

But, of course, forever meant marriage. And the idea that my father, a man who didn't know or care for me, could potentially swoop in and take it all away, was frightening. It was little wonder Iannis wanted to keep me away from my father, in light of the fact he'd been considering the possibility of marriage for some time.

Isn't knowledge power, though? I asked myself as I lathered my arms and legs with fragrant soap. I'd always considered it better to be forewarned than taken by surprise, and I didn't see why this situation would be any different. Yes, under the circumstances, it would be foolish to seek my father out and announce I was his daughter. But that didn't mean I shouldn't find out who he was. Surely, there was a way to do so discreetly, without alerting him.

I'll ask Janta to help me, I decided, switching off the hot water. Stepping out of the shower, I grabbed a fluffy towel and dried off. Janta Urama, the head librarian of Solantha Palace, had been more than helpful in tracking down the Benefactor, the powerful mastermind and financier of the Resistance. With any luck, she would prove equally resourceful in the quest to determine my parentage. Based off past I experience, I could trust her not to tell anyone else whatever she might discover.

Clean and dry, I made my way into my walk-in closet and perused the selection. Since nearly all my possessions had been destroyed when the Resistance set fire to my apartment, I'd ordered a brand-new wardrobe. These clothes were much nicer than anything I'd ever owned before, and yet the gold I'd spent on them was only a drop in the bucket compared to the treasure I'd brought back with me from the pirate island I'd been stranded on. I had new leather jackets and pants, jeans, tops in a variety of fabrics and colors, more shoes and boots than I could count, and even a selection of dresses. Iannis had strongly suggested I order robes as well, but I'd pointedly ignored him—I may have taken Resinah's advice to embrace my mage heritage, but I still had no desire to dress in boring robes. And besides, I was still an apprentice, which meant that on most occasions, I'd only be allowed to wear those ugly, dun-colored robes anyway.

Of course, once I finished my apprenticeship, I would be required to wear robes on formal occasions. But considering the average apprenticeship took ten years to complete, and that my shifter upbringing and late start put me way behind, I didn't see any need to cross that bridge prematurely. Right now, I was still primarily an enforcer, and I would continue to dress like one.

With that in mind, I pulled on a pair of leather pants and a teal-colored shirt, then strapped my weapons onto my thighs and my pouch belt onto my hips. Steel-toed boots covered my feet, and I shrugged a leather jacket on over it all despite the summer weather outside. I'd be taking my steambike out later, and it didn't pay to ride without protection.

Before I left the room, I glanced at my reflection in the mirror and smiled a little. I might have come a long way from where I'd been when I first arrived at Solantha Palace, but I was still Sunaya Baine. And I was going to show the world that I could be Sunaya Baine and a mage at the same time.

It did not take me long to reach the library, on the lower level of the Palace. "Good morning, Miss Baine," a youthful voice greeted me, and I started at the sight of an unfamiliar female mage sitting behind the front desk of the library. Dressed in grey robes, the emblem of an open book inside a circle stitched above the left breast, she had dark, glossy brown hair and a polite, welcoming expression.

"Umm, good morning." I glanced around the library, a huge room with towering bookshelves and soaring ceilings. Unlike the last time I'd been here, most of the gleaming wooden desks with their green glass lamps were occupied by mages—apprentices studying new spells, and Guild employees doing research. More grey-robed librarians moved about between the shelves, placing books that had been returned, or retrieving them for someone else. It was slightly disconcerting, but I was none-theless happy to see that a sense of normalcy had returned.

"Do you know where I can find Miss Urama?" I asked, refer-ring to Janta by last name. The last two times I'd come here to see her, she'd been manning the front desk as the only librarian present, while her subordinates were out fighting the Resistance. "I need her help with an important matter."

"I believe she's in the back, cataloguing a new shipment of books," the librarian told me. "I can see if she's available, if you'd like."

"Please."

I clasped my hands behind my back and tried to wait patiently. I could feel the gazes of several mages on me, but when I turned to return their stares, they hastily dropped their eyes back to their books. I'd always been an object of rumor and speculation amongst the mages, and even more so since my engagement to the most powerful man in Canalo. Bets were being placed to see how long it would take for the engagement to be called off, and much as I wanted to be angry about that, I couldn't blame them. A marriage between a powerful mage and a shifter was unprecedented, and my half-mage heritage was the only thing that allowed the mage community to swallow it in the first place. On top of it all, Iannis and I were also master and apprentice. I doubted we'd be able to get away with that part either if Iannis wasn't the Chief Mage.

By Magorah, what a mess this was. If I didn't love Iannis, I'd be tempted to ditch the entire affair and move somewhere else where nobody knew me.

Of course, that would mean leaving my friends behind. And Solantha itself, which I loved despite the city's flaws. The shifter community was still in shambles after the war between the Mages Guild and the Resistance. Someone had to bridge the gap between mages and shifters if there were going to be any kind of peace between us. I was starting to think that the thankless job would fall on me, since I didn't see anyone else stepping up. But not today. Today, I needed to finish putting together all the pieces of who I was. And that meant finding out the identity of my father.

"Good morning, Miss Baine." Janta's, dulcet tones drew me away from my thoughts. I turned to see her coming toward me, the front-desk librarian in tow. Unlike the last time I saw her, she wore the same grey robes with the book emblem as the other librarians. Hers were hemmed in silver at the throat, wrists and collar, marking her higher position. The outfit went very well with her silver hair, which she wore twisted into an elegant knot near the top of her head, and the silver spectacles perched on her straight nose. "What a pleasant surprise."

"Good morning, Miss Urama." I smiled, genuinely happy to see her. I didn't know her very well yet, but she was on the gradually expanding list of mages who treated me like a real person. "I was hoping you could help me with another research project."

"Certainly." A hint of worry entered her pale blue eyes. "Is it something to do with the Resistance?"

"No." I hesitated, not sure it was wise to say more when I knew that at least some of the other mages were listening. "It's regarding a personal matter. Is there somewhere private we can talk?"

"Of course. Right this way."

Janta disappeared between the bookshelves, and I followed. She led me down several rows, to a glass-partitioned section of the library. A sign across the door said 'restricted area'. She pulled a key from her belt and unlocked the door, then stepped back to let me through first.

"Why is this place restricted?" I asked as she guided me to one of the tables. Other than the partition, this part of the library looked exactly the same as the rest.

"Many of the books on these shelves are very old and rare. We keep them back here to protect them," Janta said as she sat down across from me. "Besides, some texts contain forbidden or extremely dangerous spells, and they can only be checked out with special permission."

"That makes sense," I murmured, scanning the shelves with apprehension and curiosity. What sorts of spells were so dangerous that they had to be kept under lock and key? And would I be able to learn any of them, now that I was betrothed to the Chief Mage? I imagined my new status would afford me some privileges other than riches and comfort. But that was a thought for another time—I was hardly in any position to start learning spells of that caliber.

"Now, what is this personal matter for which you need my assistance?"

"I'm looking into my parentage," I explained. "Specifically on my father's side. I'm trying to embrace my heritage as a mage, and I feel I can't do that unless I know more about that side of my family."

"I see." Janta was quiet for a moment. "Have you asked the Chief Mage about this?"

"He's been very busy," I evaded. It wouldn't do me any favors to tell Janta that Iannis didn't want me to know my father's name. After all, he was her employer, and she wouldn't want to do anything to anger him. "Lord Iannis lost a significant amount of time when he went missing, and again when he rescued me from that island, and he's still got his hands full with the fallout from the failed uprising. I don't want to trouble him, if I can find the information elsewhere."

"That's true. He must be overburdened with duties just now." Janta's voice briefly softened in sympathy, then became businesslike again. "Do you have any information that may help narrow our search?"

I thought for a moment. "My mother lived in Solantha before my birth, and did not travel during the time she would have conceived me, as far as I know. It is likely that she met my father right here, but how, and who he was, is a mystery. Hookups between shifters and mages are really rare, even in Rowanville. She would never tell me, and none of her surviving family ever said anything about him."

"Is there anyone who might remember their affair?" Janta pressed.

"My aunt Mafiela. She and I haven't had the best relationship, and she would never speak a word of anything to do with my mage heritage. But she and my mother were close, so it is possible Mother confided some detail or clue to her. Perhaps if I asked her to lunch, she might be willing to divulge something now."

"That would be helpful." Janta eyed me speculatively. "Your eyes and coloring must come from your father rather than the Jaguar Clan," she noted. "That may help narrow things down, as there are not very many mage families known for such brilliant green eyes."

"Oh!" I exclaimed as a memory popped into my head. "I did meet someone in Dara, a mage, who bore an uncanny resemblance to me. His name was Coman ar'Daghir, and, last I knew, he was the Rhodea Mages Guild's Legal Secretary. He did not act as though he knew anything when we met, and he is too young to be my father—I think. But he might be a relative of some kind."

"That is very helpful indeed," Janta replied, pulling a notepad from her sleeve. She extracted a pen as well, then wrote the information down. "We have an up-to-date genealogical section. I should be able to trace his family history and connections."

"That's great!" Excitement bubbled up inside me, but it

quickly faded as I recalled Iannis's warning about my father. "Is...is there any way my father could pose a problem for my upcoming marriage to the Chief Mage?"

"Most certainly," Janta said, her eyebrows rising. "Your father could prevent the marriage if he decides he does not want his family allied with Lord Iannis's."

"What!" I shouted, then winced as Janta frowned. "Sorry," I said, lowering my voice. "But how could my father do such a thing? He gave up his right to be my father the moment he walked out of my mother's life. Surely he has no legal authority over me."

"I'm afraid that's not how it works," Janta said, sympathy in her eyes. "Regardless of whether or not your father raised you, you are of his bloodline. You would not have your magic if that were not the case. That you no longer have a living mother only strengthens his claim, should he choose to exercise it."

"And just what claim is that?" I asked, doing my damndest to keep my voice even. Janta didn't deserve my fury—she was just the messenger. "I'm an adult, aren't I? Why does he get to decide who I do or don't marry?"

"Well, by shifter standards, you most certainly are an adult," Janta allowed, a small smile briefly curving her lips. "But mages don't reach their majority until they are thirty years of age or finish their apprenticeships, whichever comes first. If you were done with your apprenticeship, your father would not have a say, but considering your late start, I doubt that will happen anytime soon. Therefore, your father unfortunately has every right to disallow the match, should he find Lord Iannis an unsuitable candidate for any reason."

I snorted. "That's so ridiculous. He's the Chief Mage. Magorah knows that the majority of Canalo doesn't think I'm a suitable match for him, but I doubt anybody would claim that he isn't good enough for me."

Janta nodded. "That is true. However, I assume you don't wish to count on your father's benevolence, considering his track record with you."

"No," I admitted, my jaw tightening. "I have no idea what kind of man he is." For all I knew, he would gloat at the chance to strike at Iannis, should he prove to be some kind of rival or enemy. "I need to find a way around this."

"I'm not sure there is one," Janta said gently. "Even if you weren't years behind in your mastery of Loranian, any shortcuts you might take have severe consequences."

"Yeah, that's true." I winced a little—Loranian was the language of magic, used in spell casting, and I was nowhere near mastering it. "What kind of shortcuts are you referring to?" I asked, curious despite myself.

Janta pursed her lips. "They are not worth speaking of."

"Oh, come on. You can't just say that and not tell me anything." When she just stared at me, I gave her my best puppy-dog look. "Please?"

She frowned. "Very well, if only to dissuade you. One such method involves transferring the knowledge and memories of an older mage into your own mind. You would instantly gain mastery of Loranian as well as any spellcraft he knew and practiced."

"By Magorah!" My eyes nearly popped out of my skull. "You can do that?"

"Yes, but it is hardly recommended." Janta's lips thinned. "The procedure has been known to alter a person's character, and the newly gained knowledge is not always easily assimilated."

"Yeesh." I made a face at that—I certainly did *not* want to take on the personality of some cantankerous old mage. "Why was such a procedure even invented?"

"It was mostly used in wartime, when a master was near

death and had not yet imparted all his knowledge to his favored apprentice. But such a scenario has not occurred in quite some time, at least not in the Federation."

"Really? Even though war recently broke out here in Solantha?"

An uncomfortable expression flitted across Janta's face. "If it has happened as a result of recent events, I do not know of it."

I let out a small sigh. "Oh, well. It doesn't really matter—I don't think I'd be comfortable trying such a thing, even if I could find a volunteer mage."

"Agreed." A thoughtful expression crossed Janta's face, and she reached into her sleeve again. A moment later, she pulled out a small text bound in light blue cloth. The title *Spellcraft for Beginners* was embroidered across the front in gold thread. "This is a basic primer a friend of mine had printed for his daughter when she was young. He was a notable Federation mage. Not many copies exist, as unsupervised practice is generally frowned upon. I do hope you'll be careful when you practice with it."

"Oh, thank you!" I took the book carefully from her, then opened it. To my delight, it was written primarily in Northian, and the Loranian spells all had a pronunciation guide. "So this has all the basic spells that mage children learn?"

"Nearly," Janta said. "And I'm sure Lord Iannis will teach you anything that's missing."

"Is that trick where you pull large objects out of your sleeve one of those spells?" I asked, staring pointedly at Janta's sleeve. I'd seen Iannis do the same thing multiple times, and I really wanted to add it to my list of skills. I could carry *much* more food around, which would be handy because using magic always left me famished.

A knock on the door sounded before Janta could answer, and we turned to see Fenris standing on the other side of the glass.

"Sunaya?" he asked, surprise flickering in his dark eyes as Janta opened the door for him. "What are you doing here?"

I folded my arms and arched a brow. "I could ask you the same question."

He huffed. "I came here looking for Miss Urama. Lord Iannis asked me to retrieve a book from the restricted section." He smiled briefly at Janta. "I was told she was already back here, but not that she was with you."

"Miss Baine wanted to find out more about mage weddings," Janta said smoothly, saving me from having to lie to Fenris. He was a friend, sure, but he was still more Iannis's friend than mine, and he probably wouldn't approve. "I was explaining to her about the legalities involved."

"Ah." Fenris's expression cleared, and he shut the door behind him. "Thankfully, you won't have to deal with the usual contracts and endless negotiations between mage families, but you will still need to observe the proper protocol expected of any Chief Mage who marries."

My heart sank a little. "What kind of protocol?" By Magorah, I *really* did not want this to get any more complicated than it already was.

"A man of Lord Iannis's position would be expected to invite the other Chief Mages in the Federation to the ceremony," Fenris explained. "Some couples choose to have the ceremonies held in Dara when the Convention is in session, since the Chief Mages will all be gathered in one place anyway."

"Ugh." I made a face. "I'm definitely *not* a fan of that idea." I wanted my friends to come to the wedding, and I didn't know if that would be possible if we held it in the middle of the Convention. Besides, I didn't want to have to travel across the country to get married—I wanted to do it right here, in my hometown.

"Well, if that's the case, you'll need to let the Chief Mage know," Fenris said. "After all, the invitations must go out at least six months early. To send them later would be an insult."

I rolled my eyes at that. All these rules! "Is there anything else I need to know?"

"Yes," Fenris said, his lips twitching as he sensed my annoyance. "Since the ceremony is magically binding, it will be conducted in Loranian. So you'll need to improve significantly." His smile widened when I groaned. *"Thankfully for you, Iannis has instructed me to tutor you in Loranian for at least two hours a day,"* he added in mindspeak. *"So you should be more than prepared."*

"Just great," I muttered, tucking the primer Janta had given me into my leather jacket. "Thanks so much for your advice, Miss Urama. Please let me know if you have any other helpful information for me."

"I will," Janta said, her eyes twinkling knowingly. I strongly suspected that she knew of my desire to keep Fenris in the dark about my true purpose for being in the library, and I made a mental note to send her fancy chocolates or something—the woman was a true godsend.

"I'll see you later," I told Fenris as I headed for the door.

"Where are you going?"

"To Witches End," I called over my shoulder as I left. I had time to kill before my lesson with Iannis, and I wanted to check in with Comenius. Hopefully, he would have news from Annia and Elnos. I hadn't forgotten my promise to help them ensure Noria's safety, and it was about time I made strides toward that end.

3

I rode my new steambike down to Witches End, enjoying the freedom of having steampower beneath my legs once more. No, it wasn't the steambike I'd lost in Turain, the one I'd scraped and saved to own, but it was an engagement gift from Iannis, and it was pretty fucking cool. The machine belched a hell of a lot less smog, making the ride cooler and more pleasant, the seat was made of smooth, custom calf leather, and there were strong protection spells laid into it that would activate if someone tried to attack me.

I'd tested the spell myself by lobbing a fireball at the bike to see what would happen. It had deflected the threat easily, and nearly singed my eyebrows off in the process. I wondered if there was a way to make the bike absorb attacks rather than deflect them, so innocent bystanders weren't harmed. Perhaps I would ask Iannis during my lesson this afternoon.

It hadn't been long since the Resistance had been beaten back from Solantha, and their attempt to take over the city was still apparent in the damaged buildings and sidewalks I passed. However, there were plenty of humans and shifters out and about as I drove through Rowanville, and more than a few construction crews repairing the damage. The sight of the city recovering so quickly brought a smile to my lips—Iannis had heeded my advice about putting the citizens to work repairing the town, using gold from the Mages Guild's coffers. At this rate, Solantha would be back to normal within the next couple of months, and the Resistance attack would be reduced to a faint memory.

Pretty soon, the houses and storefronts of Rowanville receded, and the Port came into view—a series of piers that lined Solantha's eastern shore. It was one of the largest shipping ports in the Federation, with ships from all over Recca constantly coming and going, loading and unloading goods and passengers. As a result, quite a few shops were set up in the area, and it was a popular tourist spot.

I rode my bike all the way down Witches End, then parked it outside Over the Hedge, Comenius's shop. The front door was locked, the 'Open' sign flipped toward closed, but it was a simple matter to unlock it with an open-door spell I had recently mastered. "Com?" I called as I entered the shop, the bell on the door tinkling to announce my entrance.

At this time of day, Comenius was probably having lunch, or working in the back room where he prepared and stored extra merchandise. I could definitely smell him nearby—his woodsy scent lingered beneath the scents of herbs and sea salt that permeated the store.

"Naya?" Comenius called, his crisp, throaty accent muffled by the curtain behind the counter. A moment later, the curtain parted to reveal a tall, lean man with ash-blond hair, cornflower blue eyes, and angular features. He was dressed in a dark green tunic, most of his upper body obscured by a large box he was carrying in both arms.

"Need a hand?" I asked, coming up to the counter as he set the box down.

"No, this is just some inventory I need to put out on the shelves." He patted the box, then came around the counter and gestured to the sitting area—a group of wicker chairs and couches located in a cozy nook where customers could sit as they waited for Comenius to mix up an order for them. "Why don't you come over here and sit with me? Elania was just about to—"

The doorbell tinkled again, announcing the arrival of Elania Tarrignal, Comenius's girlfriend and the owner of The Black Curtain, a witch shop that was quietly known for its under-the-table hexes. She was a tall, voluptuous woman, her face always perfectly made up, her mass of black hair piled atop her head in an elaborate do. As usual, she wore one of her curve-hugging black dresses that made me secretly envious of her figure.

"Why hello, Sunaya!" she exclaimed in her exotic, slightly musical accent as she caught sight of me. A covered basket dangled from one arm as she used the other to shut the door behind her. "I believe this is the first time I've seen you in weeks."

"I believe you're right." Smiling, I closed the distance between us, then took the basket with one hand as I gave her a friendly hug. "You've been taking care of Comenius for me?"

"As much as I am able to." She sighed a little, her dark eyes instantly going to Comenius as we broke apart. "He is worried about Noria, and wonders constantly if he could have done anything more to stop her from joining the Resistance."

"I'm worried too," I admitted, bringing the basket over to the small coffee table in the sitting area. I sat back so Elania could set out the food and plates she'd brought, and tried to ignore the scent of seasoned pork, cabbage rolls, and cheese. "In fact, I came here hoping you'd received news from Annia and Elnos. Surely by now, they must have caught up with Noria."

"I'm afraid I haven't heard anything," Comenius said, worry

tightening his voice. "I'm not certain if that's cause for alarm—if they managed to find their way to Noria within the ranks of the Resistance, it's quite possible they simply haven't had the opportunity to send me a message safely. New recruits will be carefully watched, after all. Even so..."

"You're worried they may have been compromised," I finished for him.

"Yes."

"Here." Elania handed me a paper plate with a cabbage roll, a wedge of cheese, and the diced, seasoned pork. "You should eat."

"Oh, I couldn't." I tried to hand the plate back. "I had breakfast not too long ago, and I didn't mean to come here and eat your food. I know you didn't make enough for me."

"Well, I would have if I'd known you were visiting, but never mind that." Elania sat with her own plate, refusing to take mine. "It would be rude of me not to offer you some food, especially since I can hear your stomach growling from here." She winked at me.

My cheeks heated, and Comenius grinned a little despite the heavy atmosphere. "She's right, Naya. We know you're always hungry. Eat something."

"Fine, fine." I popped a piece of pork in my mouth, then paused to savor it—it was damn good. "Any ideas on what we should do?"

Comenius shook his head as he poked at his cabbage roll with a fork. "Without knowing which state Noria was sent to, it's impossible to determine where Annia and Elnos are headed. I suppose we can track them to the Resistance camp they initially went to, but there is always the risk of unnecessarily blowing their cover."

I sighed heavily. "It's a tough call," I admitted. "Annia would never forgive me if I blew her chances of rescuing her sister...

but I would never forgive myself if she died because I sat back and did nothing."

"You may need to risk her wrath if you do not hear from them soon," Elania said. Sadness sat heavy in her dark eyes as she regarded me. "I know Noria is important to you both, but you must not forget she did make this choice of her own free will."

I clenched my teeth against the angry retort that sprang to my lips. I wanted to shout at Elania, to tell her Noria was simply misguided, that she was too young to know better... but was she, really? She was a technological genius, far more intelligent than the average seventeen-year-old. I couldn't pretend she was simply an impressionable child, devoid of responsibility for the decisions she'd made. Especially since she was about to turn eighteen. Maybe she *was* misguided, but Annia and I had done our best to dissuade Noria from her path. The fact that she'd chosen not to listen was on her, not on us.

Not that Annia would see it that way, of course. But as fond as I was of Noria, she wasn't my kin. Objectively speaking, of the two sisters, Annia deserved to be saved more than Noria did. Not to mention poor Elnos. They didn't deserve to die for trying to rescue Noria.

"I suppose the only thing to do is keep an ear out for any news, and hope we'll get a chance to rescue Annia and Elnos, if they get themselves in trouble," Comenius said.

"You're right." Unzipping my jacket, I flipped open one of the pouches at my belt and withdrew an emerald and two rubies, all three roughly half the size of my thumb. "Here, take these."

Comenius's eyes widened as I dropped the gemstones into his hands. "*Alter Schwede*, Naya! What is this for?"

"I want you to help me buy an airship," I told him. "I absolutely refuse to go on another rescue mission in a hot air balloon, or scramble around for transport when I have money now."

"You certainly do," Comenius said, sounding more than a little bemused. He examined the gems for a moment, then tucked them into his pocket. "I know a reputable jeweler who will give a fair price for these. I'll call him today to set up an appointment."

We finished lunch, and I bid them both goodbye. I tapped my enforcer bracelet twice to activate it, so that I would receive any emergency broadcasts, and took a ride around Solantha on my steambike. I had time to kill before my lesson with Iannis, and I figured I might be able to catch a bounty while I took a look around the city to see if the other neighborhoods were improving.

Not that I needed the money, I reflected as I rode down one of the very steep hills on the main drag of Rowanville. As I'd just demonstrated to Comenius, I had plenty of it now. Even if I did somehow find a way to blow all the gold and gems I'd acquired, Iannis or the Mages Guild would likely find me some way to earn more, now that I was the Chief Mage's bride to be. Besides, all mages, even lowly apprentices like me, received a stipend in gold once a year.

I was determined to make my windfall last as long as possible, though, as I really didn't want to rely on charity from Iannis. It would be one thing if we were actually married, but until that day came, I was still a single woman. And seeing as how a year was a long way off, I might as well put away some extra money to hold me over until then.

Besides, the future might look bright now, but the turmoil I'd experienced over the past few months was proof that life was forever uncertain. My newfound wealth might come handy in an emergency. If anything happened to Iannis, or if we ended up breaking off our engagement...

No. I resolutely shoved those gloomy thoughts away. I wasn't going to let anyone, or anything, take my hard-won happiness from me. Iannis was mine, and if anyone thought they could change that, they'd be singing a different tune once I got my hands on them.

$\mathcal{I}$ rode through Shiftertown first, the area which had taken the brunt of the damage in the uprising. It had been less than two weeks since the Resistance had finally been driven out of here, so many of the buildings and homes still sported holes in their walls and roofs, and boards covering broken windows. But there were construction crews in the town square, rebuilding the town hall and fixing up the shops. The rubble had been cleared away from the streets, and shifters were walking around openly again. Many faces turned toward me as I passed, and though some gazes were still filled with mistrust and derision, there were others who were cautiously friendly, and even a few that looked happy to see me.

I stopped by Aunt Mafiela's house, located on Third Street in the wealthier section of Shiftertown, with the intention of inviting her to lunch. I hadn't seen her since I'd come to warn her about the shifter kidnappings. Though she'd been less than kind to me the last time we'd met face to face, she *had* sent me a thank-you card after I'd rescued Mika, her granddaughter. Maybe she would actually be amenable to the idea of lunch.

Hell, if she was willing to give me information on my father, I'd invite her to the wedding.

You should invite her to the wedding anyway, a voice whispered in my head.

Ugh, I thought to myself as I parked my bike on the curb outside her house. *Let's take things one step at a time, shall we? You haven't even invited her to lunch yet.*

I took a moment to study the house before I walked up the front steps. It was a three-story residence with grey siding, dark purple roof tiling, and matching purple shutters. Normally, it was immaculate, but one of the dormer windows was missing, the hole covered by parchment paper and adhesive, and the front door appeared to have been replaced recently. The neighboring houses also showed minor damage—I guessed the Resistance soldiers had bashed in windows and doors when taking over some of these residences for their own use.

I bet Mafiela was still steaming over the fact that a group of filthy soldiers had been living inside her precious home. Not long ago, the thought would have made me grin, but as I trotted up the front porch steps, I couldn't help but sympathize with her a little. She'd been through a lot recently.

I lifted the heavy, jaguar-head-shaped knocker and knocked twice, then waited. Bare feet sounded on the steps leading down from the second floor into the lobby, and to my unpleasant surprise, my cousin Melantha answered the door.

"Oh, it's you." A wary look entered her yellow-orange shifter eyes, and her hand curled protectively around the doorjamb. Like her mother, Melantha was always perfectly coiffed—her blond hair curled, her makeup done, her peach-colored blouse and cream slacks perfectly pressed. But there were shadows beneath her eyes, and her clothes hung loose on her frame. I imagined she'd lost weight during her time on Prison Isle, and she was probably suffering sleepless nights.

"Yeah, it's me." I stuffed my hands in my pockets, not sure what to say. The last time Melantha and I had seen each other, she'd practically broken down my apartment door and tried to gouge my eyes out. Her daughter, Mika, had just been kidnapped, and Melantha had blamed me. At the time, it hadn't mattered to her that I'd tried to warn her family to be on the lookout for a shifter kidnapper.

"Is your mother home?" I asked. "I wanted a moment of her time."

Melantha shook her head. "She's at a council meeting. They've been meeting almost daily since they were released from Prison Isle—there's a lot of work to do if we want to get Shiftertown back on its feet."

"Mother?" a teenage girl's voice called from out of view. "Who's at the door?"

Melantha hesitated. "It's your aunt Sunaya."

Footsteps sounded, and Melantha dropped her arm as Mika came into view. She was a stunning young girl with long, blonde hair that fell to her waist—practically a carbon copy of her mother, though she had her father's square face and wide mouth. That mouth curved into a shy smile.

"I never did get to thank you for saving me," she said, sounding a little ashamed. "And to apologize for attacking you."

Warmth spread through my chest, and I cleared my throat against a rush of emotion. "You don't have to do either of those things," I said gently. "It was partially my fault you were taken. And you only attacked me because of those horrible drugs they gave you. You did nothing wrong."

Mika shook her head, stepping out onto the porch. "I said mean things to you at first. Maybe I didn't know any better, but they were still mean." She flung her arms around me and squeezed tight. "I'm sorry, and no matter the circumstances, I'm grateful that you saved my life."

Shocked, it took me a few seconds to react to the affectionate gesture. But I did, wrapping my arms around her tightly and turning my head to the side so that Melantha couldn't see the tears gathering at the corners of my eyes. I hadn't expected to talk to Melantha and Mika, since they didn't actually live here, and I certainly hadn't been prepared for any kind of emotional reunion.

"You're welcome," I finally said when I was sure I could speak again. "I'm just glad you're safe."

"I, too, must thank you for what you did," Melantha said as I stepped back. The words were a little stiff, but I sensed no lie in them—it was just hard for her to admit the truth. "Mother told me the Mages Guild gave Shiftertown a generous sum of money to rebuild, and I doubt we would have gotten so much without your influence with the Chief Mage." Her lips curved a little. "Congratulations on your engagement, by the way."

"Thank you." I gave her a small smile in return. "I'm glad things are starting to look up."

"Me too." She hesitated a moment, then said, "Perhaps you should come over for tea sometime."

"Maybe," I hedged, not sure if I was ready for that. "Speaking of which, the reason I stopped by was because I wanted to invite Aunt Mafiela to lunch."

Melantha's eyebrows rose. "I suppose it is a good time to bury the hatchet, what with your recent engagement. Mother's been much more interested in acknowledging your relationship with our clan ever since she learned you were going to be the Chief Mage's bride."

I fought against the urge to roll my eyes—of course she was. "Well, if you can just let her know I made the offer, and to contact me at the Palace, that would be great."

"Are you inviting us to the wedding?" Mika piped up. I

turned to see her looking hopefully up at me, her eyes shining with the possibility of attending a grand wedding.

I smiled. "I'm sure I will, but it won't be for some time yet," I told her, unwilling to disappoint her. "I'll send you invitations, but for now, I've got to run."

We made our goodbyes, and I hopped back onto my steambike, hoping I could shake the cocktail of emotions rolling around in my chest before I got to Lakin's place. He lived closer to the town square, on a row of single-story, one-bedroom homes that were small and neat, but looked like someone had copied the same simple design over and over. Boring. The last time I'd been to Lakin's, a duo of bird shifters had been in the middle of trying to convince him to support the Resistance. He hadn't agreed, of course, especially after I'd informed him that the Resistance planned to turn on the shifter community once they were done overthrowing the mages. But if he was still in touch with those Resistance soldiers, he might have information that would help me rescue my missing friends.

I pulled up to Lakin's house, and the sight of his steambike parked in the drive assured me he was at home. My nerves jangled a little as I headed up the path to the front door—Lakin had a huge crush on me, and he'd made it known on more than one occasion that he wanted more than my friendship. I hoped he wouldn't react too badly to my betrothal to Iannis, and that he would still be willing to help me out.

"One second," Lakin called when I knocked on the door. It sounded like he was toward the back of the house, maybe in his bedroom. My lips twitched as I remembered the first time I'd knocked on this door. He'd answered wearing very little and looking quite embarrassed about the fact. Hopefully, he'd put on a shirt this time.

Yeah, unless that was just a strategy to get you into bed.

I frowned. I hadn't thought of that at the time. I hoped Lakin would respect the boundaries I'd set for our friendship, because I would hate to have to end it. He was Roanas's successor, after all, and responsible for the safety of Shiftertown. I didn't want things to be weird between us.

"Sunaya!" He threw open the door, a friendly smile on his rawboned face. His reddish-yellow shifter eyes glowed with pleasure, and an answering grin sprang easily to my lips. "I was just thinking of you."

"What a coincidence." I looked him up and down. His short, blond hair was damp from a fresh shower, and he wore a button-up red shirt and tight pants that clung to slightly damp skin. He'd foregone shoes, which meant he probably hadn't gone out yet. The lack of shadows beneath his eyes told me he'd gotten a good night's sleep, maybe even slept in.

"You're looking a hell of a lot better than the last time I saw you," I commented as he let me in.

"Yeah, well, I've had a bit of time to recover from my little vacation in Prison Isle." His voice darkened, but only for a second. "I hear you went on a little vacation yourself."

I snorted. "Yeah, if being stranded on a deserted island with no amenities of any kind could be called a vacation." Luckily for me, shifters were much better at surviving in the wilderness than the average human. I made my way into his living room and plopped down on the couch. He'd added a bookshelf and a side table, and there was a still-life painting on his wall that I didn't remember seeing before. "I nearly went insane trying to keep myself occupied."

"Well, I'm glad you're home safe." Lakin eyed me up and down, then cleared his throat. "And, um, congratulations on your engagement." He looked away.

"Thanks." I narrowed my eyes a little. "Something you want to say about it?"

Lakin sighed, turning back to me. "Not really. I wish you the best, but I can't help thinking that it's an impossible match."

"You and everyone else," I muttered, and this time, I was the one who looked away. I knew the huge obstacles Iannis and I were facing by choosing to publicly engage in a relationship, but I didn't really need Lakin reminding me about them.

"Sorry." Lakin lowered himself into the recliner across from me, and the chair creaked beneath his weight. "I shouldn't have said anything. And I really do hope that it works out."

"Thanks." I smiled, though it came out a little strained. Lakin's words were sincere, but there was no hiding the disappointment lurking behind them.

"So, what do you need?" he asked, curiosity overcoming his momentary wistfulness. "I'm imagining this isn't a social call."

"No, it's not," I admitted. "I was hoping you might be able to tell me where any citizens the Resistance recruited after Iannis's disappearance had gotten off to."

Lakin frowned. "You mean if I know which base they were sent to?"

I nodded. "Noria Melcott, Annia's younger sister, was one of those recruits. Her boyfriend Elnos, and Annia herself, left a couple of weeks ago to find her and drag her back home, before the mages lose their temper and start annihilating the camps wholesale. Elnos and Annia made it to a Resistance camp in Canalo that they think Noria went to, but they've been out of touch since then, and I'm worried. I may need to go retrieve them, but I can't without the location."

"I see." A troubled expression settled on Lakin's face. "I'm afraid I wouldn't have any knowledge of such a camp. I did help a number of shifters flee the city, but I wasn't sending them to the Resistance."

"Yeah, but surely you know *someone* who could tell me," I

urged. "What about those two birdbrains who visited last time? Have you seen them lately?"

"Hmm." Lakin tapped his forefinger against his chin. "I haven't heard back from them, but then again, it's entirely possible they were captured and are now awaiting sentence."

"Shit." I pursed my lips together, then brightened. "Of course. I'm so dumb. I'll just go to Prison Isle and question a few of them. Maybe the Chief Mage will let me offer reduced sentences to anyone who provides useful information."

"You could start with asking your cousin Rylan, you know," Lakin said dryly. "I'm sure he would be happy to help."

"Yeah, well, that depends on your definition of 'help'." My lips thinned as I recalled how Rylan had attempted to 'help' me, by getting a witch to cast a spell that made me forget to warn Iannis about an impending ambush. Anger ignited in my chest, and I took a deep breath and exhaled through my nostrils to expel it. He wasn't worth getting angry over.

"Is there something you're not telling me?" Lakin asked warily.

I shook my head. "Nothing worth mentioning." I checked my watch, wondering if I had time to get over to Prison Isle. "Crap, my magic lesson starts in an hour. I'd better get going."

"All right." Lakin looked a little disappointed that I was cutting my visit so short, but he smiled as he walked me to the door. "I've got to check in with Chieftain Baine soon anyway. She'll have orders for me, depending on what was decided at the council meeting."

"Oh, yeah." I hesitated at the doorstep, wondering if I should ask him to tell Mafiela I'd called. But I'd already asked Melantha to do it, and I didn't want to seem desperate. Mafiela would be curious enough about my invitation to answer, anyway. All I had to do was wait.

5

I reached the training room before Iannis, which wasn't surprising. He was ridiculously overburdened, dealing with the aftermath of what the people were beginning to refer to as the Uprising. There were prisoners to sentence, structures to rebuild, jobs to fill, agreements to hash out. It was a wonder he managed to make time for our lessons at all.

Following my usual routine, I sat cross-legged in the middle of the wooden floor, closed my eyes, and practiced a breathing drill Roanas had taught me. The breathing drill might have been a martial arts exercise, but its ability to help one focus and maintain calm had endless application. Control over one's emotions was essential when practicing magic—a flare-up of anger or a lapse of concentration at the wrong time could have disastrous consequences. Today had been particularly emotional, and I did my best to breathe it all out so I would be ready when Iannis arrived.

Footsteps and murmured voices drifted through the crack beneath the door, and I tuned them out so I could focus. But the moment Iannis's sandalwood scent reached me, my heart jumped in my chest. I took in a deeper breath than was strictly necessary, listening to the distinctive sound of his approaching footfalls, but kept my eyes closed as the door swung open.

"Hello." His sexy, slightly musical accent turned the greeting into a caress that slid along my spine like a silken scarf.

"Hello to you too." I opened my eyes and smiled at him. He looked a far cry from the gorgeous, naked man I'd woken up to this morning, dressed now in his blue-and-gold robes, his hair tied back from his stern but handsome face. "How's your day been so far?"

"Busy." Iannis placed his palm against the doorjamb and muttered a few Words. Glowing blue energy rippled outward from the door and across the walls, signaling that the protective wards had been activated. My magic wouldn't be able to harm anyone outside this room, and no one would be able to get in unless Iannis let them. "Are you ready to begin?"

"Yes—" I began, then hesitated. "Well, no. Not exactly."

Iannis's eyebrows pulled together in a frown as he came to stand in front of me. "Why not?"

I got to my feet, so I wouldn't have to tilt my neck back to look up at him. Or at least not as much—he was a foot taller than I was, after all. "You said my apprenticeship would take ten years. Is that the average length, or are you adding years because I'm so far behind?"

"It depends on the individual student, but yes, ten years is about average," Iannis confirmed, and my heart sank. "You are a fast learner, so I am optimistic you can complete it in that time despite your lack of basic mage education. However, we really must do something about your Loranian—mage children typically begin learning it at four years of age."

"Yeah, Fenris told me he was going to start giving me lessons for two hours a day." I tried not to groan at the idea. "I just hope my eyeballs won't fall out."

"I think you'll manage," Iannis said dryly, though his lips twitched ever so slightly.

"So what's the basic curriculum, then?" I asked as he pulled three brightly colored balls, roughly the size of lemons, from his sleeve.

He tossed the balls to me, and I caught them hastily. "You should practice your magic while we're talking. We cannot afford to waste time."

"All right, all right." Sighing, I tossed them into the air one at a time, then spoke a variant of the levitation spell Fenris had taught me. The first ball shot up way too fast, and I had to bring it back down slowly—I still hadn't properly recalibrated to account for my recent power increase. The second one came up more easily, the third even better.

"Good," Iannis said once I had them all levitating individually. "Now make the one on the left spin clockwise, and the one on the right spin counterclockwise."

It took me a moment to dredge up the correct Words for that, and another moment still to get the balls moving in the correct directions. Any of the other apprentices would laugh to see me struggle like this—to them, this was child's play, an exercise their mothers would have taught them when they were small.

"Basic skills that all mages are taught during their childhood include the rudimentary shields and wards, making and extinguishing fire, efficient use of magic and energy, soothing frightened animals, and blending in with your surroundings," Iannis continued. "By the time a mage is ready to begin their apprenticeship, they should have mastered the spells associated with those skills, and at least one signature spell taught by their family."

"Signature spell?" I asked, then cursed roundly as one of the balls dropped onto my head. I tried to grab it before it fell to the ground, but the motion broke my concentration, and the rest of the balls fell as well, bouncing harmlessly away.

"Start over," Iannis said mildly, and I took a deep breath to curb my frustration. Once I was calm again, I reached out with my hands and spoke the correct Words to levitate the balls back in my direction. Iannis nodded approvingly as I got them back into the air and started spinning them in circles.

"Very good. As I've mentioned before, fluency in Loranian is essential for the apprentice curriculum, and is also considered a basic skill. The general curriculum includes the history and theory of magic—which you have already begun to study— healing, offensive and defensive magic, and mastery of the elements."

"Air, earth, water, and fire?" I asked. One of the balls began to dip down, but I got it back up before my spell unraveled again. *Ha.* I was getting better at this!

"Yes, and while that sounds simple, there are many applications of elemental magic, such as spells relating to weather and agriculture. Any mage worth his salt should be able to ensure his people can grow crops and have enough food for themselves, and a surplus for trade as well."

I only nodded, not willing to disrupt my concentration again. A week ago, when we'd started this exercise, I wouldn't have even been able to listen to him talk. I would get to the point where I could hold a conversation, but not today.

"In addition to that, there are around two hundred standard spells that any mage is expected to have fully mastered before graduation, and each mage should have mastered an additional hundred spells in their specialty, if they have chosen one."

"Specialty?" I asked. One of the balls stopped spinning for a second, then started up again as I glared at it.

"Yes. Mine, for example, is healing. Another mage might be better versed in magical warfare."

"I want to specialize in that," I announced. To my delight, the balls didn't even jitter.

"I am not in the least bit surprised to hear that." Iannis sounded amused. "You have a warrior's spirit. I shall keep your wish in mind, but it's rather early to think about specialization. In the meantime, I'm afraid we won't be spending as much time sparring magically as we did in your earlier lessons, since you'll need to catch up with the basic skills and Loranian."

That *was* a little disappointing—I enjoyed the magical sparring, even if I was at a huge disadvantage against Iannis. But I held my complaints back as we continued with the rest of the lesson, finishing up with the levitation spell, then moving onto other magical exercises that were built around improving magical efficiency.

After all, I wanted to finish my apprenticeship as quickly as possible, so there was no point in bitching about what couldn't be changed.

Thankfully, we didn't spend the entire hour on mind-numbing drills. Iannis had me start practicing with water, both conjuring and directing it, which proved very difficult since it was such a slippery element. He had me start by filling a bowl, then using the contents to form patterns and shapes in the air.

"Hey, isn't that one pretty?" I asked, tracing a heart shape in the air with my finger. The water followed my direction, twisting around as it attempted to form the same shape.

"Yes—" Iannis began, but I accidentally flicked my finger a little too hard, and the water splashed right into his face.

"Sorry!" I laughed as he spluttered, his head, neck, and shoulders completely soaked. He leveled a glare at me, then flicked his hand, and I ducked to avoid the thick stream of water he flung at me. I conjured another ball of liquid, then threw it straight at him. It hit him smack dab in the chest, soaking him through.

"Oh, so you want a fight now, do you?" A devilish grin curved his lips, my only warning. He flicked his hands, and my eyes nearly popped out of my skull as a towering wave of water rushed toward me out of thin air. I tried to dodge it, but it was way too big, and I slipped on a puddle just as it crashed into me.

"Oww!" I cried, slapping at the ground as I hit the floorboards hard. Or, at least, I tried to say *oww*, but water filled my mouth, choking off my words. I sputtered and gasped, trying to catch my breath as rivulets ran down my body and into the floorboards.

"Are you all right?" Iannis was suddenly next to me, kneeling on the wet ground as he gathered me into his arms. "I didn't consider the slippery floorboards."

"I'm fine," I managed, my throat a little raw from coughing up water. Clinging to him, I looked into his face, noticing the droplets of water clinging to each of his long, dark lashes. Even with his hair plastered to his head, and his features taut with worry, he was beautiful.

"I'm fine," I repeated, reaching up to stroke his cheek.

He pulled me tighter against him as his lips found mine, and I sighed as I allowed myself to melt into his strong embrace. It felt so good to be able to let my guard down, to be able to show my feelings openly, and even better, to have them returned. Just weeks ago, Iannis and I had tiptoed around each other, and now we kissed and touched every chance we got.

His big hand slid up my blouse, and I moaned a little as his thumb brushed over my nipple. "Is this part of the lesson?" I murmured against his mouth.

"A different lesson," he admitted, nibbling at my earlobe, "but one I can always make time for."

I giggled as he rolled me onto my back, and there was no more talking for quite some time after that.

6

*A*fter our 'lesson' was done, Iannis and I adjourned to his suite, where we had an early dinner with Fenris. Iannis was going to be busy all evening, but he wanted to update us about what was going on in the Mages Guild, and I was more than amenable to that.

"I've had dinner in Iannis's rooms more times than I can count, but never with another person," Fenris remarked as he cut up the seasoned chicken breast on his plate. "It's a pleasant change of pace."

I grinned a little. "I have a feeling this isn't going to be the only thing that changes around here, now that we're engaged." I squeezed Iannis's leg from underneath the table, away from Fenris's watchful gaze. He didn't react outwardly, but his leg tensed ever so slightly beneath my hand, indicating his surprise. Obviously, he wasn't at all used to being groped around other people.

Fenris chuckled. "Are you kidding? Things have already changed drastically. Or haven't you noticed the bounce in Iannis's step as he walks the halls these days?"

"There is no 'bounce' in my step, Fenris," Iannis said mildly as he forked up some green beans. But his eyes flashed in annoyance, and Fenris and I snickered. "Now, if you wouldn't mind, let's get on to business. You may have noticed, Sunaya, that I've been getting a lot of calls from the Minister lately."

"I certainly have." I'd been wondering about it, too, but had held my tongue, figuring Iannis would tell me about it sooner or later.

"Well—and this is not to blame you, Sunaya—but when I left to retrieve you from that remote little island, I had to cancel my participation in an important mission for the task force the Minister formed after we'd rescued him."

"You mean the one that is supposed to shut down any ongoing operations of the Resistance?" I sat up straighter. "What mission did you miss?"

Iannis waved the question away. "It no longer matters. But now the Minister has another mission for me, and I cannot refuse again. He wants me to personally smoke out some secret Resistance stronghold."

"Where is it?" Fenris wanted to know.

"The Minister refused to divulge that information over the phone. He wants to brief me in person, and he is expecting me tomorrow night." Iannis turned his gaze toward me. "You will be coming along."

I frowned. "For the meeting?"

"Not just the meeting, but the mission itself. We will be leaving for the stronghold as soon as we are briefed. The minister expects me to personally lead an assault on the remaining Resistance forces in the area. Your shifter and enforcer experience will come in handy, and it will be educational for you, especially if you plan to specialize in combat magic. Consider it part of your practical training."

"But I can't go."

Iannis's eyes narrowed. "Excuse me?"

"I can't go," I repeated, feeling both angry and horrible at once for saying it. I wanted to go on this mission, of course—it was an honor to be included, and, besides, I wanted to take down the Resistance. "I've got to go after Annia and Elnos."

"You think they're in trouble?" Fenris asked, sounding concerned.

I sighed. "There's no way of knowing, since it's so hard to communicate with them. But I have a bad feeling about this, and I think they're going to need me soon. I've got to be ready to leave at a moment's notice."

"Sunaya, I understand your concern, and your desire to help your friends, but going off alone on a rescue mission is absolutely out of the question," Iannis said sternly. "You're my apprentice, and now my fiancée as well—you can't simply go gallivanting off as you please."

"Gallivanting!" I slapped my hand on the table, and the silverware jumped. "You call going after my friends whose lives are in danger 'gallivanting'? Is that what I did when I took Fenris and Annia to rescue *you*?"

"No," Iannis said, completely unperturbed about my outburst. "Perhaps I chose my words poorly. But I am still your master, and I can't allow you to go off by yourself. The Resistance isn't the only danger, you know—there are others who would sooner see you dead rather than wedded to me, or would be happy to capture you and use you for political leverage."

A shiver crawled down my spine at that. "Like who?"

"Rival mages who covet my position. Or citizens who disapprove of giving shifters more status and power." Iannis shrugged. "In any case, I am not prepared to risk your life in such a foolhardy manner."

I gritted my teeth. "Then come with me. That way I won't be alone, and I can still rescue my friends."

"I *cannot.*" A hint of anger entered Iannis's tone now. "As I just explained, I must attend to this mission. If I keep refusing missions from the Minister, he will begin to doubt my commitment. He could even try to relieve me of my position if I anger him enough, and with all the chaos the Resistance has caused, he is on edge."

"Hang on." Fenris held up a hand before I could spit back an angry retort. "There has to be a way we can come to some sort of an agreement on this. After all, Annia, Noria, and Elnos are amongst the Resistance right now. Surely, whatever camp they have infiltrated is also a worthy target. The Minister should be happy to see it shut down as well."

"I can mention it, but I doubt he would consider that a higher priority than the mission he's currently assigned me," Iannis said dryly, "especially since we have no idea which camp they are in, or what sort of operation is being run there."

"It could be a higher priority," I argued. "When Elnos sends his next ether pigeon, I may have more details regarding their whereabouts."

"Perhaps, but we cannot count on that. And we have no idea when to expect his next message."

"How about this, then?" Fenris said, turning to me. "Why don't you go with Iannis to Dara, for starters, and find out more about his mission. In the meantime, I will call Comenius daily for news from Elnos, and relay it instantly once it is received. I will also keep an eye on Director Chen and the Council to see if they learn anything, since the camp Annia and Elnos went to is within Canalo's borders. It is entirely possible that you may be finished with the Minister's mission by the time we receive Elnos's next message, and you and Iannis can go find them right away. But if not, you can make a judgment call then as to whether or not to finish the mission with Iannis, or leave and go after your friends."

"I will not allow her to go off by herself—"

"I will meet her there," Fenris said calmly, cutting him off. "I may not have your power, Iannis, but I am more than capable of watching over and assisting Sunaya until you arrive."

"Of course," Iannis said, sounding calmer now. "I did not mean to imply anything to the contrary. It's just that..." He glanced sideways at me, and I softened a little at the conflicted look in his violet eyes.

"You're protective of Sunaya," Fenris said, smiling. "I would be very worried if you were not beating on your chest like an enraged gorilla at the thought of her being separated from you again."

"I resent that comparison," Iannis said as I snickered, though he didn't sound too mad about it.

"All right. Well, I can agree to those terms," I said, the anger in my chest falling away. I couldn't bring myself to be mad at Iannis for caring about me, even if his possessiveness was becoming a bit of a nuisance. "What about you?"

Iannis found my hand under the table, gave it a light squeeze. "Very well," he said, his eyes softening for just a moment before he turned back to Fenris. "You promise that you'll send me daily reports if you and Sunaya do end up going off without me?"

"Of course." Fenris picked up his fork, then stabbed at a piece of steak. "Now let's enjoy our meal, shall we? I have a feeling this may be one of the last we'll share together for a while."

No kidding, I thought as we dug into our food. I only hoped that when all of this was said and done, things would return to normal. Or whatever 'normal' would be, in the aftermath of this disaster.

7

*A*fter dinner, I made my way toward the gardens, figuring a walk and some fresh air would help clear my thoughts. I wasn't mad at Iannis anymore—in fact, dinner with him and Fenris had been very pleasant—but I was still a little unsettled over this new change in plans. Was I doing the right thing, by agreeing to go to Dara instead of holding myself ready to go after Elnos and Annia the moment I learned their location? Or would circumstances prevent me from helping them? I would never forgive myself if this delay contributed to their deaths.

You shouldn't worry so much, I told myself. Annia was a competent enforcer, and Elnos a trained mage, even if he was on the young side. Truthfully, he was probably older than I was, but mages were long-lived, and his youthful personality made me think of him as younger, closer to my age. It was likely that the two of them could manage to get out of whatever trouble they fell into, even if the Resistance did discover who they were.

But ever since we'd confirmed that Argon Chartis, the former director of the Canalo Mages Guild, had defected to the Resistance, I was worried there would be others like him. What if the camp Annia and Elnos infiltrated had a renegade mage at their disposal, or some other magic user? They could have recruited a witch, or even a shaman if they were near tribal lands. As I'd experienced firsthand, tribal shamans were not to be underestimated—they could be just as powerful as mages. And though I didn't know much about witches, some of them might be equally formidable, even if they practiced their magic differently.

I wonder if Elania and Comenius might be willing to come, I thought to myself as I headed down the front steps of the palace and onto the garden path. If Fenris had to come out and meet me, perhaps he could take them along. The more manpower, the better.

The gardens were beautiful this time of year, with paths winding through perfectly trimmed lawns, past fountains and statues of famous Canalo mages. There were bushes and trees with blossoms in every variety of color, some of them magically enhanced. I paused to sit on a carved stone bench and glanced up at the tree above me. It had brilliant blue leaves, and instead of blossoms, tiny bells grew from the branches, ringing softly as the ocean breeze ruffled them. These bell trees seemed to be very popular in the Mages Quarter—I'd seen more than one of them on the front lawns of the mages who lived here.

"Miss Baine! There you are."

I stiffened at the sound of Director Chen's voice. She was coming down the path to my left, her pale, ivory-skinned face serene as usual, though I caught a hint of relief in her slanted eyes. She wore emerald-green silk robes with a cream sash around her waist that drew the eye to her slim figure, and her fine, straight hair was tied into an elegant knot.

"Director Chen." Resigned, I got to my feet to greet her. She was the director of the Mages Guild and Iannis's deputy, after all, and I had to show some respect even if I didn't like her all that much. "What can I do for you?"

"Would you mind sitting down with me for a cup of tea?" she asked. "There are some things I'd like to discuss with you that might be better said in private."

I narrowed my eyes. "What kind of things?" If she was going to warn me off Iannis again, I was going to punch her right in the nose. Sure, that was probably stupid, since she was a powerful mage, but I wasn't going to stand here and let her try to tear Iannis and me apart.

"Nothing bad," Chen assured me hastily, reading the look in my eye. "It's business-related, I assure you."

"All right." Biting back a sigh, I followed Director Chen inside, through the lobby, and down the hall toward the Mages Guild offices. I hated Chen's office with a passion—her visitors' chairs were incredibly uncomfortable—but I would endure them rather than chance someone overhearing us. Especially if she did want to say something nasty about my relationship with Iannis.

However, we walked straight past Chen's office and entered a lounge two doors down, commonly used by senior Guild employees for receiving visitors. The room was decorated in Canalo's blue and gold—dark blue wallpaper with a repeating pattern of the state emblem, gold couches and chairs, dark blue rugs with golden embellishments, heavy wood tables, and parquet flooring. To the left of the seating area was an unlit fireplace of white gold-veined marble, which served as a sort of accent and relieved the colorful space.

"I hope you like green tea," Chen said as we sat on the couches. She lifted a small red clay teapot with Garaian symbols painted on the sides from the silver tea tray that had been left on the coffee table, and began to pour steaming, pale yellow liquid into matching red cups. "I confess it's a favorite of mine."

"Green tea is fine," I said. I preferred my tea cold rather than hot, especially in summer, but it would have to do.

"Excellent." Chen handed me the cup, and I held it gingerly —there were no handles, so I had to endure the hot ceramic directly.

"So what's this about?" I asked, blowing on my tea as I waited for it to cool.

"Well, before I get into anything else, I would like to offer my apologies," Chen said. She picked up her cup of tea and blew gently over the top before taking a dainty sip. "I misread the situation between you and Lord Iannis. It is quite clear to me now that he is fonder of you than I realized."

"I believe the word you're looking for is 'love', not 'fondness'," I said evenly. I wasn't going to let her trivialize what Iannis and I had.

An uncomfortable expression crossed Chen's face, but she nodded. "Yes, of course. In any case, I hope there are no hard feelings."

"I can move past it if you can." I took a sip from my tea. Yowch. Still too hot. How the hell did Director Chen manage to sip hers so calmly, when it had to be scalding her lips off? Drinking hot tea had to be classified as some kind of torture, I was sure of it.

"Excellent." Chen gave me a brief smile, then her expression grew serious. "I brought you here because it's time to discuss public-relations strategies. Specifically, we need to carefully handle the media regarding your engagement."

"What?" I stared at her, baffled.

Director Chen's perfectly plucked brows furrowed. "Surely you realize that the papers and radio hosts are taking a passionate interest in your engagement to Lord Iannis. And regretfully, not all outlets are portraying it in a positive manner. It is essential that the Chief Mage's reputation should not take any damage from this unconventional relationship. As his fiancée, you can no longer stay out of the public eye. If you do not present yourself to the public in a sympathetic manner, the media will gleefully take advantage of your silence."

"So what do you want me to do?" I asked, trying not to sound irritated. After all, Director Chen had a point, even if I didn't like what she was saying. Papers all over the Federation had already printed articles speculating about my relationship with Iannis, and that was before our engagement.

"I've had my secretary set up some appointments for you. You will be meeting with important mage families and media representatives to answer questions and discuss your future role as the wife of Canalo's Chief Mage." Director Chen smiled again. "In fact, the first interview is already set for tomorrow."

"Oh." Relief swept through me. "I'm sorry to say I won't be able to make any of those appointments. I'm leaving for Dara tomorrow, with the Chief Mage."

"I'm well aware," Director Chen said, unruffled by my announcement. "Tomorrow's interview will take place in the morning, at nine o'clock. I believe your flight is not scheduled to leave until just before lunch, correct?"

"Correct," I said through gritted teeth. Dammit, but I wasn't ready for this! It was one thing to interview suspects, another thing to be interviewed myself. And I'd never been groomed for the kind of political schmoozing that Chen clearly had in mind.

"Excellent," Chen said briskly. "Your other appointments will be rescheduled if you cannot return on time. I will assign you a social secretary to help you keep up with your engagements."

"Whoa, whoa, hang on." I held up a hand, getting a little overwhelmed now. "I'm not sure I should be doing this so soon. I want to talk to Lord Iannis about this first. Does he know you've set this up?"

"I haven't had a chance to tell him about it yet, but I will, and I'm sure he would approve. With all this adverse gossip about the two of you spreading, Lord Iannis would be the first to demand that something needs to be done."

"I dunno," I said dubiously, not sure if I should trust Chen. I wasn't completely certain she had my best interests at heart. "I think I'd rather pick out my own social secretary, thanks. And I'd rather do the interviews when I'm more prepared for them."

"Miss Baine," Director Chen said patiently, but in the sort of tone one used on small children or half-wits, "the papers are currently presenting you as a sleazy gold digger, because they've never had a chance to interview you in person. Once they do, I am reasonably confident they will change their tune. But you have to be willing to talk to them."

I let out a sigh. "Fine, I'll do this interview in the morning," I agreed, knowing in my heart I would regret it. "But I still plan on talking to Lord Iannis before I agree to do anything else. Who am I seeing?"

"You will be interviewed by Gena Chanie, a correspondent from *Now*," Chen informed me. It was a celebrity-focused publication I'd seen on the magazine racks many times, though I'd never read it myself. "She'll meet you in this room for the interview, unless you would prefer to see her in your sitting room?"

"No, here's fine." I set down my teacup, ready to be done with this conversation. It was bad enough I had to meet this journalist—no way was I inviting a stranger into my private suite. "Is that everything?"

"I believe so," Director Chen said. "Unless you want to look through the list of suitable candidates to serve as your secretary now. I could advise you—"

"I'm sorry, but it'll have to be another time." I rose from my chair. "I have to prepare for the trip to Dara, and now that I have an interview scheduled for tomorrow morning, I have less time than I originally anticipated." I allowed the slightest bit of censure to enter my voice.

"Of course." Director Chen inclined her head fractionally, though she did not look contrite at the fact that she had, in my opinion, overstepped her bounds by scheduling all these interviews without consulting me first. "Good night."

"Good night." I walked out of the room, and barely, just barely, managed not to slam the door behind me. I had to improve my control over my emotions, and who better to practice on than one of the most infuriating women in Canalo?

8

Too restless to head up to my rooms yet, I went back out to the garden. By this time, the sun had set, and all that was left were the last faint streaks of purple, pink, and gold. The lanterns had turned on to help the crescent moon illuminate the darkness, and their warm, magical light gilded the plants, statues, and bushes. The evening's serene beauty was at odds with the conflicted thoughts churning away in my head.

Of course, I'd known my engagement with Iannis was going to draw public attention to me, that I would have to deal with interviews and public speculation. I wasn't stupid. But so many things had been going on when I'd agreed to the engagement that I'd pushed this aspect aside, unwilling to confront it. Now that my life was calming down a little, I was starting to experience the reality of what it meant to share Iannis's life. Interviews, photo ops, fancy dresses, parties, meetings, and more. Not to mention my calendar was no longer my own to dictate—Chen was scheduling interviews without my permission, and Iannis was roping me into missions on short notice.

You asked for these things, I reminded myself. *You wanted to take a more active role in Solantha, to provide a voice for the shifter community. This is all part of the deal.*

I rounded the corner of the palace, following the path along the side of the massive structure so I could head to the back. There was an excellent view of Solantha Bay from the rear of the Palace. I never got tired of looking at Firegate Bridge—the magical red metal shimmered mysteriously beneath the twinkling stars, drawing the eye away from the ugliness of Prison Isle that stood in the middle of the bay. I wondered how many Resistance soldiers still languished there, awaiting their grim fate.

Sunaya! a familiar voice shouted in my head, and I jumped, eyes widening. It sounded a hell of a lot like Roanas, my dead mentor. *Sunaya, move!*

"What?" I said, confused, but my body automatically stepped to the side. As it did, a flaming object whizzed past my ear, missing me by an inch. Panic burst in my chest, and I jumped out of the way as the bomb hit the ground. Even so, the explosion tossed me like a rag doll, and I went flying several feet before landing hard in a row of rhododendron bushes planted along the palace wall.

"Fuck!" I clapped my hands against my ringing ears as I struggled to sit up. The grass had caught fire, and the conflagration was quickly spreading toward the bushes. Taking a deep breath, I focused as best I could, then aimed my hand toward the flames and spoke a Loranian incantation Iannis had taught me. A jet of water blasted from my palm, and I swung my arm back and forth, dousing the fire as quickly as possible.

A magical alarm had gone off as soon as the bomb exploded, and I heard shouts from the Palace, as well as footsteps pounding through the grass. I'd just finished putting out the fire when several mages clad in red robes rushed around the corner —our new guards. Iannis hadn't found a suitable replacement as of yet for Privacy Guard, so he had hired low-level mages for the task.

"Miss Baine!" the one in the lead panted, skidding to a stop in the wet, burnt grass. His narrow face had gone stark white, his brown eyes round with shock and horror. "What happened here?"

I looked down at my clothes, which were completely ruined by the smoke and flames, then over my shoulder. My eyes narrowed at the sight of a broken length of pipe lying amongst the scorched vegetation. I crossed over to where it stood, ignoring my shaky legs and my wildly beating heart.

"I think this is a bomb, or at least what remains of it," I muttered, crouching down to examine the object.

"Bomb?" the guard echoed in disbelief. I poked at the jagged piece of pipe. It was still boiling hot despite being soaked with cold water. My nose wrinkled at the scent of gunpowder, a scent I was becoming more familiar with now that the Resistance had begun using firearms. "Who in the world would dare to bring a bomb into Solantha Palace?"

"I don't know." I glanced up at the row of second-story windows. One of them was open, the curtains flapping gently in the ocean breeze, and I pointed at it. "But whoever it was, they snuck right past you. And they had a perfect shot at me through that window."

∽

LATER, I sprawled on my four-poster bed, staring up at the canopy as I tried to relax. But it was hard to calm my racing mind after narrowly escaping death... especially considering the way it had happened.

Had it really been Roanas's voice I'd heard, warning me away from the bomb? Or had I imagined it? This wasn't the first time

I'd heard voices, but until my recent conversation with Resinah, the first mage and the mouthpiece of the Creator, disembodied voices had been few and far between in my life. I'd mostly thought of them as figments of my imagination... but after all I'd been through, I wasn't so sure anymore.

It would be just like Roanas to choose to transform into a guardian spirit in the afterlife, rather than be reborn. A smile touched my lips. It was comforting, the idea that he might be still out there, watching over me.

The entrance to the hidden passage creaked open, and I sat up to watch Iannis duck through the narrow doorway. A sigh of relief passed my lips before I could stop it—I'd been worried I wouldn't get to see him tonight.

"I wish we'd been able to locate the attacker." Frustration simmered in Iannis's voice as he crossed the room and kicked off his shoes. The sheets rustled a little as he settled onto the bed next to me. "I don't understand how they were able to evade us."

"Neither do I," I said, clenching the bed sheets in my hands. I'd rushed up to the open window as quickly as possible, hoping I could catch the assassin, or at least his scent. The window had been in an unused guestroom, which, unfortunately, had reeked of sulfur, masking the other scents in the room. It had been impossible to tell which of the human scents I'd caught had been there most recently, due to the gunpowder's stench.

At my suggestion, we'd immediately called all the palace staff together for an inspection. Fenris and I had checked them for any sulfurous odor—surely, if the room smelled so strongly of it, the assassin would as well. But the majority of the staff had already gone home at the end of the day shift, and none of those who remained on duty smelled like sulfur. A thorough search of the Palace and grounds proved equally fruitless. Whoever the would-be assassin was, they'd been fast as well as clever.

"Don't beat yourself up about it." I reached out to squeeze

his upper arm. "You've been neck deep in meetings, phone calls, and who knows what else. You can't be expected to be on the lookout for bombers too."

"No, but my guards should," Iannis said, his tone almost a growl. He scooted closer to me, took my face in his hands, and stared at me for a long moment. "I insisted you live here so you would be safe. It is unconscionable that I have not been able to keep that promise."

"Stop," I said firmly, gripping his hand. "I didn't agree to stay at the Palace because I wanted a hidey-hole. I agreed because we're going to be married, and I love you." I turned my face, so I could press a kiss into his palm.

Iannis gathered me up in his arms, and I sighed as he rolled onto his side, tucking me against his body. His strength and warmth eased more tension from my body, and my neck and shoulders relaxed.

"Whoever threw that bomb at me is probably the same person who's been giving intel to the Resistance," I muttered into his chest. "We have a spy in our midst."

"Indeed." Iannis stroked my hair softly, his hand skimming the newly shortened strands—I'd had to chop an inch off, as it had been burned by the fire and smelled like rotten eggs. My eyebrows had seen better days too, but they would grow back to normal overnight. "I wish I could continue the investigation tomorrow, but we cannot delay our trip to Dara. We will have to rely on Fenris to keep up the search in the meanwhile, and if he hasn't found the culprit by the time we get back, I bloody damn will myself."

I smiled at that—Iannis so rarely cursed, and never more than once in a single sentence. "I'm sure you will," I said, tugging open the sash of his robe. "But in the meantime, I could use some help getting to sleep. I'm still a little wired from all the excitement."

Iannis tensed as I slipped my hand inside his robe and ran it along the smooth, hard muscles of his chest. His right hand pushed up the fabric of my nightgown, and I gasped as he slid his hand between my legs, finding my sweet spot with his skilled fingers.

"Anything for you," he murmured, rolling me onto my back. His lips found my own, and I lost myself in his arms, pushing aside my troubles. I would deal with them tomorrow, but for now, I would enjoy Iannis, and be happy that I was still alive to do so.

9

"*I* must say, you're looking very well for someone who nearly died in an explosion last night!"

"Thank you." I smiled at Gena Chanie, the correspondent, who had arrived half an hour early to interview me this morning. I'd arrived in the meeting lounge at nine o'clock on the dot —which was a damned miracle considering how long it had taken me to get ready. A maid had rapped on my door at six in the morning, sent by Director Chen to help me prepare, and I'd endured over two hours of scrubbing, washing, hair pulling, and powdering as she dressed me up.

"I imagine you aren't used to wearing such feminine clothing," Gena said as her eyes skimmed the peach-colored and far-too-lacy dress the maid had crammed me into. "Considering that you're an enforcer by trade."

I smiled a little, smoothing out the skirt of my dress. "I'd have a lot of trouble catching criminals if I had to chase after them wearing ensembles such as this."

Gena laughed. "Too true! But they will look great on the photos we just took." She glanced down at her binder. "So tell me, have you and Lord Iannis picked out a wedding date?"

I froze. "Um, no. Not yet."

"Really?" Gena frowned as she scribbled on her notepad. "I know it's only been a week since you announced your engagement, but, surely, you've given it some thought. Do you plan to have the ceremony in Dara, during the next Convention?"

"No," I said automatically. The next convention wasn't for another two years, and there was no way I was waiting that long. "We want friends and family to be present, and that will be easier if we have the wedding here in Solantha."

"Family?" Gena asked, her pen poised like a viper ready to strike. "Do you mean your relatives from the Jaguar Clan? Do you plan to invite all of them, or only immediate family members?"

Fuck.

The questions came fast and furious, and I floundered badly at each one. Had I picked out a designer for my wedding dress yet? Who was going to give me away at the altar? Did Iannis have any family who would come out of the woodwork to attend? What was it like being engaged to the most powerful man in Canalo? On and on and on it went, and I had no idea if the answers I gave were damning or not to my reputation, never mind Iannis's.

"Well, I'm afraid that's all the time I have left," I announced, cutting off the correspondent mid-sentence. She'd been edging towards questions about the 'intimate' side of my relationship with Iannis, and I was having none of it. "I'm leaving for Dara today, and I'm afraid I'm not quite packed yet."

"Really?" Gena jumped to her feet as I rose, her pen and pad still clutched in her manicured fingers. "What for?"

Shit. I had no idea if our trip to Dara was supposed to be a secret or not. But even if it wasn't, I doubted Iannis would want me leaking details to the press.

"I cannot say," I said coolly, deciding it would be best not to offer any information at all. "Lord Iannis asked me to come along as his apprentice, so I am going. Good day to you."

I swept out of the room, heels clicking on the hallway floor as I hurried back to my rooms as fast as I could without running. I didn't want to look like I was fleeing from the interview—even if I was, sort of. I really did have to pack, though—between the events of last night and the interview this morning, I wasn't even remotely ready to go.

As I stepped into the Guild lobby, I caught sight of Dira, the receptionist, on the phone. Remembering my visit with Comenius yesterday, I veered toward her desk, then waited until she was off the phone.

"Good morning, Miss Baine." Dira's eyes flickered in surprise at the sight of my outfit—she'd been too busy dealing with the morning crowd to notice me when I first came in. "What can I do for you?"

"Do you have pen and paper? I need you to get a message to Comenius Genhard, at Witches End."

Dira passed me the requested items, and I quickly scribbled out a note to Com, explaining my change in circumstances. I told him to go ahead with the sale of my jewels and the airship purchase in my absence, and apologized for not being able to say goodbye in person. I also mentioned the explosion from last night, and that I was fine and not to worry.

Fenris will let me know the moment Com learns anything new, I reminded myself as I hurried on toward my rooms. Even so, I couldn't push aside the anxiety twisting in my gut, or the fear that something was about to go horribly wrong for my friends.

DESPITE THE STRESSFUL MORNING, I felt my anxiety drop away as I watched Solantha recede, face pressed against the glass of the airship window. We were off to Dara without a hitch so far, and now I had to focus on getting through this trip as quickly as possible so I could be there for my friends.

"You're very tense." Iannis, who sat facing me, reached across and tugged me from my seat. I went willingly, allowing him to gather me onto his lap. He smelled faintly of roses this morning, and I buried my nose in the crook of his neck, inhaling the scent.

"Wandering in the gardens this morning?" I asked, pressing a kiss against his warm skin. "I didn't think you had time."

"I didn't, but I wanted to check again and see if there were any clues we'd missed that could lead us to the assassin." He stroked his big hand along the curve of my spine. "Is that why you're still so tense?"

I shook my head. "No, I'm just worried about my friends. And that stupid interview this morning put me even more on edge."

Iannis stilled. "Interview? Who did you speak to?"

I explained that Director Chen had scheduled a number of publicity interviews and meetings for me, and had cornered me into doing the first one that morning. When I told him how it had gone, and how I worried I'd made a fool of myself with Gena Chanie, he only sighed and kissed the top of my head.

"I will rein in Director Chen upon our return," he promised, holding me a little tighter. "You are not ready to deal with the press yet, and she should know better. As for your interview this morning, I doubt you said anything damaging, but I will teach you how to handle them more smoothly on future occasions. You cannot simply blurt out the first thing that comes to mind when journalists ask you a question."

"I know." I scowled as I turned to look out the window again. "I fucked up. I get it."

"I'm not blaming you." Iannis's fingers curled around my chin, and he turned my head so he could look into my eyes.

There was annoyance in his violet gaze, but concern as well. "Though I do wish you'd told me about the interview last night."

"Yeah, well, my mind was a little preoccupied after nearly being incinerated," I reminded him as I poked a finger in his chest. "As was yours."

"Indeed." Iannis pressed his lips together, glancing out the window and back at Solantha's receding shoreline. "I discussed the search for your attacker with Fenris this morning. He is going to inform the staff that everyone will have to submit to a truth spell upon my return, which I will administer personally."

"That could lead to the traitor making a run for it," I pointed out.

"Yes, and if that happens, he will have made himself known." Iannis's glittering gaze turned to ice. "Fenris is monitoring the employment records very closely. We will find out who it is. They will not escape retribution."

"And what happens if the guy doesn't leave, and he somehow manages to evade your truth spell?"

Iannis shrugged. "I suppose in that case, I would have to fire all the human staff."

"You can't just put people out of jobs like that," I argued, horrified at the idea that he'd put dozens of innocent people out of work. "Your servants are incredibly loyal, and to punish them like that will only increase resentment in the human population."

"That's a risk I'm willing to take if it means keeping you safe," Iannis said firmly, his hands banding around my upper arms. "You are mine, Sunaya Baine, and I won't let anyone take you away from me."

I sighed, fighting against the urge to roll my eyes. This macho-ness was getting a little ridiculous...but it was also incredibly sweet, and I didn't want to discourage Iannis. "That's fine," I said gently, placing my hands on his broad shoulders.

"But you're going to have to replace all those humans, and it would be all too easy for the Resistance to slip in even more spies."

"Then we'll require that all new employees submit themselves to truth testing. In fact, I may make that a new-hire policy in general, at least until the Resistance has been eradicated."

"And are you going to apply that same policy to mages?" I demanded, annoyed now. "In fact, shouldn't you be subjecting *all* employees to the truth test, and not just the human ones?"

Iannis's eyebrows winged up. "I doubt it was a mage who did this. No self-respecting mage would use a bomb to assassinate someone, not when there are so many magical means of doing so."

"Yeah, that's the obvious reasoning, isn't it?" I jabbed his chest with my finger again. "If a mage *did* use a bomb, it would automatically deflect suspicion away. And don't go around telling me it's impossible for one of your mages to be in with the Resistance. Not after what happened with Chartis."

"Hmm. You do make a good point there." Iannis's grip on my arms relaxed as a thoughtful look entered his eyes. "I will consider what you've said."

"Great." Aware that Iannis didn't want to talk about the subject further, I switched topics. "So, have you made any more headway regarding the Resistance prisoners?"

Iannis nodded. "A number of them have been sent to the mines already to carry out their sentences, or back to prison until the date of their execution. There are more yet who are still awaiting trial, including your cousin Rylan."

"Right." My mood darkened at the thought of Rylan Baine, my aunt Mafiela's youngest son, and a high-ranking officer in the Resistance. He and I had been close once, but after his betrayal, I wanted nothing to do with him.

"I thought to consult with you before tackling his case, but it seems as though you do not wish to discuss the subject," Iannis noted, stroking my cheek with his thumb. "Did something happen?"

"You can give him whatever sentence you want," I bit out. "He's a traitor, not just to our country, but to me as well."

Concern darkened Iannis's eyes. "What do you mean? Has your cousin done something else that I don't know of?"

I let out a slow breath. "He hired a witch to put a spell on me so that I would forget to warn you about the Resistance's plans to ambush you." Hot anger surged in my chest just thinking about it. All those times I'd gone to Iannis, intending to warn him not to get on the dirigible, or to hire extra security, or *whatever* it took to keep him safe. Whomever Rylan had hired to put the spell on me had been damn good, because looking back on it, I still couldn't tell that I'd been spelled. Every time I'd tried to warn Iannis, something had always come up to derail the conversation, and by the time it was over, I'd completely forgotten to tell him. If Rylan hadn't admitted the truth to me, I would still have trouble believing it had happened.

But it had. And Iannis had almost been killed as a result.

"I see," Iannis said slowly, but he didn't seem nearly as angry as I'd anticipated. "So Rylan prevented you from warning me, because doing so would have put *your* life in danger?"

"Yes, but he doesn't get to make that call. He doesn't get to decide whether or not I'm allowed to protect you."

"Indeed."

I narrowed my eyes at Iannis. "You're not seriously *agreeing* with Rylan's actions, are you?"

"No, but I also can't fault him for trying to protect you the best way he knew how."

I huffed. "Men. You're all the same when it comes to women. You'd rather hide us in the closet and keep us away from the action, even if we have skills and abilities that would be useful."

Iannis arched a brow, then looked around the cabin. "Unless I'm very much mistaken, we don't appear to be in a closet. In fact, I believe I'm taking you straight toward 'the action', as you put it."

I smirked. "You're such a smartass."

"Your attitude is clearly rubbing off on me." Iannis kissed me, quick and hard. "In any case, I will do as you suggest and assign an appropriate punishment for Rylan."

"What about Thorgana Mills?" I asked, now that we were on the subject. "She's on her way to Dara now, isn't she?" I had very mixed feelings on letting her out of state—she was incredibly dangerous. But the Minister had insisted on her extradition, and since she was a resident of Dara and her crimes were national rather than local, we had no choice but to relinquish her. The Minister hoped to get her to reveal additional information on the recent plot to kill and supplant him. There were probably other plots we had yet to discover, but it would not be an easy task to drag them out of her.

"She will be leaving within the next few days," Iannis confirmed. "I don't intend to let her set foot off Prison Isle without the most stringent security."

"Damn right." He'd better have a veritable army accompanying her.

"There is also the matter of dealing with Father Calmias," Iannis said. "He is proving quite troublesome."

"How so?" Despite his vicious, genocidal gospel, the famous preacher struck me as rather harmless, physically. He had a grandfatherly air about him, and besides, he was human. The prison guards shouldn't be having any trouble with him.

"Though he obviously incited the humans to riot and rebel, as you witnessed yourself, we can find no proof that he has done anything more tangible to aid the Resistance. The law is unclear on whether that is enough grounds for prolonged imprisonment, once an emergency is over. Many of his supporters are demanding that he be freed."

"Yeah, I noticed." On my way back from Shiftertown the other day, I'd taken a ride through Maintown to see how the humans were faring. Like the other sections of Solantha, repairs were underway. But I'd seen quite a few posters plastered around town with messages like 'FREE FATHER CALMIAS!' and 'FATHER CALMIAS IS INNOCENT!'.

"He's not innocent though, and, surely, you can charge him for preaching genocide, or something like that," I argued. There was no way a man like him should be allowed to roam free in the Federation—he never mentioned the Resistance in his sermons, only the Ur-God and His plans, but it stood to reason he must be in Thorgana's pocket.

"Agreed," Iannis said. "We have offered to let him go if he promised to stop encouraging his followers to engage in mass murder, but he rejected the deal without hesitation. Exile may be the only option, though that is not likely to appease his supporters."

"Yeah, well, as far as I'm concerned, his followers should be tossed into jail or exiled right along with him," I grumbled. Normally, I didn't believe people should be punished just for having contrary beliefs, but I was getting pretty fed up with the pro-Resistance humans.

Noria is a pro-Resistance human, a voice in my head reminded me.

Iannis and I talked for a little bit more, but eventually he set me off his lap so he could review a stack of reports he'd brought along. Figuring I might as well be industrious myself, I pulled *Spellcraft for Beginners,* the primer Janta had loaned me, from my bag. I opened the book and started reading, snacking on some walnut cookies as I did so. It was an interesting text, with lots of easy yet useful spells in it, but without a safe space to practice any of them, I was soon bored. An airship wasn't a suitable place for magical experiments.

"Where are you going?" Iannis asked as I rose from my chair and headed to the front.

"I'm going to bug the pilots to give me a lesson," I called over my shoulder. "I plan on owning one of these myself in the near future, and I'd like to be able to fly it."

Iannis twisted around in his chair, and I turned to look back at him, mere inches away from the double doors that separated the pilots from the main cabin. He stared at me for a long moment, as if he were considering strapping me down into my chair to prevent me from committing such a foolish action.

"Just don't kill us," he finally said, turning back around in his seat again. "The Minister won't be happy if we fail to show up for the meeting."

"Oh, I'll get us there on time," I said, grinning. I pulled open the doors and stepped into the pilots' cabin, prepared to convince them to let me take over. After all, if Annia could fly one of these contraptions, then I sure as hell could learn how. And I might need to, if I was going to get her out of that Resistance camp in one piece.

nlike the last time we came to Dara, we didn't land the dirigible on the front lawn of the Capitol Dome. I wanted to, of course, but the pilots wouldn't let me. In fact, they shooed me back to the main cabin because they didn't want to risk me crash-landing at the airport. Disappointing, but not exactly surprising—I'd done well enough for a first lesson, but I was no pilot yet, that was for sure.

"I didn't expect you to be up there for the entire flight," Iannis remarked as I sat back down into my chair. "You'll need to freshen up a bit before we get off the aircraft."

"Huh?" I glanced down at myself, then noticed the crumbs clinging to the bodice of the satin green dress I wore. Unlike the ridiculous lacy confection I'd worn for my interview, this one was quite comfortable and easy to move in. But I couldn't go before the Minister with crumbs on it, and I probably needed to redo my makeup too.

"Here, let me help you," Iannis said, standing as I got up to retrieve my bag from the overhead compartment. He settled his hands on my waist to pull me forward, then gently slid one hand down my front, brushing stray crumbs away.

"Are you cleaning me up, or trying to cop a feel?" I asked, raising a brow.

"I can always do both," Iannis murmured, dipping his head down. He kissed me lightly, then skimmed his fingertips over my cheeks. The scent of magic tickled my nostrils as tingles skipped up my face, and Iannis smiled, stepping back.

"Perfect." He pulled a small, circular mirror from his sleeve and handed it to me. "You're all set now."

"Is there anything you *don't* keep in that weird magical compartment of yours?" I asked, examining myself in the mirror. Iannis had used magic to freshen up my makeup, and I had to admit the effect was beautiful, and much less time-consuming. My eyeliner was bold and dramatic, my lips red and glistening, and the light dusting of blush on my cheeks gave me a healthy glow. Even my hair, pulled back from my face and artfully arranged with jeweled pins and clips, looked like I had just come from the salon.

"I believe in being prepared," Iannis said, smiling down at me. "You look stunning, by the way."

"Thanks to you." Grinning, I returned to my seat, and we settled in for the landing. It didn't take us long to disembark from the dirigible, and it was pleasant to head directly into the waiting carriage without worrying about our luggage. The steward would take it directly to our hotel.

"We're only staying one night, right?" I asked as we drove along the paved streets, heading toward the Capitol Dome, which was on the west side of town. Beyond the curtains, the city rolled past—much less crowded at this late hour than the bustling city I remembered from my last visit, but still imposing and well lit. It was far later than one would generally expect to conduct a political meeting after traveling across the country. But as Iannis had told me more than once, this was an urgent mission, and holding a high office meant working long and irregular hours.

"We'll leave the moment we are done," Iannis assured me. "Of course, you understand that things can change, and if the Minister wants us to stay longer, we can hardly refuse."

"Indeed." I pressed my lips together as I thought of Zavian Graning, the Minister of the Northia Federation. Iannis and I had saved him from almost certain death the last time we were here. If not for my sleuthing skills and Iannis's healing talents, he would be rotting in his grave. That didn't mean I particularly liked Graning, or approved of his politics as the highest mage in the country. After all, he didn't seem too friendly toward shifters, judging by the fact that there seemed to be none in Dara. Then again, a nice and straightforward mage would hardly have been able to climb to such a powerful position.

The Benefactor had been the master manipulator behind the plot against the Minister—I was sure of it, even though she still hadn't admitted to the crime. Or any crime, in fact. If Cedris ar'Tarea, her would-be puppet, had managed to take power, Thorgana would have pulled his strings behind the scenes until the entire Federation came toppling down. I shuddered as I remembered just how close we had come to losing everything at the Convention. As bad as things still were, they could have turned out much, much worse.

The carriage rolled to a stop outside the Capitol Dome, and a footman opened the door for us. Iannis disembarked, then helped me down from the carriage. I managed to remember to take his hand and let him guide me instead of jumping down with my skirts flying everywhere. A damn good thing, too, because all eyes were glued on us. Given the late hour, there were a surprising number of mages about, on the steps and the grass, clustered in pairs or trios as they talked about politics, or perhaps which blend of tea their secretaries brewed for them, but whatever they discussed seemed quickly forgotten at the sight of Iannis and me.

Or maybe it was just me.

Truthfully, it was hard to tell which of us was drawing more attention, or perhaps it was the sight of us together, arm in arm, as we walked up the white marble steps to the entrance of the Dome. Unlike last time, I wasn't disguised as a mage, and my bottle-green shifter eyes were on display for all to see. Whispers ensued as we passed, some of them uncomplimentary, others simply disbelieving. They'd heard the rumors, but they hadn't been sure what to think of them until Iannis and I had shown up.

Now it was official. Now the whole world would know, without a doubt, that the Chief Mage of Canalo had engaged himself to a bastard hybrid shifter. And his apprentice, at that.

"Pay them no mind." Iannis's voice murmured in my head as he gently squeezed my forearm. *"They will settle down soon enough, once they realize you are not a passing whim and that I intend to keep you by my side."*

"Of course," I replied as we stepped over the threshold of the huge, gilded double doors. The guards bowed as we passed, and I returned their greeting with a strained smile. I didn't doubt that Iannis would stay by my side, but it was still hard to walk by these people as they tittered behind their hands. I saw coins exchanged several times, and knew they were betting on how long Iannis would take to come to his senses and call the engagement off.

Glossy mosaic tiles patterned the floors of the entrance hall, under arching ceilings decorated with runes. The center of the large space was dominated by a fountain sculpture of the Founding Trio—Jeremidah, Faonus, and Micara. The three mages stood in a circle, back to back, and water burbled into the marble basin from their outstretched hands. If one looked into the fountain itself, they could see a mosaic pattern of the Northia Federation beneath the water. The message was clear—these three, through their power, had given life to the Federation, and were forever honored for their service.

"Good evening, Lord Iannis, Miss Baine." Pamina, the receptionist greeted us. "Welcome back to Dara." Her brown eyes lingered on me, bright with curiosity and maybe a little envy. As human, I imagined she would be jealous of my position, considering I was a hybrid.

"Thank you, Pamina." Lord Iannis inclined his head. "We are here to see Minister Graning."

"He is expecting you," she said, and gestured to a well-dressed mage who had been hovering in the background. "This is Loris ar'Mengis, one of the Minister's aides. He will escort you."

The young man bowed to Iannis, somehow including me without bowing again. "If you will follow me, Chief Mage, Miss Baine."

Iannis could have easily led the way by himself, but apparently, we were required to have an escort. The aide led us down the entrance hall, then to the right. We passed the coffee shop at the corner, where I'd spent the bulk of my time during the last Convention, eavesdropping on conversations between mages in an attempt to discover the Minister's location. Toward the end of the hall, a set of carpeted stairs led toward the offices. I'd tried in vain to get up there the last time I was here, but it had been guarded too well. There was no way to get up there without drawing attention to myself and possibly compromising my disguise.

This time, however, I had no disguise to compromise. And since Iannis and I were escorted by the Minister's aide, there was nothing to stop us from going up those stairs.

Just like last time, there were two guards posted at the

entrance, and they bowed to us as we passed. My heels made barely a sound against the red carpet as we climbed the staircase and stepped into a smaller, but no less well-appointed lobby.

"Welcome, Lord Iannis." Another receptionist sat behind another glossy desk. This one had pale blonde hair pulled back from her face into an elegant updo, and she wore mage robes of moss green. "And Miss Baine," she added, her grey eyes narrowing ever so slightly as she acknowledged me. "The Minister is expecting you both."

Ar'Mengis nodded to her and led us down a long hallway. Portraits of previous Federation politicians graced the papered walls. They looked down at me scornfully, as if to suggest I didn't belong there. I ignored their judgmental stares and kept my head high as the aide rapped lightly on the heavy wooden door at the end of the hall.

"Come in," a firm, commanding voice called from the other side, and the aide pushed it open.

Iannis and I were ushered into a large office decorated in red, white, and gold—the Northia Federation's colors. It was a grand space, with a well-appointed sitting area on one side of the room, and a large desk, shelving, and chairs on the other. At the desk sat the Minister, who looked to have been in the middle of reading a report. Behind him, a trio of large glass windows provided a gorgeous view of the glittering city.

"Good evening, Minister," Iannis said, bowing. I did the same, though I stayed silent and studied the Minister through my lowered lashes. His long, yellow hair was tied back at the nape of his neck, leaving his austere features unframed. He was dressed in red-and-gold robes that I knew would help him cut a fine figure standing. It was those robes, and his commanding presence, that made others sit up and take notice—his facial features themselves were rather ordinary, nothing in comparison to Iannis's masculine beauty.

"Good evening, Lord Iannis, Miss Baine." The Minister gestured to the glossy, hand-carved visitors' chairs that perched on the red-and-gold rug in front of his desk. "Have a seat, please. There is much to discuss."

As Iannis and I obeyed, the Minister gave me a good, long look, eyes traveling up and down my body. I tensed slightly—it wasn't a sexual gaze, but a clinical one, as though he was measuring my worth based on his ocular examination.

"I appreciate you coming on short notice," he told Iannis, flicking his chocolate-brown gaze away from me.

"Of course. You said the matter was urgent."

"It is indeed." The Minister paused, his gaze turning back to me. "I have not yet had the chance to congratulate you on your engagement, Miss Baine."

I blinked, surprised he wasn't launching into the mission details immediately. "Thank you, Minister."

"You realize, of course, that a union between a man of Lord Iannis's status and yourself is a highly unusual affair, if not outright taboo," the Minister continued, his voice growing stern.

I lifted my chin a little. "A number of mages have already informed me of that."

"I imagine they would have." A faint smile crossed the Minister's face. "I have decided not to oppose the union, because shifter-mage relations are strained right now. Coming between the two of you would only make things worse." The Minister leaned forward now, his eyes narrowing dangerously on me. "But make no mistake, Miss Baine, if you fail to publicly conduct yourself in a manner befitting your new station, and embarrass the mage community in any way, I will have you exiled from this country."

"Would you? I would leave with my fiancée, in that case," Iannis said, his voice as cold as I'd ever heard it. "We came here to fight against the Resistance, not to listen to pointless threats."

His eyes bored into the Minister's, who averted his own gaze after a moment.

I kept my back ramrod stiff in my chair, my hands splayed comfortably in my lap. I wouldn't give the Minister the satisfaction of shouting at him, or clenching the fabric of my skirts. After all, he was just waiting for any sign that I was an uncouth shifter girl, slave to my animalistic instincts and unfit to sit at the table with the important mages.

Well, fuck him. I would show them all that I was good enough to sit at the table with the big kids, despite the fact that I was half-shifter. Hell, I would show them I was *more* than good enough *because* of my heritage as a half-shifter.

You are not merely the sum of your parts, Sunaya Baine, Resinah had said to me once. *Whole, you have the potential to be stronger than both your shifter and mage ancestors.*

"Are you ready to tell us why you needed our assistance?" Iannis asked. His expression was calm, but I could sense the fury thrumming under his rigid control.

"Yes, it might be best to move on," the Minister said with a slightly nervous glance at Iannis. He initialed the report he'd been reading and tucked it away before giving us his full attention. "As you know, I have recently expended a great deal of time and effort to thoroughly purge my office of anyone untrustworthy."

"Yes, I remember." The anger in Iannis's eyes died away, replaced by intensity as he focused on the subject that had brought us three thousand miles away from home. "Have you discovered something useful during said purging?"

"Indeed I have." The Minister scowled. "I managed to identify the human staff member who administered the drug which made me so ill—according to her confession, it was put into the milk I use with my coffee. I have taken to drinking it black now. Thank the Creator that you were able to cure me. It seems the conspirators were confident that no mage would be able to do so."

"Healing is one of my stronger talents," Iannis said drily. "It was not easy, even for me, especially as we caught it so late."

"Just so. After lengthy questioning, the staff member, who worked in the Capitol kitchens as an assistant cook, confessed that the substance she put in my milk came from a Doctor Elan Mitas. He's a physician with a successful practice right here in Dara." The Minister's lips twisted into a grim smile. "For some reason, the idiot human had chosen not to flee, so it was easy enough to apprehend him."

"That is excellent news!" Iannis leaned forward a little, like a bloodhound that had suddenly latched onto a promising scent. "What have you learned from him?"

"Not nearly enough." The Minister frowned, looking quite irritated now. "He has a remarkably strong mind and is resistant to truth spells, which is likely why the Benefactor recruited him in the first place. But we had his house and practice searched, and postal receipts in his house lead us to suspect that the substance might have been forwarded from somewhere in the Northwest. We did find one smallish parcel dispatched from Wacoma. However, there is no proof, and it might have contained something else entirely. Dr. Mitas refuses to say."

Iannis looked grave. "That is not much to go on, but better than nothing. You want us to follow up on the origins of this deadly substance?"

"Of course." The Minister's face tightened. "We must assume that this substance was not produced for single use only. Thorgana and her henchmen may be manufacturing more of these lethal diseases to target specific people or races. Perhaps even on a large scale. I would not have thought mere humans capable of such feats, without magic and with those short lives of theirs, but clearly we have been underestimating their cunning."

By Magorah. Icy horror spread through my chest. Those must be the secret weapons the humans had been whispering about. Some powder or liquid dropped in a jug of milk, or perhaps mixed into a city's water supply by the human maintenance crew, could not easily be defended against. I already knew the humans pulling the strings behind the Resistance were planning to kill off entire populations, but I thought that was just talk. Would they actually succeed?

"I need you to locate this manufacturing lab or plant and destroy it before the Resistance can deploy their newfangled weapons," the Minister commanded. "It would be a disaster, should they actually use them to massacre unsuspecting citizens. Not to mention embarrassing, since we've assured the country they are safe, now that we've caught the mastermind of this evil plot."

"Agreed," Iannis said, his eyes narrowed. "It is a pity Thorgana is not here yet, as I imagine she would know the exact location."

"That's true, but we can still question the doctor, right?" I asked. The men turned to look at me, the Minister blinking, as though surprised to hear me speak up. "Shifters are very good at telling truth from lies, and as an enforcer, I'm an experienced interrogator. You should let me question the doctor."

"That was my plan, actually," the Minister said wryly. "But thank you for volunteering."

"You're welcome," I said, my cheeks heating in embarrassment. So, apparently, the Minister considered me a useful tool, and not just a liability. At least that was something.

"Is there anyone else we can interrogate?" I asked. "What about Lord Cedris, or his Legal Secretary, Coman ar'Daghir?"

"They have already been questioned thoroughly. It was found they had no direct knowledge of Thorgana or their operations," the Minister said firmly. "Both have been released, upon condition that Cedris resign from public office, which he has done. He is spending more time with his family these days, and I hear he's thinking of writing a memoir."

"I see," I murmured, burying my disgust and incredulity. I would have thought the Minister would punish Cedris harshly for his not inconsiderable role in the plot to kill him and take his position. Why was he being so lenient? Did Cedris have some sort of hold over him, just as Thorgana had been blackmailing Cedris and a number of other mages in order to control them?

Fucking politics, I thought. I hated all the layers involved, and wished I didn't have to have anything to do with it. But that was impossible if I was going to be married to Iannis, and if I wanted to effect change within our unfair system.

"Well, I see no need to waste time." The Minister clapped his hands together, then rose from his seat. "Mr. ar'Mengis will take you to the doctor now, and Miss Baine can prove her worth by getting some answers out of him."

Great. *No pressure.*

11

The Minister's taciturn aide escorted us to the prison via carriage. Even though it was well after midnight, I wasn't at all tired—I was eager to get on with the job and find out everything we could. It took about half an hour before we drew up in front of Dara's main prison facility, a large, ugly building that rested right at the fork of the Motoac River. The reinforced windows and the runes set into the walls and gates suggested that it was secure, protected both magically and physically. It must be incredibly difficult to escape from there, a thought that comforted me since I knew Thorgana would be kept in this very facility once she arrived in the capital.

The aide didn't actually go with us to the prisoners' cells, but was very helpful to get us through several levels of guards without hassle. The Minister's office had clearly phoned ahead, asking for every assistance to be rendered. We were led to a soundproofed chamber the prison officials called a 'special interview room'. Iannis and I made ourselves as comfortable as we could in the cold, dimly lit stone chamber, sitting at a bare metal table on bolted-down metal chairs as we waited for Doctor Mitas to be brought in.

"So how are we doing this?" I asked quietly. "Are you asking all the questions, or are we taking turns?"

"I would prefer to take the lead," Iannis said, "but as your nose can determine whether or not he speaks truth or falsehood, you can intervene when you sense a weakness. As a human, he won't be able to tell if *we* are truthful, and he will already be predisposed to expect the very worst of mages or shifters. That may help us intimidate him."

The door opened, and two guards led the prisoner in. Doctor Mitas was a middle-aged, lean man with dark brown hair, round, wire-rimmed spectacles, and a handlebar mustache that gave him a respectable air, at odds with the black-and-white striped prisoner uniform he wore. His thin wrists were weighed down by heavy manacles. Nevertheless, he kept his shoulders straight and his chin high, and regarded us with a haughty look as he was guided none too gently into the chair across from us. The guards left us alone, but said they would be right outside, within calling distance.

"Good evening, Doctor Mitas," Iannis said pleasantly, once the door had shut behind them. "I am Chief Mage Iannis ar'Sannin, and this is my apprentice, Sunaya Baine."

"I know who you are," Doctor Mitas said in a cultured, snooty voice. His bird-like nose twitched as he regarded me, and his lip curled. "A Chief Mage and a hybrid, set to be wed. What a strange world we live in, don't you think?"

"Some might consider such a match to be progress," Iannis pointed out. "The union of a shifter and a mage is a step in the direction of equality amongst the races."

"Pah!" The doctor's eyes narrowed behind his spectacles. "Perhaps, if one agreed that equality between the races was possible. But I do not. The illegitimate mage regime must be overthrown if humans are to regain their rightful position in this world."

"How about shifters?" I asked, curious to know if he ascribed to Father Calmias and Thorgana's genocidal views. "Are they to be eradicated as well? Or do you believe that they have an equal place in society?"

Doctor Mitas's sniffed. "I don't believe you dragged me from my cell to discuss my views on shifters."

"Indeed we did not," Iannis said, his voice growing stern. "We came to ask you about disease-spreading substances the Resistance is manufacturing."

The doctor's stare did not waver. "I don't know what you're talking about."

"*Lie*," I mentally told Iannis, though it was obvious anyway.

Iannis said nothing for a long moment, while the doctor's gaze slid away and fixed on a dent in the metal table.

"This is a waste of time," I said in a bored voice. "This guy looks like a minion, the kind nobody would trust with confidential details. He probably knows nothing useful about the origin of the sickness."

A tiny smirk lifted the corners of the prisoner's mouth.

"Is that so?" Iannis said sternly.

"As I said, I don't know anything." The doctor sounded downright smug now. Iannis and I exchanged a glance.

"For all we know, what he used was nothing special, just a garden-variety poison," I declared, hoping the doctor would not know Iannis himself had healed the Minister. "Does this guy look intelligent enough to even know what he was doing? Curing shingles or ear infections is probably more his speed."

Dr. Mitas shifted in his chair, and I held back a grin as my nose detected a strong sense of indignation from him. "I object to being insulted by a shifter!" he insisted, his eyes blazing at me. "One who hasn't the remotest idea what she's talking about."

"Then prove her wrong," Iannis said pointedly. "Tell us where you got the substance used to make the Minister sick."

"Did the substance arrive via mail?" I asked while he was still off-balance.

"No!" I could smell the lie. "That is, I have nothing to say on the subject." He cleared his throat, attempting to regain his composure.

I smirked, getting in his face by leaning forward and invading his personal space. My sensitive nose picked up the cold sweat erupting on his neck. "I suspect it came from the Northwest."

Panic flashed in his eyes, confirmation enough for the moment.

"Perhaps from the town of Wacoma?" Iannis asked softly.

Dr. Mitas jerked. "Why are you asking me, if you already know?"

"Have you ever been there personally?" I followed up.

"No." He sullenly glared at me.

"*Truth,*" I told Iannis. Aloud, I said, "But you know what is being produced there, and for what purpose?"

Though he did not reply out loud, it was easy for me to read him. "He knows," I told Iannis, out loud. "Does it not trouble your conscience as a medical man, Dr. Mitas, to be involved in wholesale killing? I would not want to be one of your patients, if you are so careless of human life."

He bridled at the accusation. "My patients are human. I do not consider mages or shifters to fall under my medical oath. My loyalty is to humanity, and I'm proud of my allegiance to the Resistance."

Ha! It looked like the dam was finally breaking.

"The Resistance?" I jeered, curling my lip at him. "I hate to break it to you, but you've chosen the losing side, buddy. Now that the Benefactor is in our custody, your cause is doomed. I'm sure she would have no qualms about selling out her comrades in order to lessen her sentence."

"Pah!" The doctor looked down his nose at me, which was an impressive feat considering he was an inch shorter. "The Benefactor is far more clever than either of you could hope to be. Our cause will triumph with or without her." The firm conviction in his tone sent a shiver down my spine, but I kept my posture relaxed, determined not to let him see the effect his dire prediction had on me.

"And without you as well, it looks like," I said, arching my eyebrows. His shoulders slumped slightly at the reminder. I was pretty sure he would receive the death penalty for his role in nearly assassinating the highest official of the mage government.

"Yes, it is too bad I probably won't see it," the doctor admitted. "But I am not the only specialist working for the human race." He bared his teeth in a savage smile. "I was looking forward to the pleasure of administering diseases to all the mages in Dara."

"All of them?" I asked, hiding my horror. "You mean at once?"

The doctor laughed. "No, it will happen inconspicuously, and will look as though the mages are dying of natural causes. I don't mind telling you, as you won't be able to stop it." That expectation seemed to afford him great satisfaction. "Whatever happens to me, I shall soon be avenged."

Iannis regarded him with disgust. "What's to stop the Federation from bringing healers in, to cure the mages you and your confederates infect?"

Doctor Mitas scoffed. "I believe you noticed it was extraordinarily difficult for you to cure the Minister of his illness, wasn't it?"

So he was aware of that, after all. When Iannis said nothing, the doctor smiled coldly. "We are focusing on diseases that are resistant to magical healing. There are simply not enough first-rate healers to deal with an epidemic, and, with any luck, those will be the first to die." He smirked openly now.

"This is crazy!" I snapped, unable to hold my tongue any longer. "If these diseases can't be cured by magic, then what are you going to do when they spread to the human population as well? Or are you so keen to kill off your own kind?"

The doctor gave me a patronizing smile. "The humans will be quite safe. Shifters, of course, are another story."

My muscles coiled, and Iannis put his hand on my leg to keep me from lunging across the table and grabbing the smug bastard by the throat. "Doctor Mitas," he said in a cold, commanding voice, "You will tell us exactly where those diseases are being manufactured, right now."

I had never seen such a stern, compelling expression on his face. The doctor was staring into his eyes as though mesmerized. Iannis must be using persuasion, despite the Minister's assurance that the prisoner was resistant. Yet, what mere human would be strong enough to stand against Iannis's power, when he had Tua blood flowing through his veins? Iannis's hand on my leg was tense now, so it could not be an easy spell to maintain, whatever it was.

The staring duel lasted for over thirty seconds before the doctor's eyes fell. "I have not been there myself," he said in a strange, faraway voice. "But I am nearly certain the place is in Nika, a small town in Osero."

"Nika? That is fairly close to Parabas, isn't it?" Iannis asked, referring to Osero's state capital.

"Yes."

"Very well." Iannis released whatever spell he had employed to force the doctor to confess. The prisoner's lips thinned as he sat back in his chair.

"You may have tricked me with your thrice-damned mage

power," he spat, bitter resentment burning in his gaze, "but the information will not do you any good. No mage can breach the facility's walls."

"Why is that?" Iannis demanded.

The doctor shrugged. "I don't know, but I have it on good authority that even if your kind discovered the place, you would never be able to get into the labs." He bared his teeth at us. "So go to Osero, if you must. You won't get in, and if the Ur-God is just, you might very well end up being our first victims."

WE BRIEFED the Minister in the comfort of his home, before retiring to our rooms at the Crystal Hotel for a much needed late-night dinner. We would leave for Parabas just before noon, after grabbing a few hours of sleep. The Minister would contact the Chief Mage of Osero and ensure his full cooperation with our mission. The Capitol library would provide us a map of Nika and its environs before we left, so that we could be prepared for what lay ahead.

"It is quite possible that we may not be able to get into the lab, as the doctor suggests," Iannis said, his arm curled around me as we lay in bed, showered and fed now. He'd booked two adjoining rooms, my luggage was in the second one, but I had no intention of sleeping in a separate bed. "Certain wards are impossible to break, even for me. In that case, we may have to destroy the entire building from outside."

"And kill all the people in it?" I frowned. "What if they have innocents in there? They may use test subjects they're experimenting on, perhaps even mages, if they are trying to create a formula to target them specifically."

"It would be regrettable, but I don't see that we have a

choice," Iannis said. "We cannot risk the lives of the entire Federation for the sake of a few."

I sighed. I hated that sort of thing—sacrificing one to save the lives of many—but I couldn't argue against the logic in this scenario. If the Resistance was using innocent test subjects, they were probably going to die anyway, so blowing up the building would only accelerate their tragic fate. "Still, if there is any way to stop this madness without resorting to mass killings, we should try to find it."

"Of course."

I slept uneasily that night, despite being cradled in Iannis's warm, comforting embrace. My thoughts were too tangled up in my worries for me to settle down. How were Annia and Elnos faring? What was Noria up to? Had Comenius received any word from them? I wished I could rush to their side now, but I had to admit the news about the Osero lab was extremely troubling. If I was being fair and logical, shutting it down was more urgent than rescuing my friends.

But I wasn't an automaton. Just because I knew in my head that going to Parabas first was the right thing to do, didn't mean I felt as certain about that in my heart. I was conflicted, torn between the desire to do two things that were, in their own ways, equally important to me.

An urgent knock at the door woke me, and I shot upright, my heart pounding. Who was at the door? Was it a message from Fenris? Had something happened?

"I'll get it," Iannis murmured, placing a hand on my upper arm. "Lie back down."

I did as he asked, burrowing beneath the bedclothes while he donned a robe and answered the door. Under different circumstances, I would have balked, but we couldn't let an unknown servant see the two of us in bed together. So, instead, I hid and waited, listening to the messenger tell Iannis that he had received an urgent message from Solantha Palace.

"It's from Fenris," Iannis said, sitting down on the bed and unfolding the single sheet of paper. His violet eyes narrowed as he scanned the words. "He says that Annia is in trouble, and Elnos has lost contact with her."

"What?" I shot upright again, my fists clenching in the bed sheets as fear coursed through my veins. "What kind of trouble? How did they get separated?"

"The message doesn't say," Iannis said, his brow creasing. "Comenius received an ether pigeon from Elnos, and the information contained was rather brief. Apparently, Elnos and Annia tracked Noria to Nika, Osero, and Elnos awaits reinforcements at the local inn."

"Nika!" I exclaimed. "Do you think that Noria is in the very same plant that we're about to destroy?"

"I'm afraid it would be too coincidental for that not to be the case. She's an inventor, after all. I could see why the Resistance would find her useful there."

"Well then we can't just go in and blow it up." I threw off the sheets and began pacing next to the bed. "If Noria is in there, we have to get her out."

"As I said, we will do what we can, but remember that Noria is a traitor," Iannis warned. "She chose her side, and is assisting the Resistance in committing genocide."

"I can't believe she would willingly participate in that. Who knows what they have her doing, and what she's been told." Groaning, I shoved my hands into my mass of curly hair and tugged, hard. Why was everything going to hell right now? "Annia could very well be in there with her, and *she* certainly doesn't deserve to die. All she wanted was to save her little sister."

Iannis sighed. "That is true. And I owe Annia a debt for her part in my rescue." He stroked his chin for a moment, considering. "I have to meet with the local Chief Mage, but it makes sense to find Elnos first, and get a clearer picture of the situation. If he is staying in a local inn in a small town like that, he should be easy enough to find."

"Great. So we're leaving now, right?"

"Just as soon as you get your clothes on."

12

The aerial view of Osero was impossibly beautiful. Pressing my nose against the glass window in the dirigible's cabin, I stared out at the rolling hills and wide open valleys, covered in greenery as far as the eye could see. Lakes and rivers shimmered like liquid silver in the afternoon sunlight, and I imagined all sorts of creatures teeming in the vast wilderness spread before me.

"It's not all forests," Iannis commented from his seat across from mine. His violet eyes were fixed on the view outside the window as well. "Though it does seem that way from up above."

"I know that," I said, tracing a dirt road with my finger that was barely visible from this height. "We've seen some small towns already, and I imagine the capital will be much bigger."

"Yes," Iannis agreed, "though not as large as Solantha. I have been to Parabas—it is quite cosmopolitan for its size, and many foreign magic users have settled there. Homeschooling is quite popular, so some humans escape magical screening and end up under the tutelage of witches and other foreign magic practitioners. The local Mages Guild generally turns a blind eye, unless any of these humans get out of control and cause real damage."

"And what happens then?" I asked, very interested given my own past.

"The human has their powers stripped, and the mentor faces imprisonment or hard labor in the mines."

I winced. On the one hand, that didn't seem very fair... but on the other hand, at least these humans had a chance to practice magic.

"I know that not all humans born with magic are automatically mages, but how do you know if they're a mage or a witch or whatever?" I asked. "I've always been a little confused on that point."

Iannis sighed, rubbing at his temple. "There are varying degrees of magical ability. Mages, witches, and sorcerers just practice their magic talent in different ways. Your friend Comenius, for example, could have been a mage of middling strength, had he not been raised as a hedge-witch, as could his lady friend, Elania. But there are others who only have a very small amount of magic, and that magic tends to manifest in a certain way. That is why you have healers and fortune tellers and the like—they can perform a specific kind of magic, but nothing else."

"So then, what happens if a human who's actually a mage is mentored by a healer?"

"Those are the cases where things get out of control," Iannis said gravely. "A healer would not be able to properly control the strength of a budding mage. Though these people try to be careful about who they take in, sometimes they make mistakes and accept an apprentice whose powers are beyond them."

"I'm guessing this is why you don't use a similar system in Canalo," I said dryly.

"Indeed." Iannis let out a small sigh. "However, Parabas

suffers a surprisingly low number of troublesome cases, some-what to the surprise of other states. We are watching what is happening here with interest, as you can imagine. This particular system has only been in place the last fifteen years or so, but I would not be surprised if the Chief Mage, Logar ar'Dronach, decided to implement it across all of Osero once it has been smoothed out a little bit more."

"Huh." I frowned at that. "What does Minister Graning think of this?"

"It is not up to him, as only the Convention can impose its rules on a state government. The Chief Mages are allowed to do as they wish so long as they operate within Federation guidelines and the Great Accord, and the Chief Mage of Osero is not openly breaking any laws." Iannis rubbed his chin in thought. "Given the current upheavals that demonstrate the shortcomings of the status quo, the Convention may look at experimental government systems such as the one in Parabas with a more open mind. If Chief Mage ar'Dronach succeeds, many other states could follow his example. Or there might be a backlash against experimentation. It is too soon to tell."

"Do you think it's coincidence, then, that the Resistance chose Osero as their breeding ground for this secret weapon of theirs?" I asked. "I imagine that the idea of magic growing even stronger in the Federation would go against their plans."

"Indeed. I do wonder how they plan to deal with humans who continue to be born with magic, if they were to ever succeed in eradicating us mages. They can hardly subject them to magic wipes, with no mages left to administer them."

"I bet Thorgana would just have them killed at the first sign of any magical talent." My upper lip curled at that. No, I didn't approve of the current system, where humans had to choose between execution or a magic wipe, but it was still better than indiscriminately killing anyone who was born with magic.

A gloomy silence settled over the cabin, and we didn't speak for the rest of the flight, too caught up in our respective thoughts. Once we landed at the Parabas airport, Iannis ordered our luggage delivered to Parabas Palace, where we would be staying as guests of the Chief Mage. But true to his word, we did not go along with our bags. Instead, our carriage took us straight to Nika, a ride of some two hours, we were told.

From what we had learned so far, Nika was a small town, perhaps only eighteen thousand strong. That seemed insignificant compared to Solantha's nearly half a million citizens, and I wondered what it was like to live in such a community. From what I could observe as we drew close, it was a thriving place, mostly comprised of sprawling, one- and two-story homes on big lots, with winding roads to connect them to each other as well as the small clusters of shops and municipal buildings. We'd passed some farms on our way in, bursting with cattle, sheep, and fruit-laden orchards. The map Iannis and I studied during our ride told us that industrial buildings were located on the outskirts of town, away from residential homes. We picked out a canning factory, a sawmill, a tannery, and a shoe factory.

"Where do you think the Resistance is most likely to be hiding out?" I asked.

Iannis frowned as he studied the map, which I'd spread across my lap. His long forefinger traced the main road that wound through the town, then drew a semi-circle across the northern end, along the edge of the wilderness.

"I suspect that it might be behind one of these factories, or perhaps even *part* of one," Iannis said. "We could question the townsfolk to see if they've noticed any suspicious activity, but that would draw unwanted attention. Let's hope Elnos will provide more information."

He folded the map up. "Time to disguise ourselves, I think. A middle-aged human couple should not attract too much attention, don't you agree?

"I guess so," I said, closing my eyes as he reached for my face. It didn't take too long for him to transform me, and then himself. Judging by the thin, nondescript form he'd chosen as a disguise, I was glad I couldn't see my new disguise in full. I was having a hard enough time with the checkered blouse and tweed skirt he'd put me in.

The carriage pulled up outside the Black Lion Inn, where Elnos had instructed us to meet him. It was a two-story, stacked-stone building, with dark grey curtains in the casement windows, and four chimneys jutting from the slate rooftop. Not a particularly cheery-looking place, but a sturdy one that could withstand the rainy weather Osero was known for, and the heavy winter snows.

Iannis held the front door open, and I stepped over the threshold, out of the summer heat into the comparatively cool confines. Unlike the inn's outside, the interior was very inviting—the floors and walls were paneled with warm, honey-colored wood, and the smell of spiced tea and fresh meat pies laced the cool air. A woman in a blue serge dress came bustling forward, ready to attend us. Off to the left was a hallway that likely led to the kitchens and offices, and to the right was a large, open common room, complete with a fireplace, wingback chairs, coffee tables, and rugs. Above the hearth, I noted a wooden shield with a lion's head on it, painted in black. There were lions in other places too—the patterned rugs, the candlestick holders, and furniture carvings.

"Good afternoon," the woman said in a pleasant voice. "Welcome to the Black Lion Inn. Are you staying long?"

"We're here to meet a friend," Iannis said. "He's waiting for us in the common area."

"We could use some food though," I mentioned, holding up a finger before Iannis could drag me over there.

"Gallie, our server, should be coming around to the common room in a few moments," the woman assured us with a smile. "You go off and meet your friend, and I'll let her know that you two will want something to eat."

"As I recall, you ate three helpings on the flight," Iannis commented in my head as we walked away, a smirk in his voice. I could feel the woman's curious gaze on us as we passed through the entrance to the right.

"Yeah, but I'm still hungry. And besides, there may not be much food wherever Elnos is taking us." Any smart shifter fueled up every chance she got, and as a magic user, I needed even more energy than the average shifter.

It wasn't hard to find Elnos—he was wearing the same disguise he'd donned before leaving town, and was sitting in a chair by the fire, gazing toward the window, his features tight with strain. He turned his head as we approached and jumped a little in his chair, no doubt sensing the magic that provided our glamour.

"Hey," I greeted him quietly in my my own voice. "It's Sunaya, and Iannis."

Elnos's mouth opened in surprise, and he jumped up from his seat. "L--" He caught himself just before he shouted Iannis's name aloud. "Lord Iannis, Sunaya," he said more quietly as he enfolded me into a quick hug. "I'm so glad you were able to get here on such short notice." He looked absolutely nothing like the fresh-faced, gangly young mage that I knew—the man hugging me was more filled out, sporting a leather jacket and dark sunglasses rather than mage robes.

"As it turns out, you've landed smack dab in the middle of a mission the Minister's sent us on," I said as Iannis and I settled onto the couch across from Elnos.

"What?" Elnos's eyes widened. "Do you mean to say that the Federation has taken a special interest in the Resistance compound here?"

"Be quiet a moment," Iannis warned, lifting his hand. He muttered a Word and snapped his fingers. My nose twitched as the scent of magic laced the air, shimmering around us for an instant like a pearly soap bubble.

"There," Iannis said, sitting back and making himself comfortable. "No one will be able to overhear us."

"Really?" I arched a brow, and filed away the Word he'd muttered for later use. "That's a nifty trick."

"I should have thought to do that. Sorry." Elnos sighed, scrubbing a hand over the lower half of his face. "I've just been so... frazzled, these past few days."

"Yeah, you mentioned that you and Annia had been separated," I said, my mood dropping. "What happened?"

"About ten days ago, the Resistance transferred Noria out here to work on some highly classified project," Elnos began. He took off his shades, exposing the dark circles beneath his worried gaze. "It was pretty clear she wasn't coming back to Canalo any time soon. When Annia and I weren't able to wangle a transfer to Noria's new location, we deserted."

"So you made your way to Osero on your own?" Iannis asked.

"Yes. We obtained Noria's location from a Resistance soldier using suggestion magic, then traveled by boat to Parabas. We arrived four days ago, and, from the soldier's description, we were able to locate the compound quickly enough. It is an underground bunker hidden under a wooded hill, on the outskirts of the town."

"So it must be within walking distance," I mused, glancing out the window.

"Yes," Elnos confirmed. "Unfortunately, things grew more

difficult from there. Security around the bunker is tight. Worse, there is some sort of ward surrounding the perimeter that prevents any mage from entering."

"So Doctor Mitas wasn't lying." Iannis's brows drew together. "They really do have a way to keep mages out. I will have to investigate this ward myself, to identify the spell and perhaps dismantle it."

A server in a grey dress and apron came to our table then, and I ordered meat pies for all of us. "I hope you can break that ward, Lord Iannis," Elnos said fervently after she'd gone, "because Annia is within those walls, and I'm not sure if they've taken her prisoner or executed her."

"How did she manage to get caught?" I demanded.

Elnos took a long drink from his beer mug before replying. "She was trying to find another way into the bunker from the back. Unfortunately, she was picked up by a patrol, and they nearly killed her right then and there. There was blood on the ground, from several people, I think." Frustration sparked in his eyes. "I told her to stay near me, where I could protect her, but she didn't listen. And because she was on the other side of the wards, I couldn't get to her. She's stubborn, like her sister."

"Yes, she is." A bittersweet smile curved my lips, then faded away as I thought of Noria. "Do you think Noria knows Annia is being held in the compound?"

"It's hard to say," Elnos admitted, his shoulders slumping. My heart sank at the look on his face—I'd never seen him so discouraged. "I don't know exactly how large the bunker is, but the perimeter protected by the ward is huge. I'm afraid it's all too possible that Annia could be locked away in an entirely different section from Noria, and that Noria could be unaware of her presence, sequestered away in her technical work."

"Her work," Iannis said softly, anger burning in his gaze. "She is helping the Resistance manufacture weapons that spread disease and epidemics, you know. Some of which are specifically targeted at mages."

"No!" Elnos recoiled, horror widening his eyes. "I know that Noria is committed to the rebellion, but she would never consent to something so horrible. How did you come to such a conclusion?"

"Such a weapon was used to attempt an assassination on the Minister during the last Convention," Iannis said. "The Minister's office tracked the substance to a doctor, who is now in prison. He told us the lab that tests and manufactures these deadly weapons is right here, in Nika."

"It's possible that Noria isn't being given all the information," I consoled Elnos, who looked stricken. "She may not know exactly what these weapons do, and she's an engineer, not a chemist. I doubt she's actually producing these substances. They'll have her working on some mechanical project, most likely."

"Perhaps," Elnos said slowly, his gaze distant. "But Noria is no fool. She would figure it out eventually, and if she is willingly dedicating her time to such a horrific cause—" He broke off, shaking his head. "This is just so hard to think about. It's like my mind just freezes. I don't know what to do."

We fell silent again as the waitress returned with our food. I paid her, then stared down at the tray she'd left on the coffee table. The meat pies looked and smelled amazing, but in the wake of Elnos's distress, I wasn't quite so hungry anymore.

"Let us focus on one thing at a time," Iannis said, not unkindly. "We'll eat now, and then you'll take us to this hidden bunker. Once we get there and I can assess the lay of the land, we'll decide our course of action."

"Very well," Elnos said, reaching for his portion of pie. We all dug in silently, and I tried my best to push away the heaviness that settled onto my shoulders. I'd be damned if I was going to sit here and act like this was our last meal together. Iannis and I had faced ridiculous odds in the past—we would do it again, and get my friends home safe.

I just wished I knew whether or not I could still call Noria one of those friends.

13

*S*till disguised as humans, Iannis and I left the inn with Elnos and made our way to the hidden Resistance compound. As Iannis had predicted, it was on the northern outskirts of town. Technically, that was walking distance, but it was a good five miles from the inn, and it took us longer to get there than I would have liked. We could hardly take the carriage and remain inconspicuous, and though Iannis and I could travel much faster than a brisk walk, Elnos had no such ability.

"This is where Annia and I made camp," Elnos said quietly, leading us into a small clearing halfway up a hillside covered by dense forest. The trees provided cover, while allowing us to spy on the enemy. "I put up a special ward that repels the attention of patrols, so we shouldn't be discovered."

"Well done," Iannis murmured as we carefully crawled up the hillside to get a better view. We'd trekked through the forest to avoid the guards patrolling the wire fence that surrounded the large plot of land before us. Within that plot sat a plain greyish building, about two stories high, and I counted twelve windows that I could see from the side. The rest of the building disappeared into the cover of the trees, making it impossible to see exactly how large it was without getting closer.

"There don't seem to be many guards," I said, taking stock of the security. One man sat inside the booth outside the main gate, munching on a bag of snacks as he kept an eye on the road. I spotted two more guards making their rounds across the perimeter.

"There are more than you'd think," Elnos said. "Especially at night. The patrol that caught Annia prowls the surrounding forest. They also have guns on the rooftops."

"What?" Guns were strictly forbidden in the Federation, their possession punishable by death. To find them in use here would be more proof that the place belonged to the Resistance. Sure enough, I picked out a small, humanoid shape on the rooftop of the main building, and another on the garage port. "By Magorah," I growled, curling my hands around the blades of grass sticking up from the dirt. "These guns are really becoming an issue."

"Bullets can be shielded against," Iannis said, his eyes narrowed as he studied the main building, "though they are a nuisance. It's the ward that worries me."

"How big is it?" I asked, knowing he would be able to see it.

Iannis was silent for a moment. "It begins just inside the fence, and surrounds the buildings as well as a good portion of the wooded area. I'd say at least ten acres, total."

"Shit," I muttered, trying to wrap my head around that. "The facility must be huge, then."

"Indeed," Iannis agreed grimly. "This particular type of ward is most often tied to an object within its boundaries, usually referred to as an anchor. Getting your hands on that is the only means to shut the ward off, but of course you must first get inside. I believe Argon Chartis favors this method of warding."

"That bastard," I hissed, baring my teeth. "I wish I'd had the chance to kill him."

"You chopped off his leg," Iannis reminded me. "That is an impressive feat in itself. Chartis may be a traitor, but he is an experienced mage, and I would not feel comfortable allowing you to face him in a duel."

"Well then, you'd better kill him yourself," I retorted. "Because he seems to be tripping us up at every turn."

"I guess Director Chartis wasn't told exactly what is being produced inside the bunker," Elnos surmised. "I can't imagine any mage helping the Resistance develop a mage-killing disease, no matter how much he might hate you, Lord Iannis."

"You're probably right, but that doesn't make me feel better," I grumbled.

"I suppose you've triggered the alarm yourself, Elnos," Iannis said. "What happened when you did?"

"Nothing much." Elnos shrugged. "No guards came out. But the patrol doubled, and Annia and I could barely leave the camp after that. I believe they won't actively go after a mage, since they likely have no way to defend against magic aside from the ward Chartis set up."

"That must mean they haven't perfected the weapon they're working on," I commented.

"Yes, or they're simply unwilling to use it yet," Elnos said. "Besides, they would have to have a very fast-acting disease for it to be of any use as a defensive weapon."

"Do you think I might be able to slip through?" I asked. "Since I'm only half-mage, perhaps I won't trigger the wards."

"I doubt it," Iannis said. "This particular spell is very sensitive, and will recognize you as a mage even though you are half-shifter."

"The bracelet charm Annia wore did not set it off, so small magical artifacts and enhancements seem to go through," Elnos observed. "But hardly a person with any degree of inherent magic."

"Isn't it worth a try, at least?"

"I do not believe it would be wise to trigger the alarm again," Elnos argued. "They've just begun to relax, since nearly four days have passed since that incident."

"I agree," Iannis said firmly. "There is no use alerting them to our presence and losing our element of surprise."

"Okay, so then, what do we do to get in?" I demanded. "If you're not willing to let me try, then who else? I guess we could try recruiting a local human as our inside agent, but I doubt they'd be willing."

"Sending in an untrained human would be far too risky," Iannis said sternly. "No, I'm afraid we're going to need to head back to Parabas and confer with the local Chief Mage."

"Do you think he'll have any solutions to offer?"

"Not likely," Iannis said regretfully. "I imagine he will come to the same conclusion I have—that our only choice is to annihilate the entire place."

"What!" I nearly jumped to my feet before remembering that we were supposed to stay hidden. "You can't do that! Noria and Annia are in there!"

"I must protest as well, Lord Iannis," Elnos said, desperation tingeing his voice. "I came out here with Annia to rescue Noria. I refuse to see our efforts wasted."

"I understand, but we cannot risk the safety of the entire nation over two lives," Iannis said, his voice hard. He locked eyes on me, his gaze burning with intensity. "I told you that this might happen, Sunaya."

"Yes, and you also told me that it would be a last resort!" I said hotly, tears burning at the corners of my eyes. I couldn't lose Annia, not after all she'd done to help me, and I couldn't bear to see Noria meet her end in such a horrific manner.

"And so it will," Iannis said gently, laying a hand on my fore-arm. "I cannot take action on the compound without conferring with Lord Logar, since this is out of my jurisdiction. So no matter what we decide, I must return to Parabas and meet with him. But if there is any way I can get your friends out safely, I will see that it is done."

"Okay." I let out a slow breath. That was the best response I could hope for really. I mentally prepared myself to leave the compound and my friends behind, to return to Parabas with Iannis and try to find a solution. Hopefully, nothing else would go wrong while we were gone.

"In the meantime, you and Elnos should stay here," Iannis said, surprising me. "You can keep watch on the compound and perhaps eavesdrop on the guards and staff when they are in town. It is unlikely that Noria is allowed to go out, since she is a new recruit, but not impossible. If you find anything useful, or if you do manage to breach the wards by some miracle, Elnos can send me a message by ether pigeon." He gave Elnos a stern look. "Is that understood? I do not want to be met with any unpleasant surprises when I return."

"Yes, My Lord." Elnos bowed his head.

"How long are you going to be gone for?" I asked, torn. On the one hand, I didn't want to be separated from Iannis, but a weight had lifted from my shoulders at the news that I wouldn't have to leave. Maybe I would be able to find a way in while Iannis was gone, and get Annia and Noria out before he came back with an army of mages to flatten the place.

"No longer than two days, I estimate," Iannis said. "Lord Logar is a busy man, but he will not want to delay acting on such an urgent issue."

"Okay." I could work with that. "Should we camp here, or stay in the town?"

"Whichever is easiest for you, but it is best that you not stray too far," Iannis said. "I would like you and Elnos to confiscate and destroy any packages leaving the facility—they may contain these deadly concoctions that we are trying to prevent from spreading."

"I've been doing that already," Elnos said, nodding. "I didn't know what they were sending out, but since it's the Resistance in charge here, I knew it could be nothing good. I figured it would be too risky to ambush arriving packages, as it would make whoever is running the compound suspicious if expected packages started going missing. But it's been easy to transmogrify packages leaving the compound.

"Transmogrify?" My eyebrows winged up as I regarded Elnos with interest. "Into what?"

"Usually water, or grape juice, if it is a liquid, or bread if it is a solid." Elnos's lips twitched. "I imagine whoever is receiving these shipments is very frustrated."

"That is impressive, and lucky for us all," Iannis commented. "Were they very large shipments?"

"So far I've only done two," Elnos confessed. "One left by a rather large wagon, the other in a smaller steamcar. It was easy enough to break a wheel or flatten a tire from the cover of the trees on the side of the road, then sneak into the back and change the contents before they noticed." Elnos smiled shyly, rubbing the back of his neck as he realized how much attention he was getting. "I'm studying chemistry, which gives me quite an advantage in transmogrification."

"That is very good work," Iannis praised. "You would make a good spy."

Elnos shook his head. "I'm much more comfortable in my workshop."

We descended from the hill, back down into the warded clearing. Frowning, I looked around at the fire pit and tents Elnos and Annia had set up. "Is there going to be enough food?"

"I'm afraid not. I planned on picking some up from the market in town, but I forgot to do so before we left the inn. Annia and I stocked up when we arrived, but we're out now."

"I guess we can do that, and maybe snoop around in the local pubs and catch some useful gossip."

"Try not to get into too much trouble while I'm gone, Sunaya." Iannis settled his hands on my waist, drawing me close and dropping the disguise. "I want you alive when I get back."

"I plan to be." I framed his gorgeous face with my hands and kissed him, hard. His arms banded around me, drawing me tight to him as we savored the moment. Sparks sizzled through my veins, igniting my hunger, and I nipped his bottom lip before pulling back.

"I love you," I whispered, allowing my gaze to roam over his face. I soaked in every curve and edge of bone in his aristocratic features, every line and dent in his alabaster skin. But most of all, I soaked in the emotion blazing from those iridescent eyes, those impossibly vibrant irises that he inherited from a mythical Tua ancestor long ago.

"I love you." Iannis brushed a thumb over my cheekbones, then pulled away. "I'll be back soon," he said to me, then turned to Elnos. They locked gazes for a moment, some kind of unspoken communication passing between them before Elnos nodded.

And then he disappeared, one moment here, the next gone in a burst of wind and speed.

14

hree days later.

"Sunaya, don't be foolish!" Elnos hissed from the tree line. "Come back here!"

"No," I growled, stalking forward. My boots thumped along the dirt path that led directly to the back entrance of the compound. Or, rather, the exit, as it was a metal door sunken into the back of a hillside, with no handle. It could only be opened from the inside, as Annia had discovered when she'd tried to get in this way.

"I won't let you do this!" Elnos dashed from the trees and grabbed my arm, pulling me to a stop. "Why set off the alarm and risk exposing us, when Lord Iannis will be back any moment now?"

"Iannis should have been back yesterday!" Angry, I ripped my arm free as I whirled around to face Elnos. He was a good deal taller than I was, nearly as tall as Iannis, so I had to crane my neck in order to glare at him. "It's been three days with no sign of him, and we haven't been able to discover any way into the compound. All we've managed to do is ruin those two outgoing shipments yesterday!"

"I understand your frustration," Elnos said, and indeed, his own voice was brimming with the same emotion. "But charging in now and risking our safety is a foolish plan. We have time until Lord Iannis returns. Surely we can think of something—"

"Like what?" I propped my hands on my hips. "We're out of options. We've found no way to get past the wards, and eavesdropping on those guards in town hasn't gotten us anywhere. Impersonating them won't do us any good, because you tried to breach the wards disguised as a human and you still set them off. The ether pigeons we sent in to warn Noria and Annia didn't seem to do any good either." They'd probably fizzled out the moment they'd touched the border, though they hadn't actually set off the alarm.

"You don't know that," Elnos said tightly. "For all we know, Noria may have noticed our attempts to breach the barrier. She could be trying to engineer an escape attempt right now. What if we trigger the alarm and ruin her chances of getting out?"

"And what if triggering the alarm provides a diversion, and makes it easier for her?" I argued.

Elnos let out an annoyed sigh. "This is a ridiculous argument."

"Yes, it is," I agreed, spinning on my heel. Ignoring Elnos's protests, I stalked toward the back entrance of the bunker. The scent of magic grew thicker the closer I got. I was just inches away from butting up against the wards.

"*Sunaya.*" Iannis's voice resonated in my head, and I stumbled over a rock.

"*Iannis?*" I shot out a hand, bracing myself against a tree to steady myself. "*Are you back?*"

"*Yes. Meet me at the camp with Elnos. I have urgent news.*"

"*Damn right you do. You're late!*"

"Sunaya?" Elnos asked, puzzlement in his eyes. "What's going on?"

Sighing, I turned back to him. "Iannis is back. He wants us to go meet up with him at our campsite."

"Thank goodness," Elnos said, sounding incredibly relieved. Guess he was getting his wish after all.

We headed back to camp as quickly as we could—or rather, as quickly as Elnos could, since I couldn't leave him in the dust. About ten yards away, I caught a trace of Iannis's sandalwood and magic scent on the wind, and a smile curved my lips in spite of my irritation. But the smile faded as I caught another scent, a familiar one, and I froze.

"What is it?" Elnos asked as I sniffed the air.

"No," I growled. "No fucking way."

I took off before Elnos could ask what I was talking about, tearing up the path as fast as my legs could carry me. Voices coming from the clearing became more audible, and I burst into the campsite, my heart pumping hard.

Not from exertion, but from anger.

"That was fast," Iannis said, turning to face me from the middle of the clearing.

"Yeah, no fucking kidding." I jabbed a finger in the air at the figure standing behind him, who I could only partially see. "You wanna tell me just what he's doing here?"

"Hello, cousin." Rylan Baine stepped out from behind Iannis, an unrepentant smile on his handsome face. He was dressed in a red t-shirt, leather pants, and sturdy boots, and the gaunt, emaciated look had faded from his features. My cousin was healthy and bursting with life and energy, instead of suffering like he should have been.

"I brought him here." Fenris ducked out of Elnos's tent, and I started. I'd been so focused on Rylan's scent that I hadn't noticed his. "Iannis called me from Parabas and explained the situation. It occurred to us to use one of the Resistance soldiers that we already had sitting around in Prison Isle to infiltrate the bunker, in exchange for a reduced sentence. Your cousin Rylan was the natural choice, Sunaya."

"And I thank you profusely for that." Rylan sketched a bow, his long, straight black hair swinging forward like a curtain as he did so.

"No way. This is *not* happening." Ignoring Rylan completely, I squared off with Iannis. "How could you do this to me? How could you bring Rylan here, into our midst, on such an important mission, after knowing how he betrayed me?"

"Because Rylan loves you," Iannis said simply. "It makes perfect sense to me to bring someone in who is emotionally invested, rather than a Resistance soldier none of us know, and who is just as likely to betray as they are to help us."

"And how exactly do we know that Rylan isn't going to follow pattern and betray us again?"

"Sunaya, please." Rylan stepped forward, annoyance in his yellow shifter eyes. He reached for my hand, but I backed away. "You can be mad at me all you want, but I was only trying to protect you. And yes, I was a loyal member of the Resistance, but that was before I learned they planned to wipe out the shifters once they were done with the mages. I may not agree with the current regime, but at least the mages aren't trying to annihilate us. The human backers of the Resistance are just as much my enemy now as they are yours."

"I doubt that," I muttered, giving him a nasty look. But I detected no lie in anything he said. Much as I wanted to spurn him, he believed what he said. And we didn't have time to find someone else.

"Besides," Rylan continued, "Fenris didn't just pick me for my good looks. I happen to have inside knowledge of the compound."

"What?" I gaped. That was *way* too coincidental for my tastes. "How?"

"My unit was sent up here to guard the compound back when it was being built," Rylan said. "That was over a year ago, when there was no ward yet. Things may have changed a bit, but probably not too much. I'll be able to get in, no sweat."

"Sunaya," Iannis warned, drawing my attention back to him. "We do not have time to debate my decision to include Rylan on this mission. Lord Logar will be arriving tomorrow. We must get Annia and Noria out before then, or they will be killed."

"Fuck." I expelled a harsh breath, then closed my eyes and reined in my emotions. My feelings about Rylan weren't as important as rescuing Annia and Noria. I had to put them aside, at least until after this was over. Rylan and I would have our reckoning, but not today.

"Fine," I said, opening my eyes and pinning Rylan, my beloved cousin, my closest childhood friend and family member, with the fiercest glare I could muster. "I'll work with you. But if I detect even a whiff of anything suspicious from you, I will rip out your guts and feed them to you. Is that understood?"

"Absolutely." Rylan snapped his heels and saluted me. I bared my teeth at him, but he ignored me as he flashed another grin, looking around at everyone in the group. "So do we have a game plan, or what?"

15

*W*e waited until sunset before Elnos and I snuck over to a spot about a mile down the main road, sticking to the trees for cover so that we wouldn't be ambushed.

"Are you sure you've got the timing right?" I muttered as I crouched behind a bush. Even with the foliage to shield us, I had to shade my eyes with my hand against the brilliant sunset painting the sky in streaks of red and gold.

"I've been here long enough to memorize the watch schedule." The grass beneath Elnos' feet rustled as he tried to make himself comfortable. "The captain of the night guard spends his days with a woman in town. He should come by in the next ten minutes."

We settled in to wait for the captain to show up. My eyes were trained on the dirt road, but my thoughts were elsewhere —on Rylan, specifically. I still couldn't believe Iannis had sent for him to help us, knowing how I felt about him. Rylan had done the unthinkable—he'd hired a witch to put a spell on me. Such a thing just wasn't done in the shifter community. If someone had a problem with another shifter, they handled it according to clan customs. Using a charm or hex or other magical device on another shifter was dishonorable, and most clans considered it a punishable offense. The only acceptable excuse was if magic were required to save a life, but since shifters healed so quickly and we were immune to most diseases, such an event was extremely rare.

Maybe Rylan figured the exception applied, since in his mind, he was saving your life, a voice in my head pointed out.

I gritted my teeth at that. It would be exactly like Rylan to convolute the situation in just that way in order to justify what he had done. But by making me forget to warn Iannis, he'd ended up putting me in danger anyway. Rylan knew me better than anyone else in the Jaguar Clan—he should have known I would go after Iannis. Doing so had involved infiltrating a Resistance camp and thwarting a plot to assassinate the Minister, and shortly after that, the Resistance had put a price on my head.

So in the end, Rylan had only created more danger for me, and helped plunge all of Solantha into a terrible civil war the moment Iannis was gone from the scene.

"Sunaya," Elnos hissed, nudging my arm. Blinking, I cleared my thoughts, then caught the whistle of a steamcar coming from around the bend. "Are you ready?"

"Yep." Tensing, I watched Elnos lift his hand. In it, he held a tiny metal spike. The car came chugging around the bend, a shiny, maroon-colored vehicle that looked brand new. Clearly, the captain was being paid well—or perhaps he was skimming profits from the factory somehow.

Elnos spoke a Word, and the spike shot from his hand and into the captain's front tire. It ripped through the rubber, causing the tire to deflate instantly, with a loud hiss.

"Dammit!" the captain shouted as he pulled the car over, conveniently to our side of the road rather than his. I sprang out from beneath the cover of the trees, landing directly in the passenger seat—the fool had put the top down on his car.

Stupid, since it left him more open to attack, but I wasn't going to complain.

"W-what is the meaning of this?" the captain stuttered, his eyes widening with outrage. He was a tall, bulky man with thick brown hair and a mustache, bright red thread embroidering his dark blue uniform. "Who are you?"

"A good guy," I said, clapping a hand over his mouth. He tried to struggle as I spoke the Words to the sleep spell Fenris had taught me, but he was no match for my shifter strength. The struggle lasted about three seconds, and then he was snoring in my arms.

"Great job," Elnos said, emerging from the foliage. I hopped out of the car and walked around to the driver's side, then hefted the man out of the car. Elnos helped get him onto my back, draping his arms across my shoulders while I held his legs, piggyback style. "Give me a second to hide the vehicle, and then we'll be on our way."

"No way." I swiped at a bit of drool that dribbled onto my shoulder from the sleeping guy on my back and grimaced. "I'm not carrying this guy around for a second longer than I have to. I'll meet you back at camp."

Elnos rolled his eyes, but he let me go on my way as he put an illusion spell on the car to hide it from human eyes. It would have served the owner right for us to just destroy it, but Rylan was going to need it if he hoped to pass himself off as the man I'd just knocked out cold.

Elnos caught up with me just as I reached the camp. Iannis, Fenris, and Rylan were sitting on logs around the fire pit in the center of the encampment discussing the next phase of our operation, and they all looked up as I arrived.

"That's a big one you caught there, cousin," Rylan said, coming over to me. "Want some help?"

"No." I rolled my shoulder to the side and dumped the man

onto the ground. He grunted a little as he hit the dirt, then rolled onto his side and immediately continued snoring.

"Damn. That sleep spell really is effective. How long do you think he'll be out?" Rylan asked me.

"Only a few hours," Iannis said, coming up from behind him. He touched my shoulder briefly. "Did everything go as planned?"

"Yep," I said. "No witnesses, and the car's waiting."

"Excellent." Iannis turned his gaze to Rylan. "It's time to turn you back into a Resistance soldier."

"Hmm." Rylan glanced at the man lying on the ground. "Not sure I'm a fan of the mustache."

"Yeah, well, you're going to get it," I snapped. "So just cooperate."

Rylan frowned. "I am cooperating. Stop acting like such a bitch, Sunaya."

I bared my teeth, but before I could say anything, Iannis grabbed Rylan by the shoulders and hauled him around.

"I have no intention of meddling in your relationship with Sunaya," Iannis growled, sticking his face into Rylan's, "But she is my fiancée, and I will not tolerate insults to her. Is that understood?"

Rylan stared at Iannis for a long moment, back stiff. Surprisingly, I scented no fear off him, or anger either. Then he nodded slowly.

"Of course. I spoke out of turn." An easy smile curved his lips. "I'm glad my cousin has chosen a man who is willing to defend her honor."

"I don't need your compliments," Iannis said mildly, releasing Rylan. "But I do expect you to apologize."

"No," I said, flustered as Rylan turned back to me. I loved Iannis for sticking up for me, but all this attention was throwing me off. "You don't need to apologize. You're right, I am being a bitch, and now I'm holding up this entire operation. Let's just get on with it."

"That would be good," Fenris said, glancing at the rapidly setting sun. "We don't have much time before Rylan needs to report for his watch."

Iannis went to work on transforming Rylan into the night guard captain, while Fenris and I secured the actual captain in the tent, binding his hands and feet and gagging him so he would not be able to move when he awoke. In the privacy of the tent, Fenris also strengthened the sleep spell.

"Does Rylan know that you're not a normal shifter?" I asked, using mindspeak so Rylan wouldn't be able to overhear.

Fenris placed a hand over the man's forehead, checking for who knew what, then flicked his fingers and muttered a Word. A privacy bubble enveloped us, like the one Iannis had used in the inn's common room. "I believe he is curious about my origins, as he gave me quite a few speculative looks on the airship ride here," he said. "But I have given him no reason to suspect that I use magic."

"Good," I said emphatically. "I would hate for him to use that against you if he ever decided to defect back to the Resistance."

"Sunaya." Fenris grabbed my arm as I turned to leave the tent, and I looked back at him. His face was expressionless, but there was a pained look in his dark brown eyes. "I don't presume to know your cousin well, but I believe he regrets hurting you, and is trying to atone for his actions."

"So what, are you saying I should forgive him, just like that?" I propped my hands on my hips and glared at him. "What the hell is going on? First Iannis, and now you, both telling me I should just let Rylan off the hook for nearly getting us all killed."

Fenris rubbed a hand over his bearded jaw. "I am not saying you should forgive Rylan right away," he said, "but you might consider moving in that direction. Iannis tells me that Rylan is the only member of your family who actually loves you, and that is not an easy thing to lose." A shadow crossed his face. "I had to leave my mother and father behind in Nebara. They think me dead to this day."

"Oh, Fenris." I dropped to my knees in front of him, where he still knelt next to our prisoner. "That's horrible. Were you close to your parents?"

He smiled, despite the somber subject. "I am nearly two hundred years old, Sunaya. It's not as bad as losing your parents when you are young. But they moved back to Nebara when I became Chief Mage there to offer their support and advice, and we saw each other at least once a week. They were devastated when they learned of the Federation's decision to execute me, my father in particular. He had strongly tried to dissuade me from what he saw as a disastrous, suicidal course."

"I can't imagine faking my death, and then being unable to tell my family I was still alive." I wrapped my arms around Fenris's broad shoulders and gave him a brief hug. "Do you ever think about getting in touch with them?"

"Yes, but not as much as I used to." Fenris pushed back so that he could look me in the eye. "I did not tell you this story to elicit sympathy for me, Sunaya, but to make you reconsider your attitude toward Rylan. He may not be your only family, but he is your relative. This is your chance to mend the rift between you two."

"Sunaya, Fenris," Iannis called. "Are you coming out?"

"Coming," I called back, relieved at the opportunity to drop the conversation. Fenris and I ducked out of the tent, popping the privacy bubble, and rejoined the others near the fire pit. Standing between Iannis and Elnos was an exact copy of the night guard captain—a tall, bulky man in a navy blue uniform with red embroidery. I assumed the red was a mark of the Resistance. Since this camp was hiding in plain sight, the soldiers couldn't wear their red armbands.

"Whatcha think?" Rylan asked, wiggling his thick, dark brown mustache at me. "Do I look the part?"

My lips twitched. "You'll do." He sounded exactly like the captain too—I guessed Iannis must have put some kind of spell to help out with that part, since Rylan didn't know his voice.

"All right, let's get the scry-eye on you." Elnos pulled a gold necklace chain from his pocket, from which a large, square pendant with a tree carved into it had been attached. "Are you sure you want Sunaya to be at the other end of this?" he asked Iannis.

"I don't think it would be wise for me to do it under the circumstances," Iannis said. "If Lord Logar and his mages arrive early, or if anything else should go wrong, I want to be fully present to deal with it."

"Very well." Elnos turned to me. "Hold out your palm."

I did so, and Elnos placed the pendant in my hand. Earlier, when he'd hatched this plan, Elnos explained to us that the scry-eye was a magi-tech device he and Noria had invented, which would allow another person to borrow the eyes and ears of whoever was wearing it at the time. This way, I'd be able to see exactly what was going on around Rylan as he infiltrated the bunker, and relay important information to the others. It didn't allow for communication, but I could use my own magic to boost a mindspeak connection between Rylan and myself. Elnos was more familiar with the device, but couldn't use mindspeak.

Not for the first time, I wondered why it was that Iannis was able to communicate with mindspeak, but not Elnos. Was it an ability Iannis had cultivated over his long-lived life that Elnos had not? Or was it yet another gift of his Tua heritage?

"Close your hand around the pendant and concentrate on it," Elnos told me.

I did so, putting all my attention on the cool square in my hand. I focused on the smoothness of the glossy outer stone against my fingers, and the hardness of the metal backing. I wondered exactly what was inside it that made it function the way it did. How could a tiny piece of equipment do such extraordinary things?

Elnos covered my closed hand with his own and spoke a few Words. The pendant grew warm in my hands, and a tingle of power rushed up my arm and into my chest.

"There," Elnos said, stepping away. "Now put it on Rylan."

I did as he asked, crossing over to where my cousin stood. He might have had grey human eyes instead of yellow shifter ones, but the gleam lurking behind them as he ducked his head was all Rylan.

"This seems like an awfully pretty piece for a man to wear," Rylan said as he tucked it beneath the collar of his uniform shirt. "Hope they don't decide to strip search me for any reason."

"This particular piece was intended for Annia," Elnos said dryly.

"That makes a lot more sense," Rylan agreed. He looked at me expectantly, then back at Elnos. "So, am I supposed to do anything to make this work?"

"It'll kick in. Just give it a moment."

My vision blurred just then, and I let out a gasp of surprise. Colors swirled in a confusing pattern, then my vision suddenly snapped into focus. I wasn't staring at Rylan anymore... I was looking at myself, through Rylan's eyes. And the shock stamped across my features was almost comical.

"By Magorah, this is strange." I slapped my hand to my forehead, then grimaced as I watched myself make the motion. "Do you think you could not look at me? It's really weird to be looking at myself from outside my own body."

"Sure." Rylan switched his gaze to Iannis, and gave him a

long once-over. My gaze traveled from the hem of his robes—dark red today—up his chest, and lingered on his face for a long moment. Iannis's eyes narrowed, then his violet eyes sparkled with something that looked suspiciously like amusement.

"Oh, knock it off!" I stomped my foot, having no other outlet for my frustration. I wanted to punch Rylan in the arm, but I worried I would miss since I couldn't actually see him.

"Fine, fine." Rylan's gaze switched toward the canopy of tree branches. "Is there anything else I need to know, or can I get going now?"

"No, you should go," Iannis said, urgency entering his tone. "If you delay any longer, they might become suspicious."

"True." Rylan's gaze turned toward the hill that blocked our view of the compound. "I'll be off then."

He turned away and headed deeper into the woods. Letting out a deep sigh, I lowered myself onto the log and prepared to be a spectator in one of the most important missions I'd ever participated in.

16

*R*ylan didn't waste any time. He dashed through the trees at lightning speed, somehow managing not to make a sound as he dodged branches and roots along the way. He made it to the spot where the vehicle was hidden, then paused just at the edge of the forest.

"Drop the illusion," I said aloud to Elnos. A moment later, the car popped into view.

"Thank Magorah," Rylan said to me as he hopped into the driver's seat and pulled the key from his pocket. *"For a moment there, I thought you expected me to drive an invisible car."*

"Ha-ha," I said, rolling my eyes. It was *really* strange, feeling my eyes roll in my head while my vision stayed stationary. The sooner this was over and I was back in my own head, the better.

Rylan turned on the engine, then peeled out into the road with a loud whistle of steam.

"For Magorah's sake!" I yelped. *"Don't drive that thing around like it's a race car! You'll arouse suspicion."*

"All right, all right," Rylan groused, slowing down to a more reasonable speed. *"I wasn't going to drive the whole way like that. Just having some fun. Has becoming a mage apprentice turned you*

into a stick in the mud, Naya? I don't remember you being this uptight."

I said nothing for a long moment as he made his way to the compound. Was Rylan right? Was I turning into an uptight bitch, worrying and criticizing at every turn, unwilling to enjoy life anymore?

"I think the fact that my friends are trapped inside that bunker and are in danger of being blown up is reason enough for me to be uptight," I finally said. *"You could cut me some slack on that end."*

"That's true." Rylan paused. *"I guess things are a bit different for me, as a former Resistance soldier. We lost members all the time, charged into dangerous situations knowing that some of us might not come back. I learned pretty fast that if you didn't keep your sense of humor about you, you could quickly fall into depression."*

"I see." And the thing was, I did. Enforcers saw their fair share of death too, both amongst our own ranks and the citizens we protected. But it wasn't the same thing as going into battle, and we certainly weren't fighting all the time. Part of me wanted to ask Rylan more about his experiences in the Resistance, but this wasn't the time. And besides, I feared that conversation would open up a can of worms I wasn't ready to deal with.

Rylan came to a stop outside the gate. The sun had fully set now, only wisps of color lighting the sky, and darkness was settling over the compound. He turned toward the booth just as the guard within rolled down his window.

"Evening, Captain," the guard said. He was a short, sallow-faced man wearing the same uniform as Rylan, but with less decorative embroidery.

"Good evening, Private," Rylan said. "Anything to report?"

"No, sir. No suspicious activity up here at the front gate that I've been able to see. The day guard captain might know differently, but I haven't heard anything on the radio, so I doubt it."

"Thank you, soldier. Do you know where I can find the captain now?"

"I believe he's down below, meeting with the director. Do you need me to radio him?"

"No, thanks. I'll talk to him myself."

Nodding, the guard turned away to pull on a lever. The gate began to slide open smoothly, and I let out a sigh of relief as Rylan passed through.

"So how are you getting inside, exactly?" I asked as he drove the vehicle up the long dirt road and headed toward a garage. Elnos and I had observed a surprising number of people coming and going from this seemingly unimportant structure, so we had already suspected that it held the entrance to the bunker. But with no way to breach the wards, our theory had been impossible to confirm.

"Watch and learn."

"Good evening, Captain," a guard said as he approached the running vehicle. I half expected him to salute, but he didn't, likely because they were keeping up appearances around here.

"Good evening," Rylan replied, and the two launched into a brief conversation. The guard pulled a small remote and pressed a button, and the garage door rolled up on well-oiled hinges, exposing around a dozen vehicles—mostly industrial—that sat within. Rylan guided the car inside, and parked it in one of the spots set alongside the left wall. I looked around as best as I could through his eyes as he got out of the car, but didn't see anything suspicious—it looked like a regular company garage.

Rylan pulled out the captain's key ring as he headed to the back wall of the garage. He stopped in front of an unmarked grey door, then tried several of the keys on the ring. The third one worked, and the door revealed a dimly lit stairwell that shot steeply beneath the ground.

"*So that's where they've hidden the entrance,*" I mused as Rylan descended, closing the door firmly behind him.

"*I always hated this part,*" Rylan admitted as descended the stairs. "*It feels like I'm on my way to hell.*"

"*Maybe you are, for what you've done.*"

"*Ha-ha.*" He didn't sound amused. "*At least I'm by myself. It's worse when you've got people behind you. If someone stumbles and bumps into you, or pushes you intentionally, you'll go bouncing down this thing and break every bone in your body along the way.*"

"*Ouch,*" I said, rubbing my left arm as I imagined crashing down this set of endless stairs. Yes, shifters could heal, but that amount of damage could be debilitating. Because we healed so quickly, our bones had to be set fast if we didn't have the energy to shift. Otherwise, they healed incorrectly, and could leave us crippled unless they were broken and reset again. I'd witnessed such things myself, and it was not pretty.

It took some ten minutes for Rylan to reach the bottom of the stairwell. Toward the end, the tunnel grew brighter, light from the landing filtering upward. Four Resistance soldiers waited there, dressed in full Resistance uniform, their red armbands proudly displayed. Down here, there was no need to hide their true colors. They also carried pistols in addition to the swords strapped at their belts.

"*Wish I had one of those,*" Rylan remarked. "*Seems odd that the captain wasn't carrying one, but he probably doesn't want to scare the populace. Maybe he keeps it in his office.*"

I wrinkled my nose at that, but said nothing as Rylan conversed with the guards. I didn't want to distract him—any lapse in protocol could get him killed. But he said the required things, and, within moments, he was through those double doors and walking down a long, brightly lit, white-tiled hall.

The next hour was pretty uneventful. Rylan went to his office, retrieved the captain's gun, and checked in with the day shift captain, who went off duty. After that, he made his rounds, touching base with the guards stationed in different areas around the facility and doing the job of the man he was impersonating.

I used the time to get the lay of the land, taking mental notes and verbally relaying information about the compound to Iannis. As far as I could see, it was split into four sections. The first held the administrative offices, which was where we started. This was only a small portion of the compound, two parallel hallways lined with square rooms. All the windows were shielded with thick blinds, and there were heavy locks on the doors. The plates on those doors told us to whom the offices belonged, and I eagerly scanned each one, hoping to find Noria's name. But though several head scientists did hold offices—and Rylan even spoke to one who was behind his desk as we passed by—there was no trace of Noria.

She's not important enough to have her own office, I told myself, trying to ignore the sinking feeling in my stomach. *After all, she was only recently recruited, and looks like she should still be in school.*

The laboratory section was by far the largest. These rooms were walled off completely, protected by steel-reinforced doors and keypads. The guards posted in this section didn't have access—they simply patrolled the halls. There were no windows to see within, but every so often, a white-coated individual would emerge, usually with a clipboard in hand, and either head into another laboratory, the washrooms, or the offices.

It all looked very normal and civilized, if you ignored the faint sobs coming from the rooms. A chill rippled down my spine at the sound of a child wailing inconsolably, and anger ignited in my chest.

"*Rylan,*" I hissed. "*There are live test subjects in here, aren't there?*"

"*I'm afraid so,*" Rylan said grimly, nodding at another guard as we rounded the corner. "*I scent shifters and various small animals. When I was here before, the place was nearly empty.*" There was a hint of defensiveness in his voice.

"*We've got to rescue them,*" I insisted. "*We can't just leave them here.*"

"*Ordinarily, I'd agree with you,*" Rylan said, "*but we have no idea what condition these victims are in. If they've been injected with deadly diseases, do we really want them getting out?*"

"*Dammit.*" I dug my fingers into my hair, trying to think. It was true that we didn't want people leaving the compound only to start some deadly epidemic in the Federation. But how could I leave what sounded like a child behind in good conscience, knowing that they were being tortured?

"Sunaya?" Iannis's hand settled onto my shoulder, a comforting weight. "What is it?"

I sighed, turning my head toward his voice. His arm wrapped around me, drawing me against his chest, and I took comfort in the embrace even though I couldn't see him.

"There are people—possibly children—down there, being experimented on," I muttered into his chest. "I want to get them out, but Rylan says they might be infected with diseases."

Iannis was silent for a long moment. "If we can take over the compound, I will see to them personally, and heal them if possible. I can only hope that we manage to do so before Lord Logar arrives. He will be here soon, and when he arrives—"

"We're going to destroy the compound," I snapped. "Yes, yes, I know."

"When you locate Noria, you can have Rylan ask her about the test subjects," Elnos suggested. "You might be able to free some of them."

"*What do you think?*" I asked Rylan after I relayed that information. "*Do you think it's possible?*"

"*The subjects will definitely be separated according to what* they're being used for," Rylan said. "Judging by the different symbols stitched onto the breasts of the lab coats of these scientists, there are a variety of experiments going on. They won't want to jeopardize their results by mixing up their different test groups. It's possible we might be able to save some."

"Can we get a move on and find Noria, then?" I demanded. "What if Annia is one of the prisoners being experimented on? She could be dying right now!"

"I don't know that they would use her," Rylan said, though he sounded troubled. "She's human, so likely would not fit the criteria for whatever their experiments are. It's more likely they're just questioning her."

"You mean torturing her," I said flatly.

"I was trying to be optimistic."

I sighed, saying nothing more as Rylan finished his rounds with unhurried steps. Annia could already be dead for all I knew. But I couldn't operate as if she were. I had to have faith that, at the very least, Noria would have done something to ensure Annia wasn't executed. They might not have been on the best of terms when they last parted, but they were still sisters. Family. Blood.

Like Rylan is your blood.

"Okay, I think if Noria is going to be anywhere, it's over here," Rylan said as he turned down another corridor, past the mess hall. This section of the compound was a little less clinical, with a length of blue carpeting running the length of the floor, and softer lights set into the ceiling as compared to the harsh white lights in the other sections that left no room for shadowed corners. "This is where the staff sleeps."

"So how the hell do we find her then?" I asked. "Do we just start knocking on doors?"

"Well, we can bypass this section completely, because these are the male dormitories," Rylan said as we passed through one hall. "And *this one too. But this one....*" He stopped and sniffed, then let out a deep sigh. *"This one is all women."*

I wasn't sure whether to laugh or roll my eyes at that. I wished the scry-eye allowed me to smell the scents Rylan was picking up on, because then I could just track Noria to her room. But it wasn't built for shifters, and such a feature would be useless to humans.

Rylan walked up to the first door on the left and knocked. A woman with short blonde hair dressed in a white nightgown answered, her eyes heavy with sleep.

"Oh. Hello, Captain Witley," she said, clutching at the door-frame as she regarded Rylan. "What is it?"

"Sorry to bother you," Rylan said, sounding apologetic and a little embarrassed. "I was looking for Miss Melcott, regarding a security issue I need to discuss with her. Do you know which room she's in?"

"Oh, that little redhead?" The blonde wrinkled her nose, then pointed down the hall. "She's three doors down, on the left-hand side."

"Thank you. Have a good night."

"Anybody who's awake is going to be listening now," I told Rylan as he headed for the door in question.

"I know, but it's not like you had a better idea."

Rylan knocked on the door, then waited. My stomach sank a little when nobody answered—if Noria wasn't here, then what were we going to do? Was she working late in one of the labs? If so, which one, and was there any way to get in? Tonight was our only chance—Rylan wouldn't be able to stay here past morning.

"I'll try again," Rylan said just as I was about to ask him to. He knocked on the door. This time, we heard a muffled groan.

"Miss Melcott, it's Captain Witley," Rylan called through the door, keeping his voice as low as he could while remaining audible through the doorway. "I need to speak with you."

A rustling sound ensued, followed by footsteps, and then Noria yanked the door open. "What do you want?" she growled at Rylan. She stood there, arms crossed over her chest, looking far too thin in the cotton nightgown she wore. Her red hair was a disaster, the mass of curls flying every which way, and her skin was too pale, making the bags beneath her eyes and the freckles smattered across her cheeks stand out like beacons.

"Noria!" I cried aloud, wanting to reach out and squeeze her tight against my chest. But then I remembered I wasn't there, that I was sitting on a log out in the woods.

"You've found her?" Elnos exclaimed, hope in his voice.

Rylan darted into the room, pushing Noria back, and clamped a hand around her mouth before she could scream. She struggled mightily against him, flailing her arms and legs out as he closed and locked the door behind him.

"*Stop it,*" Rylan hissed as he dragged her away from the door. "I'm not here to hurt you. I'm trying to get you out!" He shoved her away from him, and she stumbled backward onto the twin bed in what looked to be a very sparse bedroom. There was a single nightstand, and a small dresser for clothing, but other than that, there was nothing to occupy the windowless chamber. "If you shout, somebody's going to come looking!"

"Why the hell would the captain of the night watch come to help me escape?" Noria sniped. Her voice wobbled ever so slightly, but her dark eyes blazed with defiance, and she gripped the bedspread beneath her hard enough that her knuckles whitened.

"Because I'm not the captain of the night watch," Rylan said, keeping his voice low. "My name is Rylan Baine. My cousin Sunaya asked me to get you out."

Hope flashed in Noria's eyes for a split second before she narrowed them. "How do I know you're telling the truth?" she asked. "You could be making this all up. It's no secret that I was friends with Sunaya."

Rylan popped the top button of his uniform open and pulled out the necklace from beneath his collar. "Recognize this?" he asked, swinging the pendant back and forth.

Noria's dark eyes widened. "That's my scry-eye!" Scrambling off the bed, she snatched up the pendant and held it up to the light. "This is the very same prototype Elnos and I were working on," she murmured, examining it critically.

"Yeah, he's here too, along with Sunaya, Lord Iannis, and a wolf shifter named Fenris," Rylan said. "We came to get you and Annia out before this place is leveled."

"Before the place is leveled?" Noria echoed, the last bit of color draining from her face. "What the hell are you talking about?"

17

"This is all happening so fast," Noria said as she paced back and forth alongside her bed. "One moment, I'm thinking I'm never going to be able to get out of here, and the next, I'm being told I need to leave now before the place explodes." Brown eyes, heavy with worry, lifted to Rylan's face. "Are you sure this place has to be destroyed? There is a lot of valuable scientific information here, even if so many of the experiments being done are horrible."

"You know the Mages Guild doesn't care about any of that," Rylan said. "The safety of the Federation comes before scientific inquiry."

"You mean the safety of the mages," Noria said, a tinge of bitterness seeping into her tone. But she seemed more resigned than anything else.

"Can you get a summary from her about the project she's working on?" I asked Rylan. *"We need to know if there are any factors we're not aware of."*

"Noria, what exactly have you been doing here?" Rylan asked. "When they sent you to this place, were you aware that this lab is developing a weapon to spread targeted diseases?"

Noria shook her head. "I'd heard vague rumors about secret weapons, but I thought it was just a lie spread by our enemies," she explained. "When I first arrived here, the director told me I was to invent a small flying mechanism that could spray sleeping gas on people, so they could be more easily captured while avoiding Resistance casualties. It sounded reasonable enough to me, and an interesting challenge, so I got to work."

"I'm guessing you changed your mind at some point," Rylan said, "judging by how unhappy you seem to be here."

"Well, a couple of days after I arrived, I found out the truth." Noria pressed her lips together as she momentarily came to a halt, her dark eyes growing bleak. "A chemist was flirting with me in the cafeteria, trying to impress me with his scientific achievements." She let out a humorless laugh. "He was balding and fat, and a good fifteen years older, so I don't know why he thought he stood a chance. Anyway, he got so caught up in his bragging, he let slip that my invention was going to be used for spreading deadly poisons and viruses across the nation." Noria's face twisted in disgust. "Mass murder, in other words, and not just of our enemies. Women, children, and even animals would be killed off too."

"Shit," Rylan hissed, echoing my sentiments exactly.

"I immediately went to the director's office and demanded to know if what I had learned was true. I made it clear I couldn't keep working on this project if even half of what that chemist said to me was fact. He told me to mind my own business, and continue to work on my assigned project, if I valued my life."

"Damn," Rylan cursed. "So they threatened you. I'm guessing you did continue on the project, then?"

"I tried my damnedest not to," Noria insisted. She twisted the fabric of her nightgown nervously, and the guilt in her voice was clear. "In addition to what the chemist told me, I also found out they've been keeping shifter children in the labs to use for experiments. They used to have mage children too, but I think those were too difficult to kidnap."

"That explains why we haven't seen any shifter guards around," I said to Rylan.

"Either way, I decided that the lives of children and animals were worth more than my own, so I built a flaw into the prototype to try and sabotage the project."

"Oh, so what they have doesn't work?" Rylan asked, sounding relieved.

"Well, no." Noria's shoulders slumped. "They found me out pretty quick. The director came to inspect my work personally, and he's got a sharp eye. Not long after that, Annia was captured." Noria's voice hitched. "When they first brought her in, I didn't know it was her. She was disguised as a Resistance soldier I'd seen around at the other camp, but when she was strip-searched, they removed some kind of bracelet, and the disguise failed. Has she been following me the whole time, or did she just impersonate that soldier?"

"She's been following you the whole time," Rylan said quietly. "Your sister loves you."

"I know." Tears filled Noria's eyes, and she blinked them away rapidly. "The director noticed the family resemblance between us right away, and is using her as leverage against me. If I don't complete the prototype, they'll torture and kill Annia." Noria's lower lip trembled a little, and she braced herself against the bed. "The one time I was allowed to see her, Annia told me not to listen to them, that her life wasn't as important as keeping the Federation safe. But I'm not willing to sacrifice my only sister."

"Well, it's a good thing you won't have to." Rylan came over to Noria and slid an arm around her shoulder. "We'll get your sister out, kid, safe and sound. And we'll get those shifter kids out too." He hugged her tight against him, and my chest ached. I wanted to be there for Noria, to put my arms around her, hug her, and tell her everything was going to be okay. But I couldn't, and I was grateful that Rylan was doing it in my stead.

"I don't see how," Noria said, wiping her tears. "They're all locked up in the lower level, and heavily guarded. The doors and elevators can only be accessed with a special key."

"Yeah, but I'm the night watch captain, remember?" Rylan told her, and I could hear the grin in his voice. "If the keys aren't on this fat ring I carry, I'm sure they're in my office."

"Sunaya," Iannis said, breaking my focus, and then he spoke a Word. My surroundings vanished, replaced by the campsite. Darkness had settled over the woods, the only light source the moonbeams filtering through the canopy of trees. Iannis sat next to me, his hand on my shoulder, while Fenris and Elnos sat on the two logs across from the fire pit, watching me intently.

"Why did you do that?" I cried, shrugging off Iannis's hand. "I need to be there with them!"

"I need your full attention for a moment," Iannis said simply. "I decided to eavesdrop directly on your conversation so that I wouldn't have to interrupt you. I know that you and your friends want to rescue the shifter children. But if we are to rescue anyone, we must first disable the wards."

"Right." I let out a long sigh. "Any ideas on how to do that? You said something about an object being tied to the spell?"

"Yes, the achor," Iannis said. "Though it won't literally look like one. It can be any sort of object."

"I wish I was in there," I muttered, looking up at the hill that separated us from the compound. "I could use my nose to sniff it out."

"You do have Rylan to do that for you," Iannis said. "Can you ask him if he's scented anything magical during his rounds?"

"Hey Rylan," I called—thankfully, I could still communicate

via mindspeak even if I couldn't see what he was doing. *"Did you smell any magic anywhere during your rounds?"*

"Actually, I think I did," Rylan said. *"There's a guest wing of sorts around here, and when I was passing one of the rooms, I thought I caught a whiff."*

"Why didn't you say anything?"

"I had other things on my mind," Rylan retorted. *"But you're right; I probably should have mentioned it. Aside from the wards, there shouldn't be anything else magical in here."*

I relayed the information to Iannis, who nodded. "Tell Rylan to leave Noria and get to that guest room. It shouldn't be hard for him to locate the anchor, using his shifter senses."

"Leave Noria!" I exclaimed. "But what if something happens to her in the meantime? We just found her."

"I understand your fears," Iannis said gently, squeezing my hand. "But it will be much more difficult for Rylan to do this if he has Noria with him. I doubt that the director will take too kindly to Noria running around the compound late at night, when she is already under suspicion."

"All right." I let out a hefty sigh. "Can you get me back into the scry-eye now?"

"Very well," Iannis said. "But I'm coming with you this time."

"What?" I asked, momentarily nonplussed before I understood. "Oh. You want to do that weird thing where you put yourself inside me."

"Is that some kind of sex joke?" Elnos asked, and I choked on a laugh.

"No," Iannis said, unruffled even as color spread to my cheeks. He didn't bother to explain himself further—apparently, the skill was something that came from his Tua heritage, which he kept a secret. "Are you ready, then?" he asked me.

"Yes."

Iannis reactivated the spell, and I was back in Rylan's head again, looking through his eyes and ears. He and Noria were still sitting on the bed, going through possible options on how to rescue Annia and the shifter children.

"Hey, pause for a sec," I told Rylan. *"I just finished talking with Iannis and the others. We've got to switch gears for a moment."*

"You're talking about finding the anchor?"

"Yes." I sucked in a breath as magic surged within me. Suddenly, Iannis's consciousness was inside mine, a foreign presence that sent a pleasant, though completely inappropriate, thrill through me.

"Are you all right?" Rylan asked, sensing the change in my mood.

"Yeah, I'm fine," I said, trying not to sound flustered. *"Iannis just cast a spell so that he could watch and listen too."*

"A bunch of voyeurs, the lot of you," Rylan teased, before growing serious. *"So what's the plan?"*

"Tell Noria you are going to have to leave her for a bit to disable the wards," I said, ignoring the guilty feeling squirming in my stomach. *"And that as soon as they're down, I'm coming in for her."*

Rylan relayed the message, and Noria's face tightened. "I'd rather have her come for Annia," she said. "I went into this willingly, but Annia doesn't deserve what's happened to her."

"We're getting both of you out," Rylan said firmly, standing. "Just sit tight here, okay? I'll be back for you."

Noria only nodded, her eyes filling with exhaustion. Rylan left her sitting on the bed, and my stomach sank as he quietly slipped back out into the hall. He nodded at the guard stationed at the corner, then made his way to the guest wing.

"She will be fine," Iannis said, trying to reassure me. *"Noria is a strong, capable young woman."*

"I know," I said, but the knowledge didn't make me feel better.

The guest wing was a little nicer than the staff quarters—the carpet runner was a soft, lush green, the walls papered in cream with gold designs, and the wall sconces were brass instead of cast iron. The doors were all made of dark wood instead of thin metal, and I watched silently as Rylan tracked the scent to the proper door.

"This one," he said, resting his hand on a doorknob. He tried turning it, but it was locked. *"I can smell it strongest here."*

Rylan pulled the captain's key ring from his pocket, then made an educated guess as to which key to use. Thankfully, he got it right on the second try, and the door swung open to reveal an elegantly furnished guest room.

"This must be where Thorgana or her emissaries stay when they come to visit," I said, looking at the thick carpeting and hand-carved furnishings. The room was nicely appointed, but lacked any sort of personal effects, suggesting that no one was currently occupying it.

"The scent is strongest over there," Rylan said, crossing to the opposite wall where a desk and chair sat. He picked up the writing implements and paper that sat atop the varnished surface, sniffing.

"It's the clock," Iannis told me. *"I can see the magic surrounding it."*

"I think it's this clock," Rylan said before I could relay the message. He reached up to grab the round brass object, which hung over the desk.

"Wait!" Iannis cried, and my heart rate shot up at the alarm in his voice.

But it was too late. Rylan's fingers curled around the clock, and he brought it down with a tug. As it separated from the wall, a strange red glow burst from the face, and bolts of energy struck Rylan in the chest.

"No!" I shrieked as Rylan let out a cry of pain. He toppled backward, and everything went black.

18

"*Rylan!*" I screamed as the campsite came back into view around me. I'd been unceremoniously knocked out of his head when he lost consciousness, and I had no idea what was going on. My palms were sweaty, my heart pounding with fear for my cousin. Had the shock killed him?

"Rylan, wake up!"

"I think he's alive," Iannis said quietly. His violet eyes were heavy with concern, but he didn't seem nearly as worried as I was. "That booby trap might have been strong enough to kill a human, but not a healthy young shifter. I do hope he doesn't stay unconscious for long. We need him to destroy the clock, and if someone were to happen upon him before he wakes, we could lose our only chance of getting inside."

"Fuck." I jumped up and began circling the fire pit, agitation in every step. "Why didn't you see the booby trap sooner?" I asked, unable to keep the accusation from my voice.

"Sunaya..." Fenris began, his eyes narrowing. But Iannis shook his head, and he subsided.

"Without actually being present, it wasn't possible for me to detect the trap," Iannis told me. "I was able to see the magic, but not what sort of magic it was. In my elation at spotting the key, I didn't think to warn Rylan about the possibility of a trap until it was too late."

"Crap." I kicked at a rock, and it went shooting up the hillside. Dammit, but I needed to get over there! *"Rylan!"* I shouted again, as loudly as I could, hoping that my mental voice would wake him.

"I'm... here...." Rylan's voice echoed faintly in my head. My knees went weak as relief surged through me, and I braced my hand against a tree to steady myself.

"Thank Magorah," I said, my voice a little shaky. *"Are you okay?"*

"I feel like I've been hit by lightning, but I'll live," he grumbled.

"Can you stand?"

"I'm getting to my feet now."

"Good. Iannis says that you need to destroy the clock."

"Hell no," Rylan growled. *"I'm not touching that thing again. I don't think I could survive another hit like that."*

"The trap should no longer be active," Iannis said—he was still joined with me, so he could hear Rylan. "I believe it was a one-shot spell."

"You believe?" I said testily. "Are you willing to risk my cousin's life on that?"

"If he does not destroy the clock, then everyone inside will be destroyed when Lord Logar arrives with his mages," Iannis said sternly. "There is no choice in the matter."

"Fuck." Why did I keep finding myself in these impossible situations? *"Rylan, Iannis says the spell's deactivated. You have to destroy the clock or we won't be able to get you all out."*

"Fine," Rylan said. *"But you owe me a bottle of* teca.*"*

"Done."

"We should get up the hill," Elnos said. "That way we'll be able to see if the wards come down."

We scrambled up the hill, my heart beating a rapid tattoo against my chest as anxiety chewed my gut. Was Rylan going to be able to destroy the clock? Or would it hit him with that spell again? What if he did destroy the clock, but the wards didn't come down? What would we do then?

"I smashed the fucking thing to bits," Rylan said, no small amount of relish in his voice. *"Is there anything else I need to do?"*

"The wards are down," Elnos said, his voice bubbling with excitement. "We can get in now!"

"Yes!" I crowed, a grin spreading across my face even as a strident alarm pealed across the open air from the direction of the bunker, assaulting my sensitive ears. *"We're good to go. Get out of there and go grab Noria. We're coming in."*

OUR PLAN WAS to go around to the back of the bunker, where Annia had been captured, and blast our way through the metal hatch. But as we began descending the hill, the garage doors opened, and guards raced outside with guns held ready. Their single-minded rush reminded me of a suddenly disturbed anthill. My eardrums vibrated at the high-pitched whistle of several steam engines starting up from within the garage.

"They're evacuating," Fenris growled. "They must have trained for this in case the ward ever fails."

"We have to stop them," Iannis said, changing course.

"Wait!" I grabbed the sleeve of his robe and pulled him to a stop. "I can't go with you. I have to get to Rylan and Noria."

"I can't let you go off—"

"Rylan says that he has keys to the lower levels," I said, cutting him off. "Knowing him and Noria, they'll already be rushing down there. I can't let them do this alone."

"Fine." Frustration glimmered in Iannis's eyes, but he

relented. "Take Elnos with you. And Sunaya?" he added, grabbing my arm even as I made to turn away.

"Wha—" I began, but the word was cut off as Iannis crushed me against him and kissed me, hard. His arms banded around my waist, pressing my curves against the ridges of hard muscle that hid beneath his flowing robes. My anger melted away beneath his touch, and I sank my hands into his long hair and kissed him back just as hard. I doubted this was going to be the last time I ever saw him, but then again, we were going into battle.

"Love you too," I said breathlessly, tearing my lips from his before I lost myself completely. I broke out of his grip and briefly flung my arms around Fenris. "If there are any children in there, don't let them get away."

"I won't," Fenris said, returning my hug briefly.

"Great." I locked eyes with Elnos, who was standing by, impatience sparking in his eyes. "Let's go."

Iannis and Fenris dashed for the front of the compound, and Elnos and I sprinted for the back entrance. Mercifully, the alarm had stopped ringing—I guess it was set to automatically shut off after a certain amount of time had passed. Out of the corner of my eye, I saw large, steam-powered vehicles rolling out of the garages, a hazard symbol painted on the sides. I imagined they carried the top scientists as well as their records and samples, and hoped that Iannis would be able to stop them. I wished I could see to it personally, but Annia and Noria were my main mission, and I had to trust Iannis to take care of it.

A bullet grazed my shoulder as we crashed through the trees, and I cried out as the scent of my own blood filled the air.

"Dammit!" Elnos swore, throwing out his hands. He spoke a series of Words so fast they came out almost as gibberish, and a green energy shield flared to life in front of us. More gunfire sounded from ahead, but, this time, the bullets bounced harmlessly off the shield.

"Bastards," I hissed as the trees began to thin out and the back of the bunker came into view. There were six guards lined up outside the rear entrance of the bunker, all firing rifles in our direction. Their eyes widened as we closed the distance despite the hail of bullets. Before they could run, I withdrew a chakram from my left pouch and flung it. The circular blade sliced cleanly through the neck of the first soldier, then hit the second one in his right arm at an angle. The injured man let out a bone-chilling shriek as his comrade toppled to the ground, and the other three men turned tail and ran. Elnos flung some kind of black energy bolt at the one furthest away, and it hit him square in the back. The soldier writhed and screamed in pain, and to my amazement, crumbled into a pile of ash.

"Alchemical magic," Elnos said, answering the momentary look of shock on my face.

"Yeah, well, maybe you can use that to get the door open." I yanked my chakram from the body of the injured man, who had sunk to his knees, whimpering in pain. "I'll take care of the rest of these guys." I couldn't allow any of them to live, not if it meant they might smuggle dangerous biochemical weapons out of this forsaken place.

"No, please—" the guard babbled as I drew one of my crescent knives from the holster on my right leg. I grabbed him by the hair and yanked his head back, then sliced his neck cleanly. His death gurgle echoed in my ears as I dashed up the hill and after the other soldiers, but I refused to let it bother me.

After all, these men had no mercy for me, or for my country. I would have no mercy for them.

～

WHEN I CAME BACK DOWN the hill, Elnos was standing in front of the rear entrance. The heavy door had been melted down into a hunk of glowing metal, leaving the dark tunnel entrance exposed.

"You all right?" Elnos asked, eyeing the blood staining my hair and pants.

"I'm fine." I wiped my crescent knife on my pant leg one last time, then gestured to the entrance with it. "Let's get going."

Since I now had inside knowledge of the compound, I led the way. The light filtering in from the entrance behind us illuminated the tunnel enough that I could see, but Elnos conjured a glowing ball of light anyway. The tunnel was less than a hundred yards long, and curved around the compound rather than going straight into it. My nose detected no other lurking guards, and I imagined that the rest were either in the deeper parts of the bunker, or above as they prepared to help evacuate the scientists.

"Rylan?" I called mentally as I opened a door at the end of the tunnel and stepped into a blue-carpeted hall. We were in the staff quarters. All the doors were flung wide open, the beds within them empty and unmade as the residents had hastily fled. A guard lay dead in the middle of the hall, blood seeping from a head wound into the carpet and congealing there. Rylan had probably killed him in his haste to get Noria away from the evacuation.

"Sunaya? Are you inside?"

"Yes, I'm in the staff quarters with Elnos."

"There's an elevator right outside the labs, in the north hall," Rylan told me. *"Get down here, fast."*

Elnos and I sprinted in the direction Rylan had indicated. We passed more dead guards on our way, and ran into two live ones that I dispatched with my chakrams. I didn't want to use my magic unless it was absolutely necessary—it was a drain on my energy, which I needed to preserve if we were going to get out of this bunker alive.

"Here it is," Elnos said, sounding a little out of breath as we approached the elevator door. He scowled as he noticed the keyhole in the panel, where a call button would normally be. "I'm guessing your cousin didn't think about the fact that we don't have a key?"

"Nope." I strode over to the elevator doors, then wedged my fingers into the crack and pulled. The doors screeched a little in protest as I pulled them apart, revealing the elevator shaft that dropped sharply into utter darkness.

"Looks like we'll have to float down there," Elnos said. He muttered the Words to the same levitation spell Fenris had taught me when we were in Mexia, and his feet began to lift off the ground. I did the same, and followed Elnos down the shaft, slowly descending to the next floor.

"Hey, wise guy," I said to Rylan as I lit a flame—even my eyes couldn't make out anything in this blackness. *"We're headed down the elevator shaft. Is this floor I'm coming up on the one you're at?"*

"Yes! Hurry. We're under attack."

"Fuck," I hissed aloud, wishing I could go faster. Unfortunately, this spell wasn't meant for that sort of thing, so I gritted my teeth and waited the extra twenty seconds until I touched down atop the elevator box. Using one of my crescent knives, I pried open the hatch and cut an opening through the ceiling tile, then dropped down. Elnos floated in behind me as I forced open the doors, just in time to see one of the guards grab Noria from behind, and press a gun to the side of her head.

"Don't move!" he cried, eyes darting between Rylan and me. There were four guards still standing, and two more lying dead on the floor, blood seeping from the gunshot wounds in their head. Rylan had his gun pressed to the head of the guard he held, but his eyes were glued to the guard who had Noria. Noria was still in her nightgown, which was now torn and stained with blood, and Rylan looked a little worse for wear too. A knife lay on the grey tile a few feet from Noria, and I guessed that was her weapon. Rylan wouldn't be so foolish as to take her down here without giving her any way to defend herself, but of course she was no match for trained guards, knife or no.

"Or what?" I taunted, calling on my magic through instinct rather than Words. I focused on the gun in the guard's hand, and the metal went white hot, warping the barrel. He yelped, instinctively letting go, and Noria burst from his grasp, lunging for the knife on the ground. I flung a chakram at the guard who'd threatened her life, then rushed to intercept the two who were closing in on Noria, swords drawn. Rylan shot the guard in his grasp point-blank, and Elnos magically thrust another guard back against the wall with enough force to crush his skull.

I caught the remaining guard's downswing with one of my knives, then grabbed his sword arm and twisted until the elbow joint snapped. He screamed, sword clattering to the ground, and I drove him face-first into the wall.

"*Where* is Annia Melcott?" I snarled in his ear, pressing his arm into his back as I leaned against him.

"Sh-she's in the cell at the end of the hall," the guard babbled. I could smell the tears and snot running down his face, and urine too—the bastard had wet himself.

"And the shifter children?"

"I-i-in the other rooms, sp-split up," he sobbed.

"They'll each have their own cell," Noria said, her voice remarkably subdued. I turned to see her standing next to Rylan, with Elnos's arms wrapped around her from behind. The knife was still clutched firmly in her right hand. "The scientists won't have wanted to risk skewing their data by cross-contamination."

"Shit." I glanced toward the rows of doors lining the long, grey hallway. They were made of thick, reinforced steel. No windows, though there was a slat to stick food through. "Do we get them out now?"

"We should wait for Lord Iannis," Elnos advised. "He'll be able to heal them. We can't risk exposing ourselves, especially since they're shifters. You and Rylan could catch whatever they've been infected with."

"Fine." I grabbed the guard and snapped his neck—there was no use in letting him live only to have him try to kill us again the moment our backs were turned. "Let's go get Annia then."

I dropped the guard's body and let it fall as I marched down the hall. The others hurried after me, Noria breaking free from Elnos's grip to rush to my side. She didn't look at me, her eyes firmly fixed up ahead, hope and fear etched into her pale, gaunt features. My heart pounded in my chest as we approached the final door, dreading what I might find. Would Annia be all right? Or had the Resistance broken their word to Noria and tortured her anyway? If so, I would hunt down every last person in this compound and kill them. Slowly. And with relish.

"Annia?" I shouted, pounding on the metal door. "Are you in there?"

"Sunaya?" Annia called back, relief evident in her hoarse voice. "Is that really you?"

"Yes," I cried, tears springing to my eyes. "We've got a whole welcoming committee here. Stand back from the door so we can get you out."

"Those are the best fucking words I've heard all day."

A faint shuffle in the room told me Annia was moving backward. Rylan, Noria, and I moved to the side as Elnos stepped forward, raising his hands toward the door. He spoke a few Words, and intense heat began radiating from his hands.

"By Magorah!" Rylan took another few steps back as the heat

waves rippled over us. Noria and I followed suit—my skin was close to burning. "Is he summoning the very sun itself?"

"Thankfully, even mages can't do *that*," Noria muttered. I glanced down at her, surprised to see the bitterness in her dark eyes as she watched Elnos literally melt the door. Was she seriously projecting her hatred onto Elnos, after all he'd gone through to rescue her? She should be kissing his feet right now, especially since he was rescuing her sister. I wanted to shake some sense into her and scold her for being so unfair, but this wasn't the time, so I bit my tongue and waited for Elnos to finish. Paint was melting off the walls as the steel door liquefied. Before the red-hot metal could spread across the floor, Elnos spoke another Word and began shaping it into a pile out in the hall. The heat in his hands turned to bitter cold as he worked, cooling the metal down so that it would maintain its shape.

"Holy shit, did winter come early?" Annia asked as she stepped out into the hall. She wore white cotton pants and a creased shirt, and her left arm was in a cast and sling. Her dark eyes were rimmed with shadows, but they warmed with relief and gratitude as they took us all in.

"Annia!" Noria flung her arms around her sister, careful not to jostle her injured arm. "I'm so glad you're safe."

"And I'm glad *you're* safe," Annia said, squeezing her as tight as she could manage with her single arm. Her eyes met mine over Noria's mop of red curls. "Thank you for coming after me. I thought I was done for."

"I couldn't very well leave my best friend behind," I said with a grin, fighting tears. I wanted to hug the breath out of Annia, but Noria was still clinging to her, and I was loath to break them apart.

"So this is the famous Annia, eh?" Rylan asked, looking her up and down. There was masculine appreciation in his eyes, and I raised an eyebrow.

"Yes." Annia's eyes narrowed on Rylan, and her upper lip curled in a sneer as she took in his guard uniform and moustache. "Though I don't know who the hell you are."

"It's my cousin Rylan." Rolling my eyes, I undid the illusion that still cloaked him. Annia's eyes widened as Rylan's true form was revealed. "Iannis had him flown in from Prison Isle. I guess he decided a family reunion was in order."

"Sunaya?" Iannis's voice sounded in my head, tense with concern. *"Where are you? Did you make it inside the bunker?"*

"Yes," I said, turning to look at the other doors lining the hall as apprehension settled in my gut. *"We found Annia, and the location of the captured shifter children. We need you down here if we're going to get everybody out."*

19

"This is the last one," Iannis said as he gently laid the shifter child down on a makeshift blanket on the ground. The little girl, with her blonde hair, long lashes, and tanned skin, could have been from my own clan. Laid out next to her in the camp were nine other children—two of them mages, the rest shifters like her.

"You should rest a little." I placed a hand on Iannis's shoulder as he crouched next to the child. "You just spent all this time and energy healing these children." They'd all been infected with various diseases, though apparently in muted form, so as not to kill them off too quickly. Even so, they still could have spread epidemics without Iannis's intervention. He and Fenris had joined us down in the corridor where the test subjects had been kept. One by one, Iannis had broken into each occupied cell and healed the terrified children. It had been excruciating to wait out in the hall while he attended them, but he wouldn't let any of us near, fearing we might contract the diseases.

"I would like to rest, but I cannot." Iannis briefly squeezed my hand, then stood and turned to face me. His alabaster skin was paler than usual in the moonlight, and faint lines of strain were beginning to show on his face. It seemed that Dr. Mitas's claim about these diseases being resistant to magical healing was true. "There is still so much to do."

"It's nearly midnight, Iannis," Fenris said. He sat near the mage children, his back up against a tree. "Lord Logar and his men aren't going to get here until morning. The ward you put around the garage will keep the prisoners safely confined there, even if you sleep for a few hours. I will stay up, to make sure of that." Unlike our raiding party, Iannis and Fenris had taken prisoners, mostly by using short-term immobilization spells. The majority of the scientists were currently huddled in terror in the garage, some of them still frozen as they waited for the spell to wear off.

"It's cruel, keeping them there," Noria said in a brittle voice. We turned toward her as one, apprehension sparking in my gut. She sat on one of the logs by the fire pit, staring into the crackling flame—now that we were no longer hiding, there was no reason not to have the fire for warmth. Fenris had found a blanket for her to wrap around her shoulders. Her magically shackled hands rested on her legs, glowing faintly in the darkness. Fenris had brought the shackles with him on the airship, and they would immobilize her if she moved too far away from him.

I felt a little bad that she'd been forced to wear them so soon after tasting freedom, but the truth was, she wasn't free. She'd just exchanged one prison for another.

"You said you were going to destroy the compound." She lifted her gaze to meet Iannis's. The amount of loathing in those dark brown eyes made me clench my teeth—was she still going to treat Iannis like the enemy, after all this? "By imprisoning those men and women in there, you're condemning them all to death. Don't they deserve a hearing, at the very least?"

"Of course they do," Iannis said, a hint of irritation in his voice. "I do not intend to leave them in the compound—it is simply the safest place to hold them until Lord Logar arrives with transport. They will be given a hearing, as will you," he added sternly.

Noria jerked her gaze away, staring back into the fire. Annia, who sat on the log next to her, looked stricken, and Rylan, who sat across from Noria, wore an uncomfortable expression on his face. But Iannis had only spoken the truth.

"Please remember, Lord Iannis, my sister is still not yet eighteen," Annia said quietly, clenching her hands into her lap. She looked up at Iannis, a quiet desperation in her dark eyes. "She might be a genius, but she's still a child."

"Don't, Annia," Noria protested, looking both angry and guilty all at once. "I know you mean well, but don't belittle my actions by calling me a child. I'm not one. Aside from what happened here at the bunker, if I had to do this all over again, I'd still join the Resistance." Her eyes flashed as she met Iannis's gaze, tilting her stubborn chin at him. "I'm fighting for equal rights for all, and I am willing to pay any price for that."

"If I could try her as a child, I would," Iannis said calmly. Sympathy flickered in his gaze for a moment as he looked at Annia and Noria. "But since Noria is enrolled in college, however early, she is legally considered an adult." A weariness settled across his expression, and he looked down into the fire. All that healing had probably worn him out.

"At least we managed to get these children to safety," Elnos said awkwardly, getting to his feet. He'd been putting a sleep spell on the children, to ensure they did not wake during the night—we didn't need them running off after we'd just rescued them. "You found the two mage children in one of the vehicles, Lord Iannis?"

"Yes." Iannis's violet eyes flashed as he looked down at their sleeping faces. Like all the other children, and Annia, they were dressed in simple white cotton pants and shirts. Seeing the mage children sleeping side by side with the shifter children, their eyes closed, made me realize just how similar we all were in the end. They all looked... human.

"A spell to puncture the tires and freeze the soldiers was enough to bring them all to a stop," Iannis continued. "We found the children in the back of one of the vehicles, bound and gagged, and completely isolated from the escapees." His eyes flickered toward the hill. "I must check on those wards—"

"I'll go," Elnos said, stepping forward. "I'll take Rylan with me as backup."

Rylan arched a brow. "I'll be useless if it has anything to do with the wards."

"Yes, but you're handy with a blade," Elnos said, glancing to the short sword Rylan had strapped to his hips.

"True." Rylan got to his feet, then stretched his arms over-head. "Try not to miss me when I'm gone," he said to us, winking at Annia with a roguish grin. Noria gave him a murderous glare as he turned away, and I held in a sigh.

Fenris got up too. "I'll patrol the area around our camp to make sure there are no surprises." He slipped away, no doubt to change into wolf form in the forest.

"I'm going to bed," Noria said, standing up. She stalked away toward the sleeping area, though the effect was somewhat diminished by the fact that her hands were restrained, and disappeared inside Annia's tent.

"I suppose I will go and rest as well," Iannis said, though it was clear he still didn't feel comfortable taking any downtime right now. "But someone needs to watch the children."

"I will," Annia said quietly. The firelight flickered in her sad eyes, and my heart clenched in sympathy. This was supposed to be a happy reunion, a triumphant moment, but it was anything but.

"I'll join you in a few," I told Iannis, laying a hand on his forearm.

Understanding lit behind his violet eyes, and he nodded quietly before striding off to his own tent. Iannis and Fenris had brought several more, so there were enough for everyone even if the clearing was rather cramped now. Rylan and Elnos were headed to the compound, so there was no one but Annia and me as I sat down next to her by the fire.

"I'm sorry things have turned out this way." I put an arm around her shoulder and hugged her, careful not to hurt her injured arm.

"It's not your fault." Annia let out a heavy sigh as she leaned into me. "I always knew Noria might spurn me when Elnos and I arrived to rescue her. She came here willingly, even if she didn't know exactly what she was getting into."

"And she left willingly too." I glanced over at Annia's tent, where Noria slept now. I doubt she could hear us from so far away, over the crackle of the fire, but I lowered my voice anyway. "Though I imagine she's wondering how she can escape her restraints and run off."

"I won't let that happen," Annia said, her eyes narrowing on the tent as well. "I'll be by her side the entire time. There's no way I'm going to let her run off again, not when it resulted in this fiasco." She swept her hand out, indicating the sleeping children. Her expression softened as she gazed at their peaceful little faces, and the anger sparking in her eyes gave way to sadness again. "I can't imagine the fear and pain they've been through these past weeks. Or has it been months? Do you have any idea how long these children have been down here?"

"I don't know." My eyes were drawn to the blonde girl who looked like she could belong to the Baine Clan. I didn't think we had any small cubs missing, but I would have to ask when we got back. "Their parents must sick to death with worry."

"I know I would be." Annia shook her head, returning her gaze to mine. "What kind of monsters could do such a thing, Sunaya? Steal innocent children from their beds and inject them with fatal diseases?"

"The kind that believes in the 'greater good'," I sneered, remembering Dr. Mitas's hateful, impassioned words back in Dara. He was supposed to be a doctor, a healer, yet he had no qualms about participating in such horrific activities. I didn't believe in any greater good myself, mostly because that phrase was so open to interpretation. The rulers' ideas of what the greater good meant rarely matched the ideas of the common man, after all. The Mages Guild was proof of that.

"I shouldn't really be surprised," Annia admitted. "As enforcers, you and I know better than most the lengths criminals will go to justify their actions."

"I think that the day we stop being shocked by this kind of thing is the day we should be afraid," I told her. "We should hold society to a higher standard, or the world will never become a better place." An ember popped, sending sparks shooting through the sky. I held out my palm and caught one of them as they floated back down to earth, watching as it briefly stung my palm before its orange glow faded to black.

Transient, just like everything else in life.

Annia's lips curved at that, her dark eyes sparkling. "Why Sunaya Baine, you almost sound like a sage. Is that the sort of thing that happens when one joins the Mages Guild?"

"I suppose I've gotten a little more philosophical these days," I allowed, smiling a little. I imagined my deeper thoughts were inspired by the brief, but meaningful conversations I'd had with Resinah's spirit—the first mage, entrusted with wisdom by the Creator. I glanced down at Annia's bandaged arm and changed the subject. "How did you get that?"

A shadow crossed Annia's face. "One of the soldiers broke my arm as punishment for trying to resist capture." A faraway look entered her eyes. "I killed three of them, but I was outnumbered. Even so, I don't suppose he would have broken my arm if I hadn't spat in his face." A smirk curved her lips. "The big brute didn't like that much."

"Ouch." I winced, glancing at the sling again. I couldn't imagine what that must be like for humans such as Annia, having to wait six to eight weeks for her limb to heal. Mine would have been better in the morning, so long as it was properly set and I'd had enough to eat. The bullet graze on my shoulder from earlier had already healed, nothing more than a memory now. Perhaps Iannis could mend Annia's arm once he had dealt with the current mission. I was surprised he hadn't offered already, but, then again, he was exhausted.

"You do look remarkably un-beaten up aside from your arm," I said as I looked her up and down again. Her face was clear of any bruising, and although there could be bandages beneath her clothing, the way she moved did not hint at any hidden injuries.

"Since they're a science lab using live test subjects, they happened to have a damn good doctor on staff, and some crazy medical procedures I've never seen before." Annia briefly touched her cheekbone. "The doctor who treated me was surprisingly compassionate, considering I was a prisoner. She put some kind of tingling, foul-smelling cream on my face that handled all the bruising, and she set my arm and bound it up."

"Maybe it's because you're human," I said, unable to think of any other explanation. "Or because you're Noria's sister."

Annia snorted. "Either way, I'm hardly softening up to them. Just because they treated the injuries they inflicted on me doesn't change the fact that they were planning to commit mass murder."

"No, I guess it doesn't," I said softly, looking back at Noria's tent again. And that Noria had helped us in the end didn't change the fact that she had joined the Resistance and aided them in attempted genocide, willing or not.

20

*L*ord Logar and his team arrived bright and early, just as the sun was cresting the horizon. He sent Iannis a message via ether pigeon asking us to meet him in front of the compound, so we dressed and straightened ourselves up as best we could, then went out.

Annia stayed behind again with the slumbering children, to watch over them until Logar's team came to fetch them. I hoped they had brought suitable food for children, though in a pinch, we could make them porridge.

"Good morning, Lord Iannis," Lord Logar said as we approached. For a change, he wasn't the stereotypical tall, long-haired mage. He kept his silver hair short, wore a beard of the same shade, and had a stocky, five-foot-six frame. The emerald robes he wore seemed to highlight the flecks of green in his hazel eyes. His twelve fellow mages, ten males and two females, all stood a few inches taller than him. They wore a variety of robes with the Osero Mages Guild emblem stitched to the breast, a standing grizzly bear, stitched onto their breasts.

"Good morning, Lord Logar." Iannis inclined his head courteously, and the rest of us bowed. "I am pleased to see you, and your reinforcements." He glanced over at the other mages, as well as the caravan of steam cars and carriages they had brought with them, with the human drivers keeping well out of the way. Guess Iannis wasn't the only one who'd been upgrading his fleet.

"Indeed. It looks like we'll need them." Logar swept his gaze over us. Fenris, who stood on my left, stiffened almost imperceptibly. He was uncomfortable around other chief mages, since there was always the risk that one of his former colleagues might discover his true identity. It was unlikely they would be able to tell that Fenris had once been Polar ar'Tollis, Chief Mage of Nebara, by just looking at him, but I would have been nervous if I'd been in his position.

"You have managed to accomplish quite a lot with such a small crew," Logar finally said, his eyes stopping to linger on me. "I suppose that is in no small part due to your bride-to-be." His hazel eyes warmed fractionally. "Congratulations on your engagement, by the way."

"Sunaya has been very helpful," Iannis acknowledged. "But we could not have accomplished this without the rest of our group."

"Of course not." Lord Logar turned his attention toward the compound. His eyes narrowed as he peered at the buildings through the wire fence. "So you have all the prisoners stored in these garages?"

"Yes. They will need to be rounded up before we demolish the compound."

"Pity we can't burn them all too, at the same time," the Chief Mage said with disdain. "They deserve nothing less."

"Do you consider yourself above the law, then?" Noria sneered. "That you feel it's okay to kill off all these people without a fair trial?"

"And who is this young upstart?" Lord Logar asked, turning

his gaze toward Noria. She stood between Rylan and Elnos, her wrists still magically restrained. "Is this the one you all came to rescue?"

Noria opened her mouth to answer, and Elnos kicked at her ankle. The two of them exchanged a heated glare, and Noria edged away from him, her freckled face pale with fury.

"This is Noria Melcott, the younger sister of Sunaya's close friend, Annia Melcott," Iannis said. "It is by coincidence that she turned out to be at this compound, and she was not directly involved in the production of diseases or experiments on children. She will be taken back to Solantha for trial."

"Speaking of Annia," I said quickly, before Noria exploded, "she's back at the clearing with the mage and shifter children we rescued. They're still asleep now, but they'll need water, food and clothing when they awaken, and a nursemaid to care for them until their parents can be located. There are ten in all."

"Excellent." Lord Logar turned to two of his mages, a man and a woman. "Fetch the children, then get them into the carriages. They can eat in there. They need not witness what we are about to do. In fact, they should be sent to safety as soon as possible."

"I'll escort you," Rylan said quickly, stepping forward. I suspected he wanted to personally ensure that they treated the shifter children with care, and I held back a smile as warmth spread through me. Rylan would always put shifters first, no matter what the situation. The thought eased the last of my fears about him defecting back to the Resistance—if he hadn't been convinced they were planning to betray him before, this business with the shifter children would have done the trick.

Rylan led the two mages away, and Iannis set to disabling his wards. He looked well rested despite getting less than four hours of sleep, and, somehow, his long hair and robes were perfect. I'd had to bundle my rat's nest of curly hair into a bun before coming down here, and some lovely bloodstains marred my wrinkled clothes. A great way to make a first impression as the Chief Mage's future wife.

Stop that, I scolded myself, standing a little taller. I wasn't some fucking princess; I was Sunaya Baine. Half-shifter, half-mage, *all* warrior. If the mages couldn't handle seeing me in disarray after kicking ass, that was their problem, not mine.

I glanced back at Elnos as the mages opened the gate and drove the first of the transport carriages through. He was still standing close to Noria, with Fenris flanking her other side. Conflict drew lines of tension in Elnos's youthful face. I wouldn't be surprised if he was thinking about letting Noria escape, to spare her whatever sentence Iannis decided to mete out. But would life as a perpetual fugitive be any better in the long run? I doubted Iannis would give her a life sentence, so it was probably better just to endure whatever punishment he decided upon.

"Don't let Noria out of your sight," I told Fenris. *"She looks ready to bolt, and I'm not sure Elnos has the guts to stop her."*

"I have to agree." Fenris's yellow gaze slanted toward Noria. She still had the blanket from last night wrapped around her slim shoulders. Coupled with her wild hair and gaunt, shadowed face, she looked like a lost child. But the sullen look on her face dampened my compassion for her. Yes, she'd suffered, but most of my sympathy in this messy situation was for Annia and Elnos.

"I don't know why you're looking at us like we're traitors," I said aloud to her. "You're the one who abandoned your family and friends to join a bunch of mass-murderers."

Noria recoiled as though I'd struck her, her accusatory glare briefly eclipsed by pain. "I didn't abandon them—I was trying to assure their safety." Her glare returned with a vengeance. "At least I'm not a sellout like you."

"Noria!" Elnos scolded, his eyes widening with alarm.

"Don't tell me what I can and can't say," Noria said, rounding on her ex-boyfriend. "I've had far more than enough of that since arriving here."

"Yeah, and whose fault was that?" I demanded, taking a step forward. I didn't dare close the distance completely—my hands were itching to throttle her for being such an ungrateful brat. It occurred to me that Iannis must have viewed me in a similar light, and I was amazed he hadn't killed me outright in the beginning. "You came here of your own will, ignoring all the warnings Annia and I gave you that the Resistance is corrupt. Nobody stopped you from airing your opinions in Solantha—everybody knew you wanted to join the Resistance before you left, and nobody carted you off and stuck you in a jail cell for that. It's your willful blindness that got you into this mess, nothing else, and worse, you've dragged all of us into it too. Annia almost died because of you!"

Noria opened her mouth to say something else, but no words came out. The fire died in her eyes and her shoulders sagged. "I don't want to talk about this anymore," she muttered, her dark eyes firmly fixed on the ground.

I wanted to say *tough shit*, not willing to let her run away from this conversation so easily. Anger roiled in my chest at Noria's churlishness after all we'd gone through, and I longed to rub her face in all the facts she was choosing to ignore. But Elnos gave me a pleading look, and I kept my mouth shut.

We waited outside the gates in silence as the Osero mages rounded up the prisoners, directed by Lord Logar and Iannis. The scientists, guards, and staff were marched out of the garages in single file and made to strip, then subjected to a purification spell to ensure that they carried no diseases. Iannis had forbidden me to come in with him since he didn't want me to catch anything. It was a silly fear, as shifters rarely sickened and couldn't usually catch diseases that affected humans. But I was hardly going to argue with him in front of Lord Logar.

Annia, Rylan, and the other two mages returned as the first carriage, loaded up with prisoners, rolled through the gates. The curtains were drawn over the windows, so I couldn't see any of them, but they probably weren't smiling and waving. For many of them, death was the only thing they had to look forward to, once their trials were over. I couldn't imagine that hard labor would be a sufficient punishment for conspiring to commit genocide.

Turning away from the carriage and its passengers' gruesome fate, I focused on a happier thought—that the children we rescued would get to return home. They were walking toward us, with the two mages up front, and Rylan and Annia bringing up the rear. Their little faces were anxious, eyes wide with fear, and I saw a few trembling lips.

"It's going to be all right." Annia leaned down to snag the hand of a skittish child. He was a dark-skinned little boy with ice-blue shifter eyes, and he looked like he was about to turn tail and dart back into the woods. "We're going to get you home to your parents. You're safe now."

A lump swelled in my throat, and I blinked back tears of my own as I went to meet them at the steam carriages. The two mage children were up front, between the adult mages, and I decided not to complain about the show of favoritism. I might have done the same if the situation was reversed.

"Where are you taking them?" I asked.

"They'll all be housed in Parabas Palace until their parents are found," one of the mages assured me. "Lord Logar has a soft spot for children. They'll be well taken care of."

"Good." I moved aside, giving them access so that they could direct the children into the carriages. I'd smelled no lie, and was as convinced as I ever would be that these kids would be all right.

But as I moved away, I locked eyes with the blonde shifter child I'd noticed last night. Her face was pale with worry, her slim shoulders tense, but it was her eyes that made me pause. They were yellow-orange, the exact same color as Lakin's.

"Hey there," I said, crouching down to her level and offering a hand. She hesitated for just a moment, but my shifter eyes must have decided her, because she took my hand and allowed me to briefly pull her from the group. Annia and Rylan gave me curious looks, but I ignored them.

"My name is Sunaya Baine," I told the little girl. "What's yours?"

"Tula Leoni," she said quietly. "I'm from the Leoni Clan in Parabas."

A quick sniff told me she was a jaguar shifter, and I smiled. "I think I may know a relative of yours. Does the name Boon Lakin sound familiar to you?"

"You know my uncle Boon?" Tula's eyes widened. "Where did you meet him?"

"In Solantha. He and I worked on a case together. I noticed your beautiful eyes and how similar they are to his, and I thought you might be of his old clan. He's a good man."

"He's one of my favorite uncles." The girl gave a little sniffle. Alarmed, I wondered if I'd made a mistake by mentioning Lakin, who she clearly missed. But then she smiled, her shoulders relaxing. "I guess it's good to know that you're his friend."

"He'll be very happy to learn you're safe," I told her, smiling back. I ruffled her hair, then gave her a gentle pat on the back. "I will make sure to tell him all about how I met you, and how brave you've been. Go on now."

I gave her a gentle push in the direction of the carriage, and watched the mages load her up before getting inside. The carriage let out a shrill whistle as it lurched forward, and my heart jumped into my throat as we watched the children leave.

"Small world, isn't it?" Rylan murmured, placing a hand on my shoulder as he came to stand beside me. "That you happened to have a connection to one of the children?"

"Yeah," I said, glancing sideways at my cousin. His expression was serious, his yellow shifter eyes broody for once. "It makes me realize it's not enough to ensure that Canalo is safe. We're all part of the same country, and our actions affect one another more than we realize."

Two more steam carriages rolled out of the gate, carrying prisoners, and we stepped back to give them a clear path. Iannis, Lord Logar, and the remaining mages returned via steamcar rather than walking up the long path back to the entrance. My heart began to thump a little faster as Iannis stepped out of the vehicle, a grave expression on his face as he locked eyes with me.

"It is time," he said. "We're going to demolish the compound now, and everything in it."

"Don't look so glum," Lord Logar said cheerily as he came around one of the vehicles. He surveyed us all as he spoke. "The sooner we get this done, the sooner we can get out of here and back to civilization. I don't know about you, but I missed breakfast to get here so early, and intend to make up for it with a hearty lunch."

"Yes, sir," Elnos said, and the rest of us followed suit. Normally, I jumped at any talk of food, but at the moment, my gut churned at the very thought of eating anything. There were animals still down in the labs—mice, rats, and rabbits—that didn't deserve to die. But Iannis had decided freeing them would be too risky, since an unknown number of these rodents carried deadly diseases, and Lord Logar had agreed.

As Iannis's apprentice, I was enlisted to help prepare the spell—after all, it was a rare and dangerous one, a good opportunity to learn. There was an air of suppressed excitement about the Osero mages, who seemed eager to put in practice a technique they only knew from magic textbooks and history volumes. Even Elnos looked excited to participate, despite his melancholy about Noria.

My part in the spell was simple and yet complicated. Lord Logar pulled out pouches of black stones and had several of us place them in a grid-like pattern around and inside the entire complex of buildings. Each stone was smooth and polished, about the size of my palm, and had a rune carved into it. There were four different runes in total, and Iannis explained to me that each rune stood for a different element. Each time I pulled a stone from the pouch, I spoke a Word to activate it. The rune would glow a bright, otherworldly color, and I would place it on the ground before moving onto the next location.

It was eerie, walking so close to the corridors of the underground labs as I placed my stones. The place was empty of all human life, but even from outside, I could still scent decay and despair beneath the antiseptic, and my heart clenched at the thought of the animals yet inside. My boots echoed against the paved yard as I walked above the laboratories with their rows of steel tables laden with glass beakers and cruel-looking instruments. According to Fenris, some of those tables were equipped with leather straps, clearly meant to hold down the children they kept here as they were poked, prodded, and injected. Had they killed any before we arrived, in those experiments? It seemed all too likely. I was relieved that the surviving victims had been taken away. If I had been in their position, coming out of a nightmare of being tortured and experimented on, I would not have been able to gain any peace of mind until I was as far away from this place as possible.

The thought that the Resistance was responsible for such pain and cruelty was enough to set my blood boiling again.

Burning down this compound wasn't enough. I wanted the perpetrators to burn for eternity.

Rein it in, I warned myself as sparks of magic began to sizzle in the air around me. My power was close to the surface, ready to be unleashed at the slightest provocation, and I couldn't afford to let that happen. I was in the spotlight now more than ever. Even though I knew Iannis would not allow anyone to harm or threaten me, neither of us needed the hassle that would ensue if I were perceived to be a danger to society.

The other mages and I finished placing the stones, then returned to the entrance of the compound. Iannis and Lord Logar had their heads bent together, discussing something, while the other mages were stationed at various points around the perimeter, clearly on standby.

"We've finished, Lord Logar," Gillen, one of the mages who'd gone with me, said. "The stones have all been activated."

"Excellent," Lord Logar said. "Go and take your positions."

The three mages rushed off, and I looked to Iannis. "Where am I supposed to go?"

"Stay back there with the others and observe," Iannis told me. "The rest of the spell is too complicated for an apprentice to participate in. *Besides, you should be able to use your sharp sight and excellent hearing to learn even at a distance,"* he added mentally.

"All right." I retreated to where the others were standing, folding my arms across my chest. The sun was halfway up the sky by now, shining bright rays over the green landscape as if it hadn't gotten the memo that this was a day of destruction, not cheer.

"I'm not sure if I'm excited or terrified," Annia murmured in my ear. "I mean, I want the compound wiped from the face of Recca, and I'm sure this kind of spell is rare to witness. But what if we get caught up in the backlash?"

"Lord Iannis and Lord Logar are very experienced mages,"

Fenris said. The wistful expression that briefly flickered in his dark eyes suggested that he longed to be out there with the other mages, casting this powerful spell that was so rarely used. "And like most people, they also have a strong sense of self-preservation. They would not cast this spell if they feared they would lose their lives in the process, or endanger us here."

"Of course not." Noria huffed, wrinkling her nose. "After all, sacrificing themselves for the common good would hardly be in character for them, now would it?"

"The stones they set will ensure the spell is contained," Fenris said loudly before anyone could respond to Noria's jab. "The magic will only affect what is within the boundary."

The mages raised their arms, and a hush fell over us as we watched. The world seemed to take a collective breath, the calm before the storm. As if choreographed, the mages all began chanting in Loranian at once. A faint, golden light began to emanate from around the perimeter, growing gradually brighter as the chant rose in volume. The clouds above darkened, moving closer together. The wind kicked up, whipping the mages' robes around their ankles. Iannis's dark red hair was ripped from its tie. It streamed out behind him like a banner as he stood proud and fierce, chanting the spell along with the others. I sucked in a breath, and immediately noticed that the air seemed too hot, as if someone had lit a fire that was fast spreading through the ground.

I expected the clouds to burst into a torrential downpour, the wind to spin into a violent cyclone, sparks to catch on the grass and trees and set the fire ablaze. But though I saw sparks, they weren't the kind that came from fire. Rather, they were golden and smelled like magic. They floated up from the ground and down from the sky, converging toward the area that was marked off by the stones. The golden glow that started around the boundary began to rise up as the sparks came, drawing on their strength to become more powerful.

"By Magorah," Rylan murmured, his eyes wide as he watched the stunning spectacle. "They're drawing on the power of nature herself!"

That was the closest way to explain it, I thought in agreement, as the golden glow continued to expand. A sense of awe filled me as I watched it form a dome over the compound, glowing brightly enough to give the sun a run for its money. Hell, I wasn't sure that the sun wasn't lending some of its energy to the spell in the first place.

The ground began to tremble then, and we gasped as the tremors raced up our feet, sending our hearts pounding. A muffled explosion followed, and then another tremor on its heels that nearly knocked me off my feet. I grabbed Annia, to steady her, since she only had one arm with which to break her fall.

"Get down!" I shouted to the others as I dragged her down to the grass. They followed suit, hurling themselves on the ground, belly down. We were far enough away from the trees that none would fall on us, and the safest place to be during any kind of earthquake was out in the open, away from buildings and other tall structures. Anybody from Canalo knew that. I had lived through quite a few tremors in Solantha.

Fortunately, this wasn't a real earthquake. The tremors we felt had to be caused by the bunker collapsing below the earth. Still, the sound of trees groaning as their roots were unceremoniously pushed from the ground wasn't reassuring, and I doubted the wildlife appreciated the distinction between a real earthquake and a magically induced one.

I continued to peer through the blades of grass at the compound, anxiously waiting for the spell to cease. There was nothing to see except the golden blaze and the mages standing outside of it—the wall of magic was glowing so brightly it was impossible to see what was happening within. My ears picked up groans and rumbles from beneath the ground, and muffled explosions from beyond the glowing wall. Judging by the noise, the destruction above and belowground had to be cataclysmic.

Finally, the golden glow began to fade, gradually melting back down into the ground. I waited to see if there were any residual tremors, then slowly got back to my feet, helping Annia up as I went. What would we see, now that the spell was done? Would anything remain?

Noria let out a horrified gasp as the last of the glow disappeared. Not a single building was left standing—the ground below where they once stood had sunk into a deep crater, swallowing whatever remained of the facilities. Or so I assumed. From our vantage point, all we could see was the blackened ground and the edges of the hole. Every tree and blade of grass was completely burned away. The stench of burnt carbon wafted toward me, thick and pungent in the air.

"My goodness," one of the human drivers said, his voice hushed. "That was quite a spectacle."

"A horrifying one, but yes, I agree," Rylan said, sounding shell-shocked. His tanned skin had gone pale, and I could smell the fear rolling off him. I couldn't exactly blame him, as my knees were a feeling a little on the wobbly side. But I stood up straighter and firmed my shoulders.

"It was necessary." I stared at the devastation as I struggled to overcome my own shock. "Necessary not just because of what went on inside the compound, but to demonstrate exactly what you're up against when it comes to the mages. Guns and numbers aren't enough against a race who can dish out destruction like that."

"Yeah, I get it," Noria said bitterly, her eyes brimming with unshed tears and anguish as she gazed toward Iannis. "The mages are too powerful for us to stand up against, and because they have all that power, they don't have to listen to us." She turned her bleak gaze toward me. "You win, Naya. You fucking win."

But as she turned and stomped off toward the carriages, I sure didn't feel like a winner.

21

"*I really* wish you hadn't accepted Lord Logar's invitation to this banquet," I groused as the steamcar rumbled along the dirt road to Parabas. The car had been sent to pick Iannis, Fenris, and me up from the Black Lion Inn, where we'd stayed overnight after wrapping up the destruction of the Resistance compound.

"It would have been rude to refuse," Iannis said mildly. He sat next to me on the comfortable black leather seats, with Fenris on my other side. The driver was up front alone. Iannis had cast a subtle spell to muffle our conversation, so that we could have some privacy on the ride. "We would not have been able to complete our mission without Lord Logar's assistance."

"Yeah, but it's not like he was in a position to refuse," I pointed out, staring out the window as the countryside zipped by. "He doesn't want the Resistance operating within his state borders any more than we do."

"If I can refrain from complaining about this banquet, I think you can too," Fenris said dryly. "Of the three of us, I have the most valid objections to attending."

"You know I would have sent you back to Solantha with the

others if I could have, old friend," Iannis said apologetically. "But you were specifically included in the invitation, along with Sunaya, a surprising sign of progress in the local attitude toward shifters. It could make Lord Logar suspicious if you were to refuse, and we do not wish to seem ungracious."

We subsided into gloomy silence after that, my mind heavy as I went over all that happened. I imagined Iannis and Fenris had plenty to occupy their thoughts as well. After the destruction of the compound, we had all retired to the Black Lion Inn to clean up and enjoy some much-needed food. Lord Logar had booked the private dining room, and we'd all sat around the table over plates heaped with steak, potatoes, and green beans, hashing out the next steps.

Iannis had given Rylan the choice to either go to the mines and carry out a five-year sentence, or serve the Mages Guild as a consultant for the same number of years. The work would be mostly unpaid, but he'd be given a small stipend for necessities, and he would be confined to the Palace unless accompanied by an appropriate guard or chaperone. Rylan didn't like the idea of being under house arrest too much, but the fact that I lived in the Palace sweetened the deal. Besides, it was a lot better than enduring backbreaking work in the mines.

"Oh, I'm not doing this because I'm afraid of hard labor," he'd joked after agreeing to the consultant position. "I'm mostly afraid of being forced into celibacy for the next five years." He'd winked at Annia, who grinned back at him.

I remembered how Noria's eyes had flashed, and the disgusted look she'd given Rylan. Clearly, she thought he was a sell-out. I wondered what she would do when the time came for her own sentencing. Would she take whatever deal Iannis figured out for her? Or would she spit in our faces, as she'd been doing the entire time?

Please, Resinah, I said, calling on her rather than Magorah for once. *Help Noria see sense.*

But Resinah didn't answer, and neither did Magorah. I wondered if I should appeal to Noria's god, the Ur-God, instead. But I doubted that would help—like Iannis, I suspected the Ur-God and Magorah were all just different names for the Creator, and that there was only one God. If He or She didn't answer under one name, why would they answer under another?

Besides, I doubted it would make any difference—Noria would do whatever that strong, stubborn will of hers told her to do. That stubborn streak was one of the things I liked about her—she reminded me of myself at her age. But while I had gotten into my fair share of trouble, I'd still managed to come out on top in the end. I wasn't sure Noria would be so lucky. She was headed back to Solantha now, along with Rylan, Annia, and Elnos. Annia and Elnos had agreed to accept responsibility for her. Though it pained Annia to do it, and their mother might never forgive her, I knew she would have Noria placed in a cell in the Enforcers Guild when they arrived back. And when the time came for her hearing on Monday, she would personally see to it that Noria made it there.

The alternative was that Noria would become a fugitive of the state, condemned to dodge death for the rest of her life. And Annia would be punished for allowing Noria to escape.

Parabas Palace turned out to be set close to the city center, nestled into the bend of the Millawette River that ran east-west through the state before heading north. It was constructed almost entirely of beautiful red brick, with grey slate tiles covering the roofs and turrets, and green ivy crawling up the exterior walls. Though smaller than Solantha Palace, it still cut a majestic figure against the cloudless blue sky, with the river gently flowing behind it.

The long, paved driveway leading to the front entrance was

flanked by tall trees trimmed into conical shapes. The scent of magic thickened in the air as we passed protective wards laid around the estate, dormant but ready to activate at the first sign of trouble. A fountain sculpture graced the center of the paved roundabout in front of the palace, depicting Jeremidah, Faonus, and Micara, the Founding Trio who had established the Northia Federation. This one was much bigger than the similar sculpture in Dara's Capitol building.

The driver pulled to a stop by the front steps, and a guard opened the door for us. "Welcome back, Lord Iannis," the man said, bowing. "And welcome, Miss Baine and... Fenris," he added, clearly unsure if Fenris had a last name.

"Fenris is fine," Fenris said, nodding to the man as he closed the door behind us.

As we crossed the steps and entered the Palace through the heavy oak doors, I was grateful I'd magically cleaned my leathers before departing Nika. I might not have looked as noble as everyone else here, but at least there were no bloodstains to show off, and my skin and hair were clean.

A maid in a dark green dress was summoned, and she curtsied before us. "Good afternoon," she said, her dark brown eyes wide as she surveyed me. I supposed whatever rumors she'd heard about me were flitting through her head, and she was trying to match them up with what she saw in front of her now. "Lord Logar is in a meeting. He has asked me to show you to your rooms."

She led us down a series of hallways, cutting south. Busy meeting rooms and halls gave way to carpeted floors and quiet colors as we entered the guest wing of the Palace. We were given separate rooms, Iannis's and mine next to each other, and Fenris's across the hall.

"Your evening wear has already been delivered," the woman told us. "Please let me know if any adjustments or exchanges are needed. You've only to pull the bell and I will come."

She left us with the keys, and we went to to our separate rooms. A stack of white boxes stood on my dresser and vanity table—my evening gown for tonight, I imagined. My hostess or some Palace minion must have provided it. Noticing a door that connected my room to Iannis's suite, I ignored my bed completely and went to his room instead.

A hint of steam warmed the air as my feet crossed the cream-colored carpet, and the sound of the shower running was clearly audible beyond the open door of the bathroom. My heartbeat quickened at the thought of Iannis standing naked beneath the hot spray, water sluicing down his hard body, and a grin tugged at my lips. We still had a few hours until it was time to dress for the banquet. What better way to relieve the stress and general crappiness of the week than some good, old-fashioned sex?

I stripped off my clothes as I crossed the room, leaving a trail of leather and cotton behind me. I stepped out of my underwear as I crossed the threshold, and my feet hit the cool marble tile. The fragrance of soap mingled with Iannis's natural scent, and I inhaled deeply, tingles already spreading through my body in anticipation. I could make out the hazy outline of Iannis's form through the fogged-up glass shower doors, his head bent forward as he lathered his hair.

"Hey, handsome," I said, opening the sliding glass door. His violet eyes darkened, roaming up and down my naked body as I joined him beneath the hot spray. "Thought you could use some company."

"I was using the shower time to think," Iannis said as I slid my hands up his wet, naked chest, my fingertips playing with the crisp hairs there. "But I doubt I'll get much thinking done with you in here."

"I should hope not." I reached up to tangle my fingers into

his soapy hair. The strands slipped and slid through my fingers as I brought his mouth down to mine. Our lips met, a clash of tongue and teeth and raw need, and I moaned as he devoured me with the single-minded intensity of a starving man. His hands cupped my ass, lifting me against him, and the next thing I knew, he was pushing me up against the wet tile wall. His arousal pressed against me, sending shockwaves of pleasure rippling through my body, and I groaned deep in my throat.

"Yes," Iannis growled as he tore his mouth from mine. His lips trailed a path of flame across my skin, down my jaw and over my neck. He scraped his teeth across the pulse in my neck as he rocked his hips firmly into mine, and I dug my nails into his broad shoulders as he pushed me to the breaking point, over and over, without ever quite letting me go over the edge.

"Please," I gasped, reaching between us to curl my fingers around his length. "More."

Iannis sucked in a sharp breath as I stroked him. His violet eyes blazed with desire as rivulets of water ran down his angular face. My eyes followed the trail of water down his chest, over his carved abdomen, where it disappeared into the crevice where our bodies met. Damn, but he was beautiful, especially with his barriers stripped away. Only I ever got to see him like this, naked and raw and burning, as we sought to complete each other in the purest, most basic way possible.

"Enough," he finally said, pulling my hand away. He slid his thumb over my sweet spot, sending another shock of pleasure through me, then buried himself inside me. I was already so wound up, so close to the edge, that the single thrust sent me over. Stars burst in my vision as pleasure barreled through me, and I screamed his name as I clung to him, seeking purchase in the storm we'd created together. He held me tight, but didn't stop, taking me hard and fast against the wall as water continued to drum against his back.

Magic sizzled in the air around us as he joined his soul with mine, allowing me to feel the tide of pleasure he felt as he pounded into me. My inner muscles clenched around him as I came again, and he groaned low and deep in his throat as he finally found release. His grip on me weakened, and we found ourselves sliding to the floor of the shower. Thank Magorah the hot water was powered by magic, or the spray would be ice cold by now.

"I love you," Iannis murmured in my ear, gently stroking my back.

"Love you too." Smiling, I snagged the bar of soap, which had fallen to the ground, and began lathering it up in my hands. "Now why don't we get ourselves cleaned up?"

22
_____

The banquet hall was buzzing with chatter when the three of us walked in, nearly full despite the fact that we'd arrived a few minutes early. The entire Parabas Mages Guild must have shown up. Though everyone was dressed in finery, it was easy enough to pick up on who was a peon and who was a high-ranking mage, based on body language. The grand, open space had high ceilings and a wide, carpeted floor. Gold was the dominating color, featured on the drapes hanging from the walls, the molding that edged the ceiling, and the legs and backs of the chairs gathered by the tables arranged in a semi-circle around a glossy wooden dance floor. Toward the back, there was a stage, where the first part of the evening's entertainment was already set up. A pianist was playing a light and lively tune, pleasant enough, but not too loud, so that the guests could enjoy their conversations.

Those conversations dimmed as heads turned toward us, and I was glad I was properly dressed for the occasion. Iannis wore a version of his Canalo state robes, and Fenris a well-cut black tunic that flattered his yellow eyes. But I was the star of this show in my sapphire-blue silk dress with silver butterflies embroidered over the bodice and across the voluminous skirts. My curls were pinned back from my face with butterfly clips accented with tiny sapphire-blue crystals. A maid had helped me with my hair and makeup. I was well-dressed enough to hold a candle to any of the female mages who looked me up and down, and I lifted my chin a little higher as I noticed the disapproval in some of their eyes.

"Lord Iannis!" Lord Logar called, drawing our attention to him. He was seated at the table at the top of the semi-circle, but he stood to greet us. The other mages sitting with him did the same—three males, three females. "Please, come join us here."

"Thank you," Iannis said as we approached the table. He shook Lord Logar's hand. "We appreciate your hospitality."

"You have already met Lord Iannis," Lord Logar said to the other mages, "but let me also introduce you to the lovely Miss Sunaya Baine, Lord Iannis's betrothed, and also his... advisor, Fenris. Miss Baine, Fenris, let me introduce you to the others."

He started with his wife, Lady Talari, a lovely brunette who wore the green and gold Parabas colors, just like her husband. She waved away my thanks for providing the lovely dress. Next was Jolen Tular, the Director of the Osero Mages Guild. Then came two of the secretaries who headed the departments in the Guild, followed three of the senior council members who acted as advisors to the Chief Mage. These gave me the stuffiest looks of them all, as if their old bones could barely stand to be in the presence of an upstart like me.

I made sure to give them the widest smiles.

"How unusual, for a Chief Mage's party to consist entirely of shifters," Resa Boran, the Finance Secretary, said with a sly smile. She was a gorgeous woman with flame-red hair and deep blue eyes, dressed in shimmering silver robes that were tailored to emphasize rather than hide her curves. I wanted to rip that sexy little smirk off her face, and maybe claw out her bedroom eyes too.

"We might as well embrace diversity, considering this changing political climate," Iannis said. His hand drifted to my lower back, and I calmed. Just because this woman was sex on a stick didn't mean that I had anything to fear. But it was difficult not to punch her in the face when she was ogling Iannis right in front of me. "Besides, Miss Baine is not only a shifter. She is a mage, too, and will be quite formidable when she is done with her training."

"Why don't we sit down?" Lord Logar suggested, obviously sensing the tension that had thickened the air. "Everyone knows about our mission in Nika, but they are anxious to hear the tale straight from the horse's mouth, as it were."

We sat and talked, and though the council members and Resa pretended that Fenris and I did not exist, the others were amiable enough. No, they didn't treat us as equals, but they were friendlier than the Solantha mages had been when they'd first met me. I imagined this was because of Parabas's more progressive stance toward non-mages, a stance that would hopefully expand to the rest of the Federation.

"It is most disturbing to realize that the Resistance has been organizing and plotting under our noses the entire time," Carsid, the Legal Secretary, remarked. He was a black-skinned mage who wore his long, black hair in thin braids, his yellow, orange, and black robes easily the most colorful ensemble in the room. "We have clearly underestimated them."

"Yes," Iannis agreed, taking a sip from his glass of wine. "If not for Sunaya, I am not certain we would have unearthed the Resistance's campaigns in Canalo in time to prevent them from doing even more damage." He smiled, lifting his glass to me in a toast. "She has quite the nose for sniffing out trouble."

"To Sunaya Baine and her superb sleuthing skills," Lord Logar declared, lifting his glass in a toast. The other mages around the table followed suit, and then drank. Embarrassment at the attention warmed my cheeks, and I tried to hide behind my glass. It was too bad that the wine did nothing for me—it would have been nice to have something to calm my nerves.

On the other hand, I mused, glancing sideways at Fenris, it was probably for the best that we weren't served any spirits that could affect shifters. Fenris needed to stay on his toes around these mages lest he slip and reveal his true identity. The mages of Parabas might be more tolerant, but I had little doubt that Lord Logar was loyal to the Federation and would not hesitate to turn Fenris in. And if that happened, Iannis would be charged with treason as well, both for harboring him, and for using a forbidden spell to turn Fenris into a shifter. The Solantha mages might have started warming up to me, but I had no doubt the Council would cry for my execution again as soon as Iannis was no longer around to protect me.

"So, how is Miss Baine's training to be taken care of, now that the two of you are betrothed?" Resa enquired after our entrées had arrived. "I can't imagine that you will continue to apprentice her."

"And I can't imagine that's any of your business," I said as I cut a piece of my steak. Resa's painted lips formed a surprised 'O' at the fact that I was addressing her directly, and her eyes flew to mine.

"I am simply concerned about propriety," Resa said stiffly, leaving her salmon untouched as she lowered her fork. "You would not want others to gossip about what happens after hours between a master and an apprentice."

"And *I* am concerned about your obvious desire to engage in 'after-hours' activities with my fiancée," I said dryly.

Gasps ensued from around the table, and Resa clapped a

hand over her mouth in shock. Iannis's eyebrows winged up, but I caught just a hint of amusement in his eyes, and knew he wasn't angry with me for calling out the trollop across the table.

"How *dare* you!" Resa cried, her pale cheeks mottling. "Lord Iannis, I have never in my life been confronted with such rude behavior. I expect your apprentice to apologize immediately."

"Actually, I believe you are the one who should apologize," Lord Logar said. His voice was mild, but the stony expression on his face said he was not pleased with this turn of events. All heads swiveled in his direction, and I imagined this was like watching a match of tennis to the other mages. The rest of the room had quieted some too—the attention of others had been drawn to the altercation.

"But, My Lord—"

"These are our guests," Lord Logar said sternly. "Regardless of whether or not you intended to be rude, you have clearly offended Miss Baine. You can either apologize, or you can leave this table."

The table was deathly silent for several moments. The other mages went still, astonishment in their eyes—clearly, they hadn't expected him to take it this far. Resa's face turned to stone. Like all mages, she was good at schooling her expression, but I could smell the anger and shock rolling off her in waves. I half expected her to flounce away from the table in anger, like a spoiled child.

Instead, she wrestled her emotions back into place and gave me a small smile. "Please accept my apologies, Miss Baine. I did not mean to offend you." She inclined her head fractionally, and I refrained from snorting. I was certain she fully intended to offend me—she just hadn't expected to get her ass slapped for it.

"That is quite all right," I said graciously, lifting my glass to her. "Now what do you say we enjoy the rest of this meal?"

"That sounds like an excellent idea," Lord Logar said.

"I heard you had a young mage amongst your party who specializes in alchemical magic," one of the secretaries said, addressing Iannis. "Does he know anything about *xingou shaun*?" she asked, referencing a Loranian phrase I didn't recognize.

"It's *xinghòu shaun*."

All eyes snapped to Fenris. My heart began to thud faster in my chest, and by the way Fenris's cheeks blanched slightly, he wasn't the only one who realized his mistake.

"So it is," another mage said, his eyes narrowing.

"How do you know that?" the secretary asked curiously. Her gaze turned to Lord Iannis. "Are you teaching shifters our spells now?"

"Fenris keeps me company a lot," I said, my brain racing as I tried to come up with a convincing explanation so Iannis wouldn't have to. "I often practice my Loranian while he's around."

"I see." The secretary frowned, looking at Fenris again. "I suppose it does no harm since shifters cannot use spells, but I must admit that is rather unorthodox."

"I agree," Iannis said, narrowing his gaze on Fenris. The warning in his eyes was clear.

Before he could say anymore, an apprentice rushed up to Lord Logar's elbow. "My Lord," the young man said, bowing deeply. He wore the same dun-colored robes that the apprentices in Solantha did. "I apologize for disturbing you, but the interrogator that the Enforcer's Guild has assigned to the prisoners has discovered some very distressing information, and asked me to inform you without delay."

"Well, out with it," Lord Logar demanded. "You can speak freely before us. What did they learn?"

"The head scientist of that disgusting installation has confessed that there is a sister lab in Southern Garai that is also working on producing the same type of secret weapons. In addition to the diseases, it also supplies the guns that the Resistance is using lately." He handed over a folded-up paper. "There are additional details here."

"You cannot be serious!" Lord Logar took the paper from the apprentice and scanned it, his brows drawing together in a deep scowl. "It seems the other lab is in Leniang Port," he told Iannis, a hint of disgust creeping into his tone. I could understand why —in addition to Garai being out of our jurisdiction, Leniang Port was one of the more lawless ports in that huge empire, where anything could be bought with enough gold.

Including weapons for killing shifters and mages wholesale, apparently.

"My director, Lalia Chen, is Garaian," Iannis said thoughtfully. "I believe she has family back there, and influential connections that may be useful to us. I will need to speak to the Minister before any action is taken—our trade deal with Garai is due to be re-negotiated, and it would be unfortunate if we accidentally upset things. But destroying this danger is even more important."

I groaned inwardly at the thought of having to take another trip to Dara, but I wasn't about to complain. We had to stop this madness, no matter what it took.

"If you'll excuse me, I think I will retire," Fenris said. He pushed back his chair and stood, then bowed stiffly to everyone. "I'm afraid I am not feeling very well."

"Of course," Lord Logar said graciously. "Let me know if you need us to send a healer. We have one in residence, of course."

"Thank you." Fenris disappeared, and I wished I could have joined him. I could tell from the turmoil churning behind his dark eyes that whatever ailment he suffered was mental rather than physical. Clearly, he couldn't stand to be around the other mages any longer. I toyed with the temptation of retreating as well, but it would raise eyebrows if the two of us left together, and besides, I belonged at Iannis's side. So, instead, I turned back to the table, intending to check on Fenris as soon as this torturous banquet was over.

23

Home at last. A long sigh escaped me as I shut the door of my bedroom suite in Solantha and leaned against it. A weight lifted from my shoulders, and I closed my eyes, savoring the much-needed solitude. After everything that had happened, and the long, tension-filled ride back in the dirigible, I was happy to be back where I belonged.

I kicked off my shoes by the door, then passed through my sitting room and into my bedroom. I flopped onto my enormous bed, intending to do absolutely nothing but lie here and de-stress for the rest of the day. Life could wait for at least twenty-four hours. I was beat, both physically and emotionally.

The banquet had run late last night, and I'd been forced to schmooze and dance with the locals. Dancing with Iannis had been enjoyable enough, but dancing and conversing with dozens of strange mages was a different story. The banquet was supposed to be in our honor, but it felt more like an opportunity for Lord Logar to put me on display in front of his mages so they could examine me from all angles. They'd all been very polite—no one would dare say anything rude with Iannis around, not after what happened to Resa—but being under constant scrutiny had been exhausting.

We'd managed to make it back to our guest rooms around one in the morning. I went to check on Fenris before turning in, but his door was locked. I could hear him snoring lightly beyond the door so I decided to leave him be. I'd hoped that a good night's sleep would lift his spirits, but he and Iannis had been silent the entire dirigible ride home, barely speaking to one another. Apparently, Iannis had gone to talk to him before I was up, and the outcome of the conversation hadn't been good. Neither of them would tell me what it was about, which pissed me off because, at the very least, Iannis should have told me. If it turned out that he'd been hard on Fenris for his slip-up, Iannis and I were going to have some serious words.

But right now, I was tired of fighting. I'd done more than my fair share, and I still had the outcome of Noria's hearing to look forward to.

Not.

Snuggling deep into my mattress, I closed my eyes and sank into sleep. I wasn't sure how long I was out, but it seemed like only seconds before someone was knocking on my outer door.

"Go away!" I grumbled loudly, burying my head under a pillow to block out the noise.

"But Miss Baine, it's nearly six o'clock in the evening! Please forgive the disturbance, but I have some important things to go over with you."

I scowled. Important things? What important things? And who the hell was this anyway? I certainly didn't recognize her voice—she sounded young, around my age, but a lot more innocent. Realizing the intruder wasn't going to give up, I threw off the bedcovers, then trudged through the sitting room and opened the door wide.

"What do you want?" I growled at the petite blonde standing

outside. She wore black-framed glasses and was dressed in a navy-blue pantsuit. Very professional looking, and one-hundred percent human. You didn't see too many of those in the Palace.

"Oh goodness, it's so nice to finally meet you, Miss Baine," the woman gushed, her fresh face lighting up instantly. She stuck out a hand, and I took it automatically, surprised by her enthusiasm. "My name is Nelia Thrase. I'm your new social secretary."

"Social secretary?" I scowled as she pumped my hand. I yanked it away from her before she tore it off. "I didn't hire a social secretary."

"Director Chen hired me on your behalf." Nelia's wide smile dimmed beneath the onslaught of my displeasure. "Did she not inform you? I was given to understand..." She trailed off, sounding genuinely distressed. "I assure you, I am qualified and eager to work for you. I used to write for a magazine, and before that, I interned with a local radio station."

"The director may have mentioned it," I said between clenched teeth, deciding against telling the girl I'd wanted to hire my own social secretary, and that I hadn't even decided if I needed one. "I've been a little busy the past couple of days, so I forgot."

"Oh, yes, of course." The million-watt smile returned in full force, and Nelia hefted her binder a little higher. "I've already organized your calendar and made some appointments for you. I've also made some additions to your wardrobe for your social engagements."

"You what?" Whirling around, I darted into my room and headed straight for the walk-in closet. Sure enough, space had been made in the front for a variety of conservative but very expensive-looking robes and dresses in all kinds of colors and fabrics. I instinctively cringed at the thought of how much all this stuff had to cost as I riffled through it, before remembering I was rich now, and also engaged to one of the wealthiest men in Canalo. But still...

"Are the clothes not to your liking, Miss Baine?" Nelia asked. I turned to see her standing just outside the entrance to my closet, worry stamped all over her heart-shaped face. Guilt twanged in my gut as I realized I was being incredibly rude to her.

"No, they're fine," I said, letting out a sigh as my hand fell away from a dark pink dress with a high collar and gold buttons. There was nothing here that I would hate wearing, even if these more conservative fashions weren't something I would have picked off a rack myself. As Iannis's future wife, I needed to expand my wardrobe and style choices a little bit. I wasn't going to ditch my leathers and boots, but I had to have the correct outfits for many different occasions on hand.

"Oh good, I'm so glad to hear that." Nelia smiled, then lifted her binder. "May we adjourn to the sitting room, so we can go over a few things? I promise this won't take long."

"Sure," I said, shoving my hands into my pockets. I followed her out to the sitting area, and settled onto one of the pastel green couches. Nelia perched on the chair next to me, crossing her well-toned legs as she flipped open her binder. She pushed her glasses up her narrow nose as she scanned the pages with her dark grey eyes, lips pursed.

"I took the liberty of dealing with all the mail you received after your article was printed," she told me.

"Article?" I echoed dumbly, my mind racing to catch up with hers.

Nelia smiled, pulling out a newspaper page from the binder. "Director Chen told me it might have slipped your mind. You did leave almost immediately after the interview for *Now*." She handed the paper to me, a full-page article of my interview with Gena Chanie. To my surprise, the reporter had painted me in a sympathetic rather than patronizing light, and had included two flattering photos—one from the batch her photographer had taken that day, and another someone had snapped of me in the street in my enforcer leathers. According to the write-up, I was adjusting to my new role well, bringing dignity and light to the Mages Guild while continuing to stay in touch with my "street roots", as she called it.

"I will be keeping a scrapbook of these," Nelia informed me as she tucked the article back into her binder. "So that we have a record of all printed media."

"Thank you," I said, with feeling. I had to admit, I hadn't thought about how much administrative work would come with my new social status, and it was a relief to know that someone else with experience was going to take care of it. Director Chen had chosen my secretary well—maybe she wasn't out to get me after all. I supposed I would have to thank her later.

Nelia then explained my schedule for the next four weeks. There were meetings and interviews Director Chen had already set up, though many of them had been rescheduled due to my unexpected departure. I imagined this would be a common occurrence, as I doubted this would be the last time Iannis and I would be off on a mission. Still, I would not be able to duck out of these entirely, so I guessed I was going to have to get used to it. The first interview had gone really well, so maybe I was ready for the press after all. But I would make sure to get some tips from Iannis before I did any more, on how to handle personal and inconvenient questions. I told Nelia not to schedule any more interviews for the time being.

"By the way, Chieftain Mafiela Baine called to respond to your invitation for lunch," Nelia said to me. "I penciled her in for Wednesday the eleventh, in the Winter Garden."

"Oh." I let out a surprised breath—I'd forgotten about that too. The Winter Garden was a pretty salon on the second floor of

the Palace, filled with mirrors and evergreen plants. It was sometimes used for small dinner parties by the Chief Mage, but
would do just as well for a private lunch catered by the Palace
cook. "Did she sound happy about it?"

Nelia paused, as if trying to recall. "She didn't sound
*un*happy," she decided.

I held in a sigh. Oh well. Guess that was the best I was going
to get out of my aunt. Hopefully, this lunch wouldn't be a total
disaster.

A knock at the door interrupted us before Nelia could
continue. "I'll get it," I said, rising from the couch and gesturing
for Nelia to sit. There were still some things I wanted to do
myself, and answering my own door was one of them. "Who
is it?"

"Lanyr Goldrin, Miss. I'm your new bodyguard, here to
escort you to dinner."

"Bodyguard?" I echoed. What the hell? Why were all these
new employees being sprung on me out of nowhere? Annoyed, I
threw open the door to see a Palace guard, decked out in blue-
and-gold livery, standing in the hall. As I had suggested, Iannis
had hired locals to guard the Palace, and this one was a handsome, orange-eyed tiger shifter with golden-brown hair and a
tall, lean frame.

"It's me, Sunaya." Rylan's voice echoed in my head, and I
nearly fell over.

"By Magorah," I hissed, dragging Rylan inside. "What are
you *doing*, dressed like this?" I slammed the door behind us.

"Well, I am a guard, so I'm dressed in uniform, naturally."
Rylan grinned, giving me an extravagant bow. "Lord Iannis
suggested this look. *He felt it would be better not to walk around the
Palace looking like I normally do, under the circumstances,"* Rylan
added in mindspeak.

"I see." So he'd cast a spell on Rylan to make him look and

smell like a tiger-shifter, then dressed him up as a guard and assigned him to me. "I hope this means you're not going to be hovering above me while I sleep."

"That would be rather improper," Rylan said dryly. "No, I am to accompany you around the Palace, and around Solantha as well, by Lord Iannis's orders."

I bit back the protest rising to my lips—I didn't need a babysitter. But it occurred to me that I was babysitting Rylan as much as he was me. He couldn't leave the Palace without an escort, so without me, he would be stuck to the confines of these walls. Besides, Rylan was resourceful and handy in a fight, so I couldn't say that he would hamper me by tagging along.

"Don't worry—I'm sure I won't be shadowing you when your fiancé spirits you off for a romantic evening," Rylan said dryly in my head. His grin widened as he craned his neck around me and met Nelia's gaze. "And who is this?"

"This is Miss Nelia Thrase," I said, turning to see her staring wide-eyed up at Rylan. To my surprise, and discomfort, I caught the fascinated attraction in her dark eyes. "She's my new social secretary."

"Pleased to meet you," Nelia said, getting to her feet. A faint blush spread across her cheeks as Rylan approached, deliberately looking her up and down.

"Oh, the pleasure is all mine." Rylan took her hand and pressed a kiss against her knuckles. Nelia's eyelashes fluttered, and, for a moment, I thought she might actually swoon. "Hopefully, your position means I will be seeing you more often."

"Hopefully," she agreed, sounding more than a little breathless.

"All right, Bodyguard," I said, barely managing not to roll my eyes. "Can you take me to dinner, then? I'm starving."

"Of course." Rylan dropped Nelia's hand. "See you later, Miss Thrase."

"If you break Nelia's heart, I will send you off to the mines myself," I warned as we all exited the room. I loved Rylan, but he was a player, and I wasn't about to let him mess with my employee.

My employee. How weird is that?

"Don't worry," Rylan said, sounding completely serious now. *"I intend to serve out my sentence in peace, so that I can eventually rejoin the clan. My place is with our family, and I've neglected it for far too long. I want to get back to it someday."*

I mulled Rylan's words over in my head, my heart growing heavier as we walked. Rylan *did* have a place in our family, that was for sure. Mafiela might be angry with him, but he was her son. She would welcome him back into the fold as soon as he made things right with her. But I wasn't sure there had ever been a place in the Jaguar Clan where I'd fit in the past, and now that my life had changed so much, I wasn't sure there ever would be in the future.

$\mathcal{I}$ expected Rylan to take me to the large dining hall where all Mage Guild employees gathered to eat. But, instead, he led me past it and into the smaller, private dining room that was used to entertain guests, as confidently as though he were thoroughly familiar with the warren of a palace. I wasn't really surprised, though—Rylan had always had a good sense of direction.

Iannis and Director Chen were already seated at the glossy, oval-shaped wooden table, enjoying wine and bread as they waited for the first course to arrive. Fenris was there too, as well as Cirin Garidano, the Finance Secretary.

"Good evening, Miss Baine," Director Chen greeted me with a smile. "I am pleased to see you looking well."

"Thank you." I gave her a small smile in return as I seated myself in the empty chair to Iannis's right. My stomach growled as I caught sight of the bread basket, and I took a roll for myself as Rylan left the room at a gesture from Iannis. I figured it would be weird to have him hover over us and listen to us talk about sensitive information. Maybe he'd head down to the kitchens and get himself some food in the meantime.

"I hope I didn't miss anything important while you were waiting for me," I said to Iannis. It was the closest I would give to an apology—after all, I hadn't been told we were having a dinner meeting, though I supposed it wasn't surprising.

"We were just discussing the interrogation of the Palace staff," Iannis told me. "Fenris was running it before he joined us in Osero."

"Oh, right." The bomb attack had almost slipped my mind in the last few days. I turned to Fenris. "So did you find anything before you left?"

"Three humans fled the Palace after I announced we would be subjecting the staff to a truth spell," Fenris said. There was no hint of the tension he'd radiated earlier, but then again, he was talking to me rather than Iannis. "I was in the middle of tracking them down, with the help of the Enforcer's Guild, when I was called away."

"One of them was Darca, one of my better accountants," Cirin said irritably, his dark blue eyes narrowed. "As you can imagine, finding out that I may have been employing a traitor has not improved my staff's morale."

"I imagine not," I said, sympathizing with him a little. It was probably a fucking nightmare, knowing that a Resistance spy had access to the Palace's financial documents. If Darca *was* in fact a spy, she could have passed all sorts of confidential information about the state's finances to the Resistance, information the Benefactor could have used against us. "Who were the other two suspects?"

"A groom from the stables named Tadir, and a maid called Cralia."

I frowned. "Those are all very different positions. Do you think all three of them could be spies?"

"I don't see why not," Director Chen said. "If I were organizing the Resistance, I would want my spies to be set up in different areas of the Palace, in order to get as much intel as possible."

"Yeah, you're right." It bothered me that there could be so many enemies hidden amongst us, inside the very walls I'd trusted to keep me safe. "Still, I wonder if they were all in on the assassination attempt, or if it was just one of them. And if we catch the wrong one, will they still lead us to the other?"

"All excellent questions," Iannis said as dinner arrived. "But I suppose only time will give us the answer."

The servants set out racks of lamb, and large bowls filled with salad, grilled asparagus, and new potatoes. Hunger took over, and I put my worries aside as we dug into the meal. Dinner was a surprisingly comfortable affair, despite the tension between Fenris and Iannis, and the fact that Chen was here. We all managed to be civil, and even had some pleasant conversation.

"Well, I must be going," Director Chen said when our plates were cleared. She rose from the table and bowed, her eyes meeting mine as she straightened. "I trust you have found your social secretary to be satisfactory?"

"Yes, so far." I gave her a real smile. "Thank you for finding her for me."

"You're welcome." Director Chen's stern expression softened into a smile.

"If I didn't know better, I would say that you and Director Chen are finally beginning to get along," Iannis said as we walked back to our rooms. Rylan trailed behind us at a respectful distance—he'd been waiting for me outside the banquet room.

"It might be a little early for you to jump to that conclusion," I said, twining my fingers with his. "But I'm willing to give credit where credit is due, and Nelia seems competent."

"I am happy to hear that." Iannis squeezed my hand. "You

two may have gotten off to a rocky start, but Director Chen has an excellent track record. I would not have chosen her for her position if I did not feel she could be trusted."

"Sure." A thought entered my head, and I checked that no one was within hearing distance before turning my head to look at Rylan. "Hey," I called.

Rylan lengthened his stride to catch up with us. "Yes?"

"Any chance you were provided with a list of the spies who were planted here, or in any other areas of the Federation?"

"No. That information was need to know, and I, sadly, did not need to know. I know for sure that at least one spy was planted here in the Palace, but for security reasons, their identities were closely guarded."

"Of course," I muttered under my breath. That would have been far too easy.

"However, just because those three have fled the Palace, doesn't mean you're out of danger, Sunaya," Rylan continued, his eyes sharp. "In my experience, deep-cover operatives are not so easy to spook. The three staff who ran off might have something else to hide that has nothing to do with the Resistance, while the real spy still lurks among us, waiting for another opportunity to strike."

"Indeed," Iannis said, his voice hard. "That is why you must not allow Sunaya to leave your sight, unless she is either with me, or Fenris."

"Yes, sir," Rylan said, saluting, and I forced myself not to grit my teeth. Bitching about this wasn't going to handle the situation—finding the traitor was.

"So what can we do to smoke this bastard out?" I asked as we stopped in front of my bedroom door. Rylan's room was right across the hall—as my bodyguard, he would remain close at all times. Luckily, my room was warded, so it wasn't necessary that he sleep inside.

"I suggest you assist Fenris with questioning the list of suspects he's gathered," Iannis said.

"You mean the people who went missing?" I asked, frowning.

"No," Iannis said dryly. "He made a list of all the Palace staff who were not on duty the night you were attacked, but who were on duty the day before. Most likely, the attacker simply stayed behind after the end of his shift."

"Gotcha." That was smart. Somewhere in there, we might find a connection to the spy, or even the real spy himself. "What do you think?" I asked, turning to my cousin with a grin. "You up for a little sleuthing tomorrow?"

"I'll do anything to avoid having to put myself between your body and another incendiary device," Rylan said. He gave me a quick, firm hug, and I smiled, happy we'd moved past our differences. "If I get up tomorrow morning and find out that you're dead, I'll bring you back to life, just so I can kill you myself."

"Love you too," I said with a laugh as I disentangled myself from his arms. And with no one else around to see us, I took Iannis's hand and allowed him to lead me into the safety of his bedroom, and ultimately, his arms.

25

I was up bright and early the next morning, full of energy and ready to track down the traitor. Rylan was a little grumpy about being dragged out of bed before nine, but the idea of getting breakfast while it was still hot was appealing to him, so he dressed and showered quickly before heading down to the dining hall with me.

I had hoped to find Fenris sitting in his usual spot near the buffet tables, but he wasn't there. I scanned the rows of wooden tables, filled with mages who chose to get their breakfast here rather than at home before starting work at the Guild. No sign of him at all.

"Maybe he's sleeping in," Rylan suggested as he wolfed down his third plate of bacon and eggs. "You know, like any self-respecting shifter would be."

I shook my head. "Fenris is an early bird, like Iannis." I imagined that even as a shifter, his old habits as a mage, and a Chief Mage at that, would be hard to break. "Well, maybe not quite like Iannis, since Iannis is already at some meeting or another," I amended. "But he's usually here this time of day."

Rylan nodded. "You would know," he said easily, buttering a

piece of toast. "Just as I imagine you would know where to find him."

I sighed. "I'll start with his room. If not there, he could be in the library." I'd found him there more than once in the past— Fenris liked to study magical texts discreetly, to keep up on his spell lore even though he wasn't officially a mage anymore. But the library wasn't open for another ten minutes, so unless he snuck in, I doubted I'd find him there.

It was a little annoying, having to walk all the way back to the west wing after already coming from there. Fenris's room was located a few doors up from Iannis's, on the same side as Rylan's. I sniffed the air as I knocked on his door, and his scent was strong enough that I was certain he was present.

"What is it?" Fenris called, his voice uncharacteristically irritable.

I frowned, really concerned now. Fenris was normally so unflappable, and he usually was the one calming *me* down. I wasn't totally sure how to handle the role reversal.

"I need to get the list of suspects from you," I said through the door. "Iannis said I should help you interview them."

"Did he now?" Fenris asked, sounding downright petulant.

Okay, enough was enough. "Wait here," I told Rylan as I pulled a set of lock picks from one of my pouches. I selected the right one, then unlocked the door and opened it.

"Hey!" Fenris snapped, tossing a sheet over his naked body as I stepped inside. To my surprise, he was still abed and looking *very* scruffy, with bags under his dark eyes and a serious case of bedhead. "You can't just break into my room like this."

"I can damn well do whatever I want," I told him, kicking the door shut behind me. "After all, you're too busy moping around in bed to stop me, aren't you?" I grabbed his desk chair, then flipped it around so I could straddle it.

"Don't be so overconfident," Fenris growled, his dark eyes

flashing. "I may not be a full mage anymore, but I can still wipe the floor with you without ever leaving this bed."

"Then do it," I challenged, crossing my arms over the back of the chair and meeting his stare without fear. "But until you either kick my ass, or tell me what the hell is going on with you and Iannis, I'm not leaving this room."

Fenris glared at me for a long moment, then sighed and raked a hand over his hair. The sheet dropped, exposing a muscular torso dusted with dark hair. I didn't know what Polar ar'Tollis had looked like under his state robes, but Iannis had made him damn good looking when he'd transformed him into Fenris. Strange really that I'd never been attracted to him that way—he was more like a brother, or maybe an uncle-type figure, to me. But as I looked at him now, so closed off, I wondered if he felt lonely. He deserved someone to love, and for someone to love him.

Eventually, he dropped his gaze. "It isn't what you think," he finally said, staring down at his dark red bedspread. "Iannis didn't reproach me for slipping up at the banquet. He came to check on me, and to reassure me that my identity is still secret."

"Good." Relief swept through me at that—I didn't have to be angry with Iannis after all. "So if that's the case, then what did the two of you argue about?"

A look of pain flashed across Fenris's face, his fists clenching in the sheets. "About my leaving Solantha."

"What?" I grabbed the edge of the desk to keep myself from toppling sideways off the chair. "Leave Solantha? What the hell for?"

Fenris finally met my gaze, and the pain and sadness in his dark eyes nearly stole my breath. "I'm sure you can empathize more than most, Sunaya... but I do not belong. I sit on the sidelines here, in the shadows, watching other mages walk freely in the sunlight, able to practice their magic without fear and pursue their ambitions and dreams. These past few years following my faked execution and transformation into a shifter, I've mostly focused on staying alive and out of the spotlight. But I have had no real goals, no ambition, no... direction in my life." Fenris waved his hand in the air, a frustrated motion. "I am not truly a shifter, as I have no clan and was not raised with their customs, and before you came here, I did my best to avoid real shifters. And I am no longer allowed to be a mage, even though I still retain some power, and all of my knowledge."

"Oh, Fenris." I abandoned the desk chair for his bed, then wrapped my arms around him in a tight hug. "I'm sorry." A lump began to swell in my throat. "I'm sure this is very hard for you."

It was easy to empathize with Fenris—after all, my own hybrid status had made me an outcast, and until Iannis had taken me under his wing, I'd lived every day under the fear that I would be found out and executed. But at least those fears no longer plagued me. I was still learning to integrate myself into mage society, but it *was* happening. And if my lunch with Aunt Mafiela went well, perhaps I could find my way back into shifter society as well. But Fenris wasn't able to do either of those things.

"I know I said to you not so long ago that my place was by Iannis's side, and by your side," Fenris said roughly, his arms tightening around me as he returned my hug. "But after nearly exposing my true identity in front of all those mages, I was reminded that my very presence here puts you both in grave danger. If it was ever found out that the two of you were knowingly harboring me here, and that Iannis had used illegal magic to transform me into a shifter, all three of us would be executed. You are my friends, and far too important for me to allow that to happen."

"Stop this." My nails dug into Fenris's upper arms as I pulled back to glare at him. "Fenris, you stop this bullshit right now.

Yes, Iannis and I might be part of the Minister's task force, but don't think for one second that you haven't been instrumental in *everything* we've done so far. You're important too, Fenris, and I fucking need you. *Iannis* fucking needs you. The entire Federation needs you, even if they're too blind and ignorant to know it." My voice broke a little as anger scalded my chest, and maybe a hint of fear too, at the thought that Fenris might walk out of our lives. "I can't stand to lose another friend right now, Fenris," I whispered. "I just can't."

Remorse flashed in Fenris's dark eyes, and his expression softened. "I understand," he said quietly. "We've been through quite a lot recently, haven't we?"

"You could say that," I said tiredly, running a hand over my face. "I was just getting over Roanas's death, and now I'm faced with the likelihood of losing Noria. I don't know what I would do if I found out you were leaving too."

"Knowing you, you would probably come up with some harebrained scheme to chase after me, and get yourself into considerable trouble that I would have to help you out of," Fenris said dryly, a grin tugging at his lips.

I grinned back. "Well, that is what you're around for, isn't it?" I asked, smacking him on the shoulder.

"It would seem so, at least for now." Fenris shook his head, his smile fading. "I suppose that so long as there is still need of me, it would be a disservice to you and Iannis for me to disappear," he said. "I will stay then, and help however I can. But if there is any sign that my presence puts either of you at risk, I will leave, and you must promise not to stop me." Fenris's eyes darkened as he locked gazes with me. "Promise me, Sunaya Baine."

"I promise," I said, trying to sound as normal as possible as the lump in my throat threatened to resurface. But what else could I say? "Now can you get your ass out of bed and help me get this list of suspects? We don't have all day."

"Yes, but it would help if you gave me some privacy," Fenris pointed out. "I am far from decent."

"What else is new?" I muttered, opening the door and walking out. Shifters didn't really have a button on nudity, but as Fenris wasn't born a shifter, I had to forgive him for being a prude. And I didn't really need the image of his naked ass branded in my mind anyway.

"By Magorah," I muttered as Rylan and I trudged back inside. We'd just finished questioning the head gardener, which had turned out to be just as fruitless as all the other interviews. "I'm starting to think you're wrong, and the spy did flee the Palace."

"Nobody ever said I was infallible," Rylan admitted as we turned right, heading to the east wing. Fenris had taken half the suspects, leaving us with around thirty to question—and we'd just finished number eighteen. "It's always possible the spy did bolt."

"I really hope not," I said as we headed for the guest bathing rooms. The next suspect on our list was Harun Zuric, one of the Palace's handymen, and we'd been informed he was currently fixing a leak in one of the showers. "I'd rather not find out we wasted our entire morning on this."

"It isn't a waste," Rylan pointed out. "Eliminating these suspects is important."

I growled under my breath, but said nothing. He was right, but I was impatient to find my would-be killer *now*. I wanted to look him in the eye myself, dammit.

The sound of metal clanging against metal caught my ears as we rounded the corner, followed by the scent of sweaty male human. I pushed open the door to the bathroom to find a balding, heavyset man leaning half-in, half-out of the shower. His belt wasn't doing a great job of holding up his workpants, and I wrinkled my nose at the sight of his hairy crack peeking out from beneath his powder-blue work shirt.

"Good morning, Mr. Zuric," I called, and he shot straight up, banging his head against the metal doorframe.

"Dammit!" he cried, backing out of the shower stall as he rubbed his head. His eyes were wide as he turned to face us, and the sweaty stench emanating from his body turned sour with fear. "Couldn't you knock first? You scared the hell out of me!"

"Is that so?" I smiled, my fingers grazing the crescent knives strapped to my right thigh as I walked toward him. "And what exactly is it that you have to be scared of?"

"Nothing," he said quickly, his meaty hand drifting to his tool belt. "You just startled me."

"I would think you'd know it's stupid to lie to a shifter," I began, and the man let out a battle cry. He charged me with surprising speed for his bulk, pulling a silver knife from his tool belt, and I moved into a fighting stance, ready to take him.

"Oh no, you don't!" Rylan pushed me back, then twisted around to Zuric's side and slammed him against the wall. Several of the blue tiles cracked beneath the force of their bodies, and Zuric cried out as Rylan grabbed his knife arm and twisted it behind his back. The knife clattered to the ground, and Rylan kicked it away as he hiked the spy's arm up higher.

"Fuck!" the man screamed as his shoulder popped from his socket.

"I can do worse if you keep struggling," Rylan said calmly. "Or you can give up, and let me restrain you."

"Never!" Zuric hissed, then screamed louder as Rylan pulled again.

The sound of heavy footsteps outside the hall drew my

attention, and I turned to see three more guards burst through the door. "Is everything all right, Miss?" the first one asked me, his sword already drawn.

"We're good," I said, gesturing to Rylan and Zuric. The spy had stopped struggling. He was sagging against the wall, tears of pain streaming down his ruddy face. "As you can see, my bodyguard has things under control." I was slightly annoyed that Rylan had gotten to the bastard before I did, but I couldn't fault him for it—he *was* my bodyguard. And his reaction time had always been a shade faster than mine. I was going to have to enlist him as my sparring partner—it had been too long since I'd done physical training with any real dedication.

"Actually, I would appreciate a hand from one or two of you gentlemen," Rylan said as he restrained Zuric. "This man is a spy and would-be assassin who tried to kill Miss Baine with that bomb just a few days ago."

"*This* is the spy?" one of the guards asked incredulously, looking Zuric up and down. "I never would have guessed."

"Well, that's why I'm her bodyguard and you're not," Rylan said with a grin as he spun Zuric around and shoved him into the guards' waiting hands. "Now, let's get this fat bastard out of here."

"This isn't over!" Zuric shouted as they led him from the room. "You may have won the battle, but the war is far from over!"

As we followed him out, listening to his shouted protests all the way, I couldn't help but fear he might be right.

26

*I*annis insisted on holding Zuric in the Palace dungeon rather than taking him to the Enforcer's Guild, intending to interrogate the spy himself. Since Warin Danrian, the bank manager who'd been running the Shifter Royale, had been assassinated in his cell, it seemed better not to send high-risk prisoners there.

Iannis and I didn't have another lesson scheduled until dinner, and Fenris had cancelled our Loranian lesson for today. So, with some free time on my hands, I rushed over to the library to see if Janta had made any progress with her investigation into my family tree.

"Are you nervous about finding out who your father is?" Rylan asked as he lengthened his stride to keep up with me. I'd hurriedly filled him in on the basic details via mindspeak, so no one would overhear, and he looked intrigued. *"And what will you do once you know his identity?"*

"Yes, and I don't know," I replied as we stopped outside the tall, wooden doors that closed the library off from the rest of the Palace. *"I probably won't be able to make any kind of decision until I do know who he is, and why he abandoned me."*

"Makes sense," Rylan said as he pushed open the door, going ahead to make sure there were no assassins lurking on the other side. Despite my suggestion that he do so, Iannis wouldn't dismiss Rylan as my bodyguard even though we'd captured the spy. He claimed we couldn't be certain there weren't more like him skulking about inside the Palace walls, and he wanted Rylan to stick close to me for now.

I asked the young librarian at the reception desk for Janta, and was told she was meeting with someone but would be available soon. Rylan and I settled down at one of the tables to wait, me with my spellbook primer and Rylan with a history text he'd snagged from one of the shelves. It didn't take very long at all for Janta to show up.

"Good afternoon, Miss Baine," Janta said, giving me a small, but friendly smile. She wore lavender robes today, her silver hair rolled up into a high bun, and a smile lit her eyes. "Thank you for the box of chocolates. They were a most welcome surprise."

"Oh, it was the least I could do after all you've done to help me. And please, call me Sunaya," I added with a smile. "Anyway, I was hoping you had some news for me?"

"Of course. Please come back to my office, ah, Sunaya." She cleared her throat. "You may also use my first name, if you like."

She led us between the shelves and to the back, to her administrative office. It was a comfortable space, with powder-blue curtains, cityscape paintings hanging from the walls, and, of course, book-laden shelves. The shelves were made of birch wood, as were her desk and chairs. She gestured for me to have a seat.

"Are you certain you wish to have your guard present?" Janta said as she pulled a file from one of her desk drawers. "This is a private matter, after all."

"I can wait outside," Rylan said, bowing to us both. "So long as I can trust you with Miss Baine's life."

"You can," Janta said, smiling. "We will only be a half hour or so."

Rylan disappeared back into the library, shutting the door behind him. I wondered if he would tune out our conversation, or if he would listen in beyond the wall—his shifter hearing would be able to pick up our conversation easily. If I knew him, he would listen in. It didn't matter either way—we were family, and I trusted him not to use this information to hurt me.

"So," I said, settling back into my chair, "what have you found out?"

Janta opened the file in front of her, revealing a photograph of Coman ar'Daghir, the dark-haired Legal Secretary from Rhodea who shared my hair and eye coloring, and who I'd suspected was related to me in some way.

"I started by tracing back the lineage of your friend here," she said, tapping the facsimile of Coman's slightly hooked nose. "His dark hair and green eyes, which you share, come from his mother's side of the family, which is far more distinguished than the ar'Darghirs. Something of a misalliance, in fact. His mother is a scion of the noble ar'Rhea family in Castalis."

"I see." Excitement shot through me at the mention of an actual name—we were getting somewhere! Castalis, I dimly remembered from school, was a peninsula at the southwestern edge of the Central Continent. "So this family is well known?" If they were, it might explain why Iannis had suspected my lineage from the get-go.

"Very," Janta confirmed. "They are particularly notable for their green eyes, strong magic, and the fact that their lineage boasts a direct descent from the First Mage, Resinah."

"Wow." My eyes widened. "Does that make them more noble than other families? I have to admit I don't really understand how classes amongst the mages work."

"All mages who have the prefix 'ar' in their surnames are

direct descendants of one of Resinah's twelve original disciples,"
Janta explained, clasping her hands together as she rested them
atop the desk. "These are the nobility in our society. There was a
time when only mages of noble birth could hold influential
positions, but that is not the case today. Our current director of
the Mages Guild, Lalia Chen, is a good example of this, as was
her predecessor."

"Right." I nodded, recalling that neither Chen nor Chartis
had the "ar" in their last names, nor did Minister Graning. "So
how is it that the ar'Rhea family is directly descended from
Resinah?"

"Two of Resinah's children, her son and daughter, were disciples of hers. Her daughter, Miyanta, is the ancestor of the
ar'Rhea family." Janta's nose twitched ever so slightly in disapproval. "According to history, Miyanta was as gracious and noble
as her mother, but the same cannot be said of all her descendants. The families descended from Resinah consider themselves to be superior to all the other noble mages, and the
ar'Rhea family is particularly snobbish. The purity of their
blood means everything to them."

"Great." I rolled my eyes, trying not to show Janta that,
inside, my heart was sinking. If my father was an ar'Rhea, it was
no wonder he'd chosen to abandon me. As a shifter-mage
hybrid, I had to be even more of an abomination to him than I
was to ordinary mages. And considering how I'd been treated
when I arrived at Solantha Palace, that was really saying
something.

"Since the ar'Rhea family is so ancient and proud of their
heritage, there is plenty of information about them in the histor-
ical and contemporary records." Janta flipped the photo of
Coman to the side, revealing a page filled with elegant hand-
writing—research notes, from what I could read upside down. "I
checked the Foreign Mages' Log to see if anyone from the

ar'Rhea family had visited Solantha in the year before your birth."

"That's smart," I said—I would have done it myself, if I'd known which name to look for. Any foreign mage visiting a Federation state for longer than a month was required to go to the local Mages Guild and fill out a form. My heart rate jumped up a notch, and I had to restrain myself from squirming in my seat like a little kid. "So what name did you find?"

Janta smiled a little, amused at my enthusiasm. "For some reason, the relevant page was missing, but, fortunately, we keep a duplicate that was still intact. A mage by the name of Haman ar'Rhea filled out the form about a year before your birth. He came from Castalis to Solantha to study for some months with Jonias Ballos, an eccentric old mage who is well known for his mastery of divination and binding magic. According to the form, Haman ar'Rhea lived in Ballos's house the entire time. That would have been the only way to learn from him, because Ballos has not left his home in several decades." Her nose twitched again. "He seems to be something of a hermit."

"Well, I guess Haman probably didn't stay in Ballos's house the whole time," I said dryly, "or he never would have met my mother."

"No, I imagine not," Janta agreed with a sigh. She pushed her spectacles up her nose, then flipped over several notes of research until she came upon a photograph of a man who resembled Coman. He had thick, curling dark hair that brushed his broad shoulders, and his handsome, aristocratic features shared the shape of my eyes and my full mouth. He wore some kind of ceremonial robe with a thick chain across his chest, and looked as though everything he surveyed belonged to him. Smug bastard. So *this* was supposed to be my father? I wanted to deny it, but the resemblance was unmistakable.

Janta did not notice my reaction. "Ballos cannot have been

very stimulating company for a comparatively young mage, used to exclusive parties and entertainments. And perhaps Haman enjoyed the anonymity of a foreign place where nobody knew his ancestry, where he thought he could let his hair down safely."

Yeah, I could imagine that.

"I surmise that your father visited Rowanville during his stay here, as many tourists do. The experience must have been especially exotic for him, as there are no shifters in Castalis."

That shocked me. "What—none at all?"

"There never were all that many, and one of Haman's ancestors, the High Mage of that time, drove them from the country about two hundred years ago. They were given one week to leave, taking only what they could carry. It is in all the Castalian history books."

"No wonder none wanted to go back," I muttered. Already, I hated the whole fucking ar'Rhea family.

"It is said the edict was issued in anger at an affair of his daughter with a shifter. The daughter was also exiled."

My cheeks burned hot with anger, and it was all I could to do hold my tongue. Somehow, this knowledge made Haman's affair with my mother even worse.

"Be that as it may," Janta said briskly, after clearing her throat, "Haman must have run into your mother somehow, then engaged in an affair. There is no way to prettify it—his actions were most reprehensible."

"Affairs between consenting adults are common enough," I admitted reluctantly. I was definitely not entitled to cast the first stone there, and my mother had been older than Haman. But the fact that he'd abandoned *me*, his child…

"Yes, but what makes it so dishonorable," Janta lowered her voice, "is not the affair as such, but that he was *engaged* at the time."

"What?" I leaned forward, gripping the arms of my chair tightly. I'd known it was highly likely that my father had a family of his own by now, but the idea that he'd dallied with my mother when he'd been promised to another stung. "He had a fiancée?"

"Indeed," Janta confirmed, disapproval clear in her voice. "As you are aware, betrothals between mages are an extremely serious matter, and even more so in his case. His bride, and current wife, was the daughter of the former High Mage of Castalis. For the last ten years, Haman himself has held that office. Those two families have more or less monopolized the power in Castalis for several centuries."

I snorted—I could easily see how the other mages in Castalis chafed under that cozy arrangement, not to speak of the humans.

"I can only imagine your mother must have been very alluring to Haman," Janta went on, "because jeopardizing his future marriage and career through an affair with a shifter was an extremely foolhardy move. He must have taken great pains to hide his relationship with her, so that neither his own family nor his betrothed's would ever find out."

"I guess that explains why my clan never knew who he was," I said, though I wasn't entirely certain that Mafiela didn't know my father's identity. She and my mother had been very close. "So he returned home and married the woman he was engaged to?"

"Yes, Lady Aria Ragir," Janta confirmed. "They married the year you were born, and have three children now." She pulled an article from a celebrity Northia magazine in Dara and pushed it across the table to me. "Here is a picture of them."

I looked down at the well-dressed family, standing on the front steps of the Capitol Building with Zavian Graning, the Federation Minister. My father's wife was a stunning woman with almond-shaped eyes and dark skin, who must have had

Sandian ancestry somewhere, and their children shared a healthy mixture of both their traits. Two daughters and a son. I couldn't tell their eye color from the black-and-white photo, of course, but the lightness of their irises suggested they had green eyes, just like mine. I wasn't sure how I felt about the idea that I had half-siblings running around, halfway across the world somewhere.

"What would happen if the truth of my parentage came out?" I asked, pushing the article back to Janta. "If some journalist discovered that Haman ar'Rhea is my father? Would it be a big deal?"

"Well, as I said, Haman is the High Mage of Castalis—the equivalent of a Chief Mage, except that Castalis is one country and not split up into different states like the Federation. That means he technically outranks Lord Iannis, though Canalo is just as big. He wasn't the High Mage when he was here in Solantha, as his father-in-law had not stepped down from the position, but he was being groomed for the job. It would have been a terrible scandal if it had come out he had an illegitimate daughter with a shifter. His brother, Daram, would have almost certainly gotten the position instead of him, and he would not have been married to his lovely and extremely wealthy bride."

"That makes sense," I reluctantly conceded even as resentment bubbled inside me. I could understand my father's decision, though that didn't change the fact that he was a selfish bastard. He should have fucking kept his dick in his pants if he didn't want to face the consequences.

But if he'd done that, then you wouldn't exist, a voice whispered in my head.

"So now that he's all happily married and has been the High Mage for over a decade, would you say that it's no longer a big deal if the world found out I was his daughter?" I wondered aloud. I needed to pin this down for sure, because I wanted to be absolutely certain that my father wasn't going to decide to come out of the woodwork and claim me before I married Iannis. He could do whatever the hell he wanted after that, but for now, I wanted him as far away from my life as possible.

"Oh no, I wouldn't say that at all," Janta said, her silver eyebrows winging up. "As I mentioned, the ar'Rhea family prides itself very much on the purity of their lineage. If it were found out that you were his daughter, it might not only ruin his social and political status, but also that of his children. The loss of reputation, the lack of integrity and judgment he demonstrated, would taint the entire family. Lady Aria herself would be humiliated and furious beyond belief, her family eager to avenge her. No," Janta concluded, shaking her head, "I don't believe your father would risk claiming you, if he even knows of your existence. He does live across the ocean, after all."

"True," I agreed. "I'm glad he lives so far away—we'll probably never run into each other." There was little chance of the two of us meeting so long as he stayed away from the Federation and I stayed away from Castalis. I put that country on my list of places to never visit, which was a shame because I'd heard it was very beautiful there.

"That does not mean there is no cause for concern at all," Janta warned. "Of course I will not tell anyone about your heritage, but as technology continues to expand, we have exposed ourselves to more eyes around the world. It is entirely possible that someone may see your face in the paper and notice your strong resemblance to Haman. You should be aware of that, and perhaps try to minimize the number of photos taken by the press until after you are married."

"All right," I said, though I had no idea how I was going to do that. Sure, I could refuse to take photos at interviews, but there would be celebrity photographers lying in wait on the streets, hoping to snag a shot of me.

"I'm afraid that is all I have for you," Janta said, closing the file. "I daresay you will want to discuss it with Lord Iannis, who may know more of the ar'Rhea family. Would you like to take this with you, or shall I keep it?"

I hesitated, my fingers hovering over the file. "No," I decided, pulling my hand away. "You keep it. That information is probably way safer under lock and key here, than it is in my rooms." I stood, then inclined my head to her. "Thank you very much for your assistance, Janta. Once again, you have proven to be an invaluable ally."

"You're welcome, Sunaya," Janta said, a twinkle in her pale blue eyes. "I could say the same about you, considering the success of your recent mission. Do let me know if you need anything else."

I left the library, wondering if maybe I should just set fire to every single camera that was pointed in my direction. Sure, that seemed a little extreme, but my relationship with Iannis was worth any price. Guess I'd have to ask him about it during our lesson and see if he had a better solution.

27

"*So where exactly are we going again?*" Rylan asked in my head as we raced through the Mages Quarter on my steambike. "*And why couldn't we have grabbed some food first?*"

I rolled my eyes, even though nobody would be able to see them behind my bike helmet. "*I already told you—we're going to Jonias Ballos's house to see if he can tell me more about my father.*"

"*I would have thought you'd want to draw as little attention to your relationship with your father as possible, after what Janta told you,*" Rylan said, tightening his grip around my waist as I whipped around a corner faster than strictly necessary. I could feel the disapproving glares of the residential mages on my back, and I grinned a little. I knew they hated the sight of my rebellious steambike racing through their genteel streets, and I made a point of doing it as often as possible to let them know I wasn't going anywhere, and they were just going to have to deal.

"*That's true, but since Ballos is a hermit, he isn't going to run around and tell everyone. And since Iannis cancelled our lesson, I don't have anything better to do.*" Some dignitary had unexpectedly popped in for a visit, leaving me with a bit of free time. Rylan and I could have sparred or something, but my need to learn more about my father had been gnawing away at my thoughts until I could think of nothing else. Better to get this over with now, so I could move on to more important things.

"*I hope this doesn't backfire on you somehow,*" Rylan said, uncharacteristically serious. "*After all that you've been through, I just want you to be safe.*"

"*I know.*" My heart warmed, and I found myself once more grateful for the fact that I had a family member who loved me. "*I just think you might be being a little optimistic, considering my track record.*"

Rylan laughed. "*I guess you're right.*"

We arrived at Jonias's house in short order. It was on the outskirts of the Mages Quarter, close to Maintown, and sat on an acre of land that looked like it was in serious need of a gardener. The grass was several feet high and had swallowed up the foot-path leading from the gate to the house. Ivy grew up the walls with reckless abandon. The house itself was large and stately looking beneath said ivy, though the pale yellow siding was chipped in places, and many of the white roof tiles were cracked. The wrought-iron gate that surrounded the place was showing signs of rust, and made a loud screeching noise as I pulled it open.

"Nice digs," Rylan remarked as we waded through the grass. He sneezed as the scent of magic grew stronger. "If not for my nose, I wouldn't have guessed this was a mage's residence."

"I told you he was a hermit," I said, shrugging. I didn't understand why Ballos's house looked like crap either. I mean, yeah, maybe he didn't go outside much, but surely he had the funds to hire a gardener and repaint the walls every once in a while. Or did he just not care?

I grabbed the heavy brass doorknocker and pounded on the door once, twice, three times. My nose caught the faint, but fairly recent, whiff of an elderly human male, so I assumed there was at least one servant around to answer the door. When no one came, I knocked again.

Eventually, I heard the shuffle of footsteps in the hall, and the scent of elderly human grew stronger. The locks disengaged, and the front door slowly opened to reveal a skinny, white-haired man with rheumy eyes, dressed in an ancient-looking black suit.

"Good evening," he said in a warbling old-man voice, and I suppose it was, since it was nearing five o'clock now. "How can I help you?"

"I'm from the Enforcer's Guild, here to speak with Mr. Jonias Ballos." I held up my bracelet as proof. "Is he in residence?"

"Yes," the old man said, squinting as he eyed us up and down. "Though I don't think he'll see you."

"Tell him I just need to ask him a few questions." I held up my bracelet, and he leaned in closer so he could peer at it. "My bodyguard and I won't take up too much of his time."

"An enforcer with a bodyguard, eh?" he said, shaking his head. "My, how times change. I will go and see if he will speak with you. Please wait here."

To my annoyance, he closed the door on us instead of letting us in to wait in the hall. Sighing, I tapped my foot as I looked around, wondering where the strong magic smell was coming from. Did Ballos keep a lot of magical artifacts in the house? Or was there some kind of spell set upon the grounds? I wondered if there was a spell that would magically keep a garden trimmed. If so, this guy seriously needed to learn it.

Nearly ten minutes went by, and I was about to explode in frustration when at last I heard the butler's footsteps shuffle back down the hall. Was he only capable of walking at a snail's pace?

"I'm sorry, but Master Ballos is in the middle of an important research project and cannot be disturbed," the butler said. "You

may feel free to call another time when he might be more
available."

"I'm here by order of the Chief Mage of Solantha," I said
through gritted teeth, even though that wasn't strictly true. If I
had to suffer through this yearlong engagement, I was at least
going to throw around the Chief Mage's title every once in a
while. "He will be very displeased if he has to come down here
himself."

The old man hesitated. "I will relay this information," he
said reluctantly, moving back inside again. "Please, wait here—"

"Oh, hell no," I growled, planting my foot on the threshold. I
wasn't going to wait another ten minutes to get another bullshit
answer! "I'll just come with you—"

A loud buzzing noise sounded as the air super-heated
around me, raising the hairs on my arms as a ward activated
around the perimeter of the house. Before I could get clear of
the threshold, an unseen force threw me back, and I went flying.
I grunted as I hit the ground, hard, the overgrown grass cush-
ioning my fall somewhat.

"Oh, dear," the butler said as Rylan hurried over to help me
up. "Master Ballos has set a spell on the house that bars access
to all individuals he has not given express permission to enter.
You cannot get inside."

"A little warning would have been nice!" I shouted, accepting
Rylan's offer of a hand up. I dusted off my leather pants and
straightened my jacket, then approached the man again. "If not
for your overgrown lawn, I might have broken something!"

"I do apologize," the old man said, bowing stiffly. "I'm afraid I
am not as young as I used to be, and we are terribly understaffed
here. Please wait just a little longer, and I will get the Master
for you."

"Thanks," I said, softening my tone a little. The butler disappeared back inside, and as I listened to him shuffle off, I couldn't

help but feel a little bad for him. Was he seriously the only servant here? If so, no wonder the place was in such disrepair. What was Ballos thinking, leaving it up to one elderly man to take care of this big house? I wondered why the old butler hadn't simply retired at this point. Maybe he needed the money, or felt some sort of loyalty for the mage who'd employed him all these years.

Eventually, the butler came back again. This time, he seemed more relaxed. "Master Ballos will see you," he said, opening the door wider. "Please, come in."

I stepped over the threshold cautiously, waiting for the ward to kick in. But, thankfully, it didn't, and Rylan and I passed into the foyer unscathed. The butler led us down a hall, and we passed through rooms of expensive, but dusty furniture and rugs. My nose twitched as I fought against the desire to sneeze, and Rylan looked like he was pretty uncomfortable too. I didn't smell a single other person in this place aside from the butler, and another male scent that I imagined belonged to Ballos.

"Master Ballos," the butler said, knocking on the door we stopped at. "Your visitors are here."

"Very well," a gruff voice barked. "Let them in."

The butler opened the door into a large study filled with bookshelves and several desks piled high with leather-bound notebooks, stacks of paper, and what looked to be manuscripts. The place seemed to be in some kind of organized chaos, with Ballos at his desk in the center of the storm, bent over a long piece of aged parchment as he peered at it, muttering to himself. He was as unkempt as the rest of the house, dressed in a pair of faded brown robes. His grey hair and beard were in urgent need of a brush—no way would a comb get through that tangled mess. A pair of horn-rimmed glasses perched on his hooked nose, and though he had the appearance of a madman, the dark eyes behind those glasses were sharp and brimming with intelli-

gence as he immersed himself in whatever magical research he
was conducting.

"Yes, so what is it?" he asked irritably as he straightened up
from his desk. His eyes widened as he caught sight of me, and he
stumbled back a step. "You!" he shouted, pointing a gnarled
finger at me. "No, you cannot be in my house. You must leave
at once!"

"You know who I am," I guessed, narrowing my eyes as I
stepped over a stack of books to close the distance between us.
"You know why I'm here."

"I am not interested in speaking with you," Ballos said firmly,
crossing his arms over his chest. "I am in the middle of some
very important work."

"You're not getting rid of me that easily." I pulled out a chair
from in front of his desk. It was piled high with books, and I
lifted them, intending to dump them somewhere so I could have
a seat. "I'm parking my butt right here, and I won't move until
you tell me about my father."

"Don't touch those!" Ballos barked, his paper-white cheeks
reddening. He spoke a Word, waving his hand, and the books
levitated out of my hands. I sat down on the chair as he guided
them over to a patch of empty space on one of the other desks.
When he turned back to me, he looked half-resigned, half-
resentful. "I read about your engagement to Lord Iannis in the
papers, and perhaps I should have expected some repercussions
from that. But I did not expect you to have the audacity to show
up on my doorstep yourself." He looked down his hooked nose
at me.

"Yeah, well, I guess you haven't heard the stories about me," I
said, resisting the urge to be belligerent and kick my feet up on
his desk. "I'm pretty audacious."

"Clearly." The old mage sniffed, then looked above my head
at Rylan. "I suppose you won't leave until I tell you the sordid

tale, but this young man must wait outside in the parlor. I do not wish for him to overhear our conversation."

I turned in my chair to meet Rylan's scowling face. "Go," I told him. *"I'll fill you in later. He's more likely to open up if we do as he says."*

"I feel like this is becoming a pattern," Rylan grumbled, but he nodded, then left the room. The butler closed the door behind him, leaving Ballos and me alone in the messy study.

Ballos carefully rolled up the parchment and returned it to its storage tube, then set it aside so he could sit down. "All right," he said, meeting my gaze. "Ask your questions."

"What do you know about my father's affair with my mother?"

"Not very much," the old mage said stiffly. "Haman was—and still is—a young mage. He was only fifty years old when he came to study under me. So it was not surprising that he spent his evenings gallivanting about the city. I always thought he was socializing with other young mages in society, seeing as how he is of noble birth, but as it turns out, he was spending time in the seedier areas of Solantha."

I gritted my teeth at that, unsure if he was implying that my mother was a whore, or that everything outside the Mages Quarter was 'seedy'. But I decided not to press the issue, or point out that he had no room to talk with the dilapidated state of his own house. Doing so would only derail the conversation and make him less likely to want to talk to me.

"Okay, but you knew that my father had an affair that resulted in a child, or you wouldn't have reacted the way you did when I walked in," I insisted.

"I did not find out about the affair until after Haman had returned to Castalis," Ballos replied. "Your mother came to my doorstep asking for Haman's address, because she was carrying his child. I remember the day well, because it was the first time a shifter had ever come to call upon me. I was so startled that I let her in, and she told me how Haman had been seeing her as a human male. Apparently, he'd disguised both his looks and his scent, which only confirms my theory that he was infatuated. I don't know why he would have gone to such pains otherwise." His voice was thick with disgust.

"I see." I frowned as a question popped into my head, and I voiced it aloud before thinking better of it. "How is it that they were able to conceive? Even during heat, it is hard for shifters to get pregnant—we usually have to take a special potion to maximize our chances. It doesn't sound like my mother did that."

"I suppose not," Haman said, shrugging. "The pregnancy was unexpected, and initially unwelcome, from what she said. She was very dismayed to learn that Haman wasn't here, after going through considerable trouble to track him down. She was angry at his deception, for she might have used stronger protection had she had any idea he was a very powerful mage. That can make a difference, and there might have been a full moon." He shrugged. "I am hardly an expert though."

"No, that makes sense." The full moon boosted a shifter's power, and it helped increase the chances of conception; that was why the heat always coincided with a full moon. Coupled with my father's mage powers... *oh*. Iannis was a powerful mage too. I would have to remember to track down some kind of potion or spell to prevent pregnancy the next time I was in heat, as it would create a huge scandal if I got pregnant before Iannis and I were married.

Of course, the idea of bearing and raising children with Iannis was a whole other topic that needed to be thought about. But now was not the time for it, so I firmly pushed it aside.

"So, did you give her my father's address?" I demanded. "And did they get in touch? Does my father know about me?"

"I did tell her your father's address," Haman said. "Given his family's prominence in Castalis, it is common knowledge. But I highly doubt Haman knows anything about you."

"What!" I nearly came out of my chair. "Are you saying she decided not to tell him?"

"I convinced her not to," Haman declared. "I explained that if she approached Haman, it would create a terrible scandal. His engagement would be broken, and his entire family would be disgraced. Of course, your mother was very surprised to hear this, and that he was engaged. For her, it had just been one of the usual ruts that shifter females engage in to get through their heat."

That note of disgust entered his voice again, and I wanted to punch him in the face. Who was he to judge us? Did his race not create us to be like this?

"In any case, your mother did not want anything particular from him; she simply felt you ought to know your father."

"Clearly, you didn't feel the same," I said, bitterness creeping into my voice.

"Don't look at me like that," Ballos protested. "I was doing your mother a favor! Your father might have taken you away from her, to Castalis, and hidden you away in shame. More likely, given their attitude to shifters, he would have repudiated you altogether. As a mage-shifter hybrid, you would not have had much of a future anyway, and I told her so."

I opened my mouth, anger burning like hot coals in my stomach, then closed it. What the hell could I possibly say to that? Ballos was right—all of those things were very possible futures for me, had my mother told Haman about my existence. But still, what if there was a chance he would have loved me? After all, Ballos seemed to think my father had been infatuated with my mother. Surely, there had been a chance.

"If my father doesn't know that I exist," I said slowly, curling and uncurling my fists in my lap, "then who put the binding on my magic?"

"I did," Ballos said. "As a favor to Haman, who was one of my better students. I told your mother that in exchange for her silence regarding your father's name, I would bind your magic so tightly that it would go undetected by the school tests. I performed the spell shortly after your birth, though it was difficult since, even then, you showed evidence of very strong talent." Something like regret passed in his eyes. "It is too bad that you were not born a full mage—you would have made Haman proud."

"Yeah, pity that." I sneered, unable to keep the scorn from my voice now. "It's clear to me that everyone would prefer I wasn't a hybrid."

"Well, it would make the lives of everyone much easier," Ballos said with another sniff. "But I suppose what's done is done, and you have made yourself a good life, all things considered."

With nothing more to say, I gave Ballos one last look, then collected Rylan from the parlor and left. Stepping out into the last rays of the setting sun, I tried to feel grateful that, for the most part, I had come out on top. But as I stared out at the dilapidated yard, and the horizon beyond, all I could feel was sadness.

"You okay?" Rylan asked, setting his hand on my shoulder. "Seems like you might have gotten more than you bargained for out of the old man."

"I just feel unwanted," I admitted, turning to face him. "I mean, I don't doubt that my mother loved me once I was born, but I was clearly the result of an accident."

"Maybe, but your entrance into our lives was wonderful all the same," Rylan said, giving me a hug. "You're a treasure, cousin, and judging by the entirely inappropriate looks the

Chief Mage gives you when he thinks no one is looking, I'm not the only one who thinks so."

I laughed, smacking him on the chest. "You're not serious!" I said, stepping back to see the twinkle of mischief in Rylan's eyes. Iannis had an incredibly good poker face—no way would he let that sort of thing show in public.

"One-hundred-percent serious," Rylan said, grinning. "He's got the hots for you."

"Oh, stop." I laughed again, shaking my head as we began heading down the steps. "You're ridiculous sometimes."

"Yeah, but you love me anyway. Now, where are we going next?"

I thought about it for a moment. "I'd like to go to Com's," I said. "I want to tell him about what I learned, and see if he's checked on Noria at all."

"Oh, yeah," Rylan said, his face sobering as he held the gate open for me. "Her hearing is coming up pretty soon, isn't it?"

"In two days," I said as we got onto my steambike. "Noria doesn't want to see me, so I haven't tried to visit her. Hopefully, Com has talked some sense into her."

"I wouldn't bet on it," Rylan warned as I started up the engine. "She's stubborn, that one."

"So you are a direct descendant of Resinah?" Comenius asked, sounding very impressed. We were sitting around his dining table along with Elania, eating pot roast—by lucky chance, Rylan and I had shown up just in time for dinner. "It's a pity you cannot use that information publicly. I'm sure many of the mages who look down on you would be changing their tune."

I shrugged as I forked up a piece of carrot. "I don't know

about that," I said. "I feel like there will always be a few who are determined to look down at me no matter what."

"Perhaps," Elania said, dabbing daintily at her lips with a napkin. She looked gorgeous as usual in one of her tight, black dresses, and for once had left her long, black hair unbound. "But even so, it must give you some measure of relief to finally know your father's identity, regardless of whether or not you ever meet him."

"It does," I admitted. "It just sucks that I still have to keep this all under wraps."

"The one thing you can take comfort in," Rylan said as he mopped up some of the pot roast gravy with a hunk of bread, "is that your father didn't willfully abandon you, or put that spell on you. I know the chances are low that the two of you would get along since he comes from such an uppity family, but maybe he's not as much of an asshole as you always thought he was."

"Maybe," I conceded. I still didn't love the fact that he'd knocked my mother up while pretending to be a human, and while engaged to another woman. But at least he'd never intended to create me as a by-blow, or abandon me to an uncertain fate.

"I hope things will settle down somewhat now that you've returned," Comenius said. "I am very grateful your rescue mission was so successful, and that no one was severely hurt. And I am relieved Noria was recovered alive from that hellhole."

"Me too." I smiled, though it was a little strained. "I'm not sure if we should be celebrating yet, though. We still have that hearing to get past."

"Ah, yes." Comenius sighed, his cornflower-blue eyes filling with sadness as he turned to look out the window. "I visited Noria yesterday at the Enforcers Guild to see how she was faring. She is being treated as well as can be expected in a prison cell, no doubt because she is Annia's sister. But Noria was very pale and tight-lipped, and would not speak much." Frustrated, he ran a hand through his ash-blond hair. "I wish we could go back to when she was simply a carefree teenager who worked in my shop downstairs."

"So do I," I said, sadness pooling in my chest. I put down my fork, no longer quite so hungry, even though I'd only had one serving. "I have a feeling she's not going to be working here again for quite a while though, Com. Likely not ever. Even if Iannis does go easy on her, she'll still be facing some sort of punishment for what she did. He can't just pardon her."

"At this point in time, we must trust Noria to determine her own fate," Elania said sagely. "She is a strong young woman, and will handle whatever happens in her own way."

"That's true," I said, smiling a little. Noria was smart and resourceful as hell. She might be sulking now, but surely she'd figure out how to come out on top. She had to.

"On a happier note," Comenius said, reaching across the table to link fingers with Elania. "Elania and I have decided to move forward with our relationship. We're to be married in three months."

"Married!" I nearly fell out of my chair. "In three months?"

"Yes." Elania beamed. "We hope to start a family soon too."

"That's great." I smiled at them both. "I'm really happy for you two." In truth, I was also a little envious of them—they had it so easy, not having to wade through all these stupid mage customs. "Guess we're both going to be married soon, huh?" I said to Comenius.

"Who would have thought it?" Comenius joked, but his smile dimmed a little. "In all seriousness, you should discuss the issues regarding your family with Iannis as soon as possible. I assume he already knows and has planned for the various contingencies, but it doesn't hurt to be sure."

"I will," I promised, but honestly, there was no rush. I'd bring it up when the time was right. "By the way, what ever happened to those jewels I gave you?"

"Oh, right!" Comenius's face brightened. "I sold them for a good price, and bought you a used but very serviceable airship. I can arrange for you to see it tomorrow, if you'd like."

"Well, look at you," Rylan teased. "First, you're engaged to the Chief Mage of Canalo, and now you're the proud owner of an airship. Moving up in the world."

I rolled my eyes at him, smiling.

"That sounds great, Com. I'd love to see it." I'd hire an instructor to teach me how to fly it too. After all, I didn't want the task-force missions to be the only occasions when I got to travel around the Federation. Now that I had time and money, I wanted to see the world. And hopefully, if everything turned out well with Noria, I'd be able to take her and my other friends along with me.

28

I didn't have a whole lot of time to think about Noria's upcoming trial the next morning—I was back to work in the Mages Guild as an apprentice. Now that I was Iannis's fiancée and he'd given orders to include me in all magical tasks, I was no longer doing paperwork for the Agricultural department. I actually got to spend the morning out with one of the maintenance crews, checking on the various spells that helped regulate the city's water and sewage systems. It was educational, if rather gross at times, and I came back with a healthy appetite.

Unfortunately, Fenris wasn't available to tutor me in Loranian in the afternoon—he had an appointment somewhere. So I found myself in my rooms, studying my primer and getting bored out of my mind that I wasn't doing any actual spellcraft.

"Screw this," I said, closing the book and tossing it onto my side table. I wanted to practice some magic! Closing my eyes, I tried to recall some of the spells I'd recently seen, figuring if I could remember the Words well enough, I could recreate them.

The image of a glowing ether pigeon popped into my head, and I opened my eyes with a grin. That was perfect. I'd seen both Elnos and Iannis use magic to create the glowing magical birds that could be used to send messages. They seemed really useful and fun, and I wanted to try my hand at making one.

Grabbing a piece of paper and pen, I sat cross-legged for a moment and tried to recall the exact Words. I checked them against the primer, but unfortunately, at least half of the incantation's Words weren't in there, so I had to guess at those as best I could. Oh well, if I didn't get the spell right, then it just wouldn't work. It wasn't like I would blow up the Palace.

Would I?

"Whatever," I grumbled, scanning the Words again. Iannis had safeguards set up around the Palace to prevent that kind of thing from happening. Besides, I was ninety-nine point nine percent certain that I had the incantation right.

Taking a deep breath, I focused in on the glowing ball of energy in my center that was the source of my magic. Since Iannis had taken the seal off it completely—a seal I now knew had been set by Ballos, not my father—it was much bigger, and I had to be careful not to draw too much too fast.

Once I was certain I had a good hold on it, I held up a palm and spoke the incantation.

Wisps of magic floated up from my palm, twisting together to form a glowing blue ball. The ball rose higher and higher into the air as it slowly shaped itself into a bird, and I grinned. Yes, it was slower than the other times I'd seen the spell performed, but it was working! My grin faded as the shape kept changing, the feathers growing longer, the beak becoming much bigger and more hooked than that of a pigeon...

"Oh shit," I breathed as it fully formed into not a pigeon, but a parrot. An honest-to-Magorah fucking parrot.

"Oh shit!" the parrot squawked, perching on the footboard of my bed. It cocked its head at me, then swiveled around to regard me with one glowing eye. Damn, but it looked incredibly real—I could see each individual feather cover its glowing body, and man did the claws curling around my footboard look sharp! "Oh shit!"

I groaned, flopping back against my pillows. "No!" I whined at the parrot, flicking my hand in a shooing motion. "This is wrong. You're not supposed to be a parrot! Just be gone already."

The parrot cocked its head to the opposite side, then vanished in a flash of light. I let out a sigh of relief that I hadn't had to resort to using magic to get rid of it. Clearly, I'd been a little too optimistic about my memory of the incantation. I was lucky my pigeon had turned into a parrot and not, say, a hippopotamus. Those things were mean as hell, from what I'd heard, not to mention downright huge.

Oh well, I thought, curling up on my mattress. I might as well take a nap until my lesson with Iannis. With any luck, he'd never find out about this little incident.

After our usual warm-up exercises, Iannis took pity on me and offered to do some combat training. We suited up with magical armor, and with Fenris acting as referee, we launched into three-minute rounds of magical combat. As in our previous mock fights, we stuck to fire and ice, but this time, we added shielding to our arsenal, which enabled me to deflect Iannis's ice blasts.

Of course, I quickly found out that since he could also do the same, our fights devolved into something more like a match of tennis, with the two of us bouncing balls of fire and ice back at each other.

"This is so frustrating!" I shouted as I shielded against another ball of ice. "What is the point of doing this if we're never actually going to hit each other? Why do mages even duel in the first place?"

"Good question!" Iannis shouted as he lobbed the ice ball back at me. I shot a fireball at it to melt it, then another one directly at his head, hoping to catch him off guard. No such luck; he simply bounced it back at me again. "Mage duels are difficult and frustrating, and should never be undertaken without good purpose."

Growling, I changed tactics. Instead of shielding against the ball, I ducked and allowed it to hit the force field protecting the wall. I shot out two more fireballs, hoping that three missiles would be more than Iannis could comfortably deal with, or at least enough of a distraction that I could figure something else out.

"Oh shit!" a familiar voice squawked, and my mouth dropped open as I saw the ether parrot materialize right next to Iannis's head.

"What in the world—" Iannis exclaimed, startled, and he missed one of the fireballs. It slammed into his chest, and he grunted as the force of the blow knocked him against the wall.

"Time!" Fenris called, and I lowered my shield. He rushed over to Iannis. "Are you all right?"

"I'm perfectly fine," Iannis said, barely even looking at Fenris. His attention was firmly fixated on the parrot, who was now perched on his shoulder. "Although I would very much like an explanation for this creature."

"Um, that's kind of my fault," I said sheepishly as I crossed the room. To my annoyance, the parrot turned his head up at my approach. "I was trying to create an ether pigeon, but I created this guy instead."

"Did you really?" Iannis laughed. "I suppose you didn't get the Word for 'pigeon' quite right."

"That would be my guess," Fenris said, who also looked

highly amused. "Does it usually drop in on you at unexpected times?"

"I don't know," I groused, annoyed that my blunder had been found out after all. "This is the first time it's happened. I created him about an hour ago, and he disappeared immediately afterward. I thought I'd seen the last of him, but I guess I was wrong."

Iannis and Fenris both laughed this time, and I felt a smile tug at my lips even as my cheeks reddened. It was good to see them together like this again, without tension between them. Fenris must have laid his misgivings about staying at the Palace to rest for now, and hopefully for good. He belonged here with us—that much I was certain of.

"Well, I must say, he makes for an unusual pet." Fenris passed a hand along the parrot's ghostly foliage. His fingers went right through, of course, as the parrot wasn't corporeal. "At least he shouldn't produce droppings."

"Yeah, that'll make me feel a lot better when he wakes me up in the middle of the night yelling 'Oh shit!'"

Iannis and Fenris burst into laughter again, but it was cut short by a knock on the door. "May I come in, Lord Iannis?" Director Chen called, and I stiffened. She had a bad habit of breaking up my lessons with Iannis early, and I was becoming less and less willing to tolerate it. I leveled a glare at Iannis, who nodded and mouthed that he understood.

"Yes, come in, but make it quick," he called.

Director Chen stepped inside and closed the door behind her. "Thorgana's convoy was attacked on its way in to Dara this evening."

"What?" Iannis and I both shouted at the same time.

"Did she escape?" Iannis demanded. "And what of the guards? Are any still alive?"

"No, she did not escape," Chen said, and I sighed as a wave of relief washed over me. "There were a few casualties, as the party that attacked our convoy was very large—over twice the number of guards. If not for the mages accompanying them, the attackers would have been able to successfully free Thorgana. In any case, she has been checked into the prison facility, and is safe once more."

"Well, that is good to hear," Iannis said, sounding much calmer now. "And after this, her air of injured innocence will look much less credible. It's all the confirmation needed that she is indeed the Benefactor. Did the attackers make contact with Thorgana in any way? And did our people capture any of them?"

"Unfortunately not." Chen shook her head. "The ones who survived fled, and the guard captain sensibly decided it would be foolish to pursue them—his top priority was guarding Thorgana in case there was a second attack. Also, they had several wounded to look after."

"Very well," Iannis said, sounding disappointed. "I will contact the Minister to ensure that she is thoroughly searched and isolated for a time— we must be certain that the attackers did not manage to slip any sort of weapon or disease to her."

"I think you will be discussing that with him in person," Chen said. "The Minister wishes for you to return to Dara immediately. To discuss *the Garaian matter*, he said." She looked at him questioningly, and I surmised that Iannis had not yet told her about the other Resistance lab.

"I cannot," Iannis said firmly. "I have a hearing tomorrow morning. But I shall leave immediately after that."

"I will let him know, sir, and I will convey your suggestions regarding the prisoner as well." Chen bowed, then swept from the room, closing the door behind her.

"Damn," Iannis muttered when her footfalls had receded. "I had hoped to have at least a week at the Palace before being called away again. I have much to catch up on."

"I'm sure Director Chen will help you pick up the slack

while you're gone. And Fenris and I will do what we can do to help." I took off my armor, then cupped his face in my hands and kissed him. "Try to get some sleep tonight, okay? I don't want you to smite Noria because you're too grumpy to deal with her attitude."

Iannis smiled at that. "I think if I've managed to deal with *your* attitude for this long, I can survive Miss Melcott for a single morning."

I snorted. "I sure hope so," I said as I left the room. Because if not, Noria was going to be in *big* trouble.

29

The morning of Noria's hearing dawned bright and cold, hinting at the coming fall. I stood on my veranda, sipping coffee while I watched the sun rise, and prayed to Magorah and Resinah and the Creator and whoever the hell else was listening, to make Noria wake up with a clear head rather than anger in her heart.

I knew now that if I'd shown up at the Palace for my own hearing with a reasonable attitude, things might have gone easier for me. I was lucky Iannis had shown me compassion despite his stony exterior, and also that he was presiding over Noria's case. With any luck, he would show her similar compassion, and she would have the sense to take whatever deal he offered her.

I bathed and dressed, then made my way down to the audience chamber, where Iannis and Fenris already waited. This was the room where Iannis heard complaints and conducted hearings, where I had experienced my first encounter with the fearsome and mysterious Chief Mage. I stepped into the spacious chamber, which was more like a hall than a room. A long blue-and-gold carpet carved a path through the center of the parquet floor, and tall, gleaming mahogany columns held up the soaring ceiling as I walked up the path. The walls were pale pink granite, as was the huge desk Iannis and Fenris stood behind. A thick, leather-bound logbook stood open on the desk, as well as a file, and there were legal texts on hand as well, should they prove to be necessary.

"Good morning," I murmured, twining my fingers briefly with Iannis's as I took my place to his right. We hadn't slept together last night, and I strongly suspected Iannis hadn't slept at all, though he looked the same as ever.

"Good morning." He squeezed my hand briefly, then let it go as the double doors opened. My heart skipped a beat as Annia and two guards brought Noria in. They were both wearing conservative dresses, Annia's a pale green and Noria's a dark red —probably their mother's idea, as I doubted Noria would have dressed up for the occasion. I was glad her mother, a rather difficult woman, had elected to stay away from the hearing. Perhaps Annia had persuaded her to stay behind. Noria held her head high as she was escorted down the aisle to stand before the Chief Mage with Annia at her side.

Comenius and Elnos were also there, trailing behind the guards—they had agreed to come as character witnesses and to provide moral support. Comenius gave me a small smile as he and Elnos stood off to the side, and I nodded. I was glad they were here, not just for Noria, but for me as well, selfish though that was.

"Good morning, Lord Iannis," Annia said, bowing. Everyone but Noria did the same. "We are ready for the hearing."

"Are you?" Iannis asked sternly, addressing Noria directly. She locked eyes with him, and I was both proud and apprehensive at the defiance blazing in her dark eyes. "Are you ready to proceed with this hearing, Miss Melcott?"

"Ready as I'll ever be," Noria said, straightening her shoulders.

"Very well." Iannis pulled a piece of paper from the file on the desk, then briefly scanned it. "Noria Melcott, are you aware that you have been charged with treason against the Federation, and for attempting to commit genocide?"

"I am," Noria said stiffly.

"And do you have anything to add to the testimony you have already given, which is on record?" Iannis asked.

"No." Noria hesitated. "Actually, yes."

Annia glared at her, but Noria refused to look at her sister. My stomach sank, and I had a feeling that whatever she was about to say wouldn't help her case.

"Very well. What do you wish to tell us?"

"I want to make it clear that even though I don't support the Resistance any more, I still don't recognize your authority over me." Elnos sucked in a sharp breath, and pain flashed in Annia's eyes. "You have no empathy for the human race, and do not attempt to understand our troubles or needs. Whatever you decide to do with me, you're still a tyrant. Nothing is going to change that."

I clenched my hands at my sides, thankful the desk shielded them. Where the hell did Noria get off saying any of that shit? There was a kernel of truth there, but after everything I'd told her, and all that had transpired, she should know better than that by now. And unlike me when I'd arrived here for my hearing, Noria had actually committed crimes against the Federation.

"Noted," Iannis said, without a hint of emotion. "Now, do you admit that it was wrong to aid the Resistance in producing the kind of weapons they were asking you to make?"

"I do now," Noria admitted. "I didn't realize the real purpose they intended to use my device for when I started working on it, or I never would have agreed. That's why I tried to stop them," she added, glaring at Iannis.

"That, too, has been noted, and it is the only reason why you haven't already been sentenced to death," Iannis said. Noria's face paled at that, making her freckles stand out, but she did not react otherwise. "Even so, I cannot let you off without any punishment at all. You must either face three years in the mines, or take a legally and magically binding oath not to engage in any sedition or revolutionary activities for the next twenty years."

I stifled a huge sigh of relief, and did not miss the expressions of relief on the others' faces. Noria was getting a huge break, and we all knew it.

"Are those my only choices?" Noria demanded.

"Yes."

"Fine. Then I choose the mines."

"What!" I shouted, slapping my hands on the table. "Noria, you can't be serious!" I couldn't contain myself anymore—this was ridiculous. "Quit being so stubborn and just take the deal!"

"I am taking the deal," Noria said, her eyes still on Iannis— she refused to look at me. "*Lord* Iannis's three-year sentence is much lighter than what I expected from him, and I'm taking it. I won't agree to the oath."

"Noria, please." Annia took her sister's arm and turned her, her dark eyes pleading. "You know Mom will be devastated."

A look of sadness briefly crossed Noria's face before it hardened again. "I'd rather die before I make a promise I can't keep," she said. "And I have a feeling that I literally *would* die if I took that oath and broke it," she added with a bitter smile, turning back to Iannis. "No, it's better this way."

"Noria—" Elnos tried, his voice filled with pain, but Iannis cut him off.

"Very well," Iannis said, his voice ringing with authority. "It has been decided. Noria Melcott, you will serve three years' hard labor in the mines as punishment for your crimes against the Federation. You are dismissed."

Tears stung my eyes as I watched the guards march Noria from the room. She left with her head held just as high as it was when she entered, pride and anger emanating from her every step of the way. Annia gave me one last stricken look, then followed her sister out to escort her back to the Enforcers Guild.

"*Zum Donnerwetter*," Comenius muttered darkly as the doors closed behind them. He shook his head. "How did it come to this?"

"I don't know," I whispered, and, to my horror, the tears started streaming down my face. I wasn't sure if it was the fact that Noria had refused to look at me, or the way Elnos was still standing there looking defeated, but something inside me broke. "It's just that it's such a fucking waste," I choked, swiping at my tears with the back of my hand.

"It is indeed." Iannis took me into his arms, his voice low and soothing. "But you are not to blame for Miss Melcott's life choices, Sunaya. They are hers to make, just as your choices and mistakes were yours to make."

I clung to Iannis as he held me for a long moment, doing my best to get my tears under control. The fact that I hadn't been able to stop this from happening, despite all the effort I'd gone through, was crushing. What good did all my work do, if I couldn't even save my friends?

"Sunaya," Elnos said, and I lifted my face to meet his gaze. His eyes were sad, but they held no anger as he looked at me. He had to be feeling even worse than I was. "I want you to know that I appreciate all you've done to help Noria."

"Thanks." I cleared my throat, then wiped at my tears again as I remembered everyone was still looking at me. As I turned to look at them, I was comforted by the fact that I wasn't alone, and I hadn't let down all my friends. Most of them were here with me, alive and well, in part because of my struggle to stop the Resistance and help keep our city safe.

"This is not the end for Noria," Fenris said gently as I stepped out of Iannis's comforting embrace. "She will pay her penance, and at the end of the three years, she will be older and wiser."

"Or, she might come out even more bitter than when she went in," I pointed out, though I knew dwelling on that possibility wasn't productive.

"Perhaps," Comenius said, "but at least she will be safer in prison than in the hands of the Resistance. With any luck, within three years, the Resistance will be eradicated. Noria will have to find a more constructive use for her talents at that time."

"That's true," I said, but I wasn't sure if I believed the words. Noria was far too clever and inventive not to find a way to escape the mines within those three years. Nor would she put her revolutionary ideas aside just because the movement she had joined was no longer active. I only hoped that when she eventually fled, she would end up in a safe place, and not in another dangerous hellhole far away, where none of us would be able to rescue her again.

EPILOGUE

*L*ate in the afternoon, I sat out on my veranda and leafed through the mail Nelia had brought to me. It had been two days since Iannis had left for Dara, and since he still wasn't back, that meant no lessons. Rather than risking the creation of another ether parrot, or worse, I decided I would catch up on my social duties.

Nelia had been delighted to assist, and she'd helped me prepare for my interview with a mage society matron, scheduled for late afternoon, before leaving me with the stack of correspondence. She'd already sorted through it herself, separating the messages by tabs in a big folder. There were invitations, bills, and even fan mail from citizens praising my efforts in stopping the rebellion.

The bills I set aside for Nelia to take care of—I had more than enough money to handle them, so they weren't the source of concern they would have been even a few weeks ago. The invitations I marked off with a check or an *x* as to whether or not I wanted to attend, and I set those aside for Nelia to answer as well. The fan mail I kept for myself, intending to start a collection of them. I would put them in a shoebox to take out and look at whenever things got rough and I started questioning myself. It was the desire to help people that kept me going, that fueled my fight against injustice and evil, and I vowed to never forget that.

My fingers settled on a tab marked 'Personal Correspondence', and I flipped it open. Inside was a single elegant cream envelope with my name on it, and the hand-printed words *Private and Confidential*. The letter was sealed with wax, into which some kind of heraldic device had been imprinted.

I tore through the seal and pulled out the letter inside. My heart skipped a beat as I noticed the signature and address—the letter was from Isana ar'Rhea, Malian Sumer Palace, Castalis.

Fuck. My eyes raced down the handwritten lines of the letter, my heart pounding.

DEAR MISS BAINE,

MY NAME IS ISANA AR'RHEA, *eldest daughter of Haman ar'Rhea, the High Mage of Castalis. I recently saw your picture in a magazine article reporting your betrothal to the Chief Mage of Canalo, Lord ar'Sannin, and I could not help but notice that you bear a strong familial resemblance to me. It sounds strange, considering how far away we live from each other, but is there any possibility that we are related?*

I find it most remarkable that, according to the article, you are a shifter-mage hybrid, and have earned your living as an enforcer in the past. How I envy you all the adventures that the paper hinted at!

Would you be willing to send me an invitation to your wedding, so that I might be able to meet you? Or if not the wedding, I would love to meet you sooner.

Best wishes on your upcoming marriage. I do hope to hear back from you!

Sincerely,
Isana ar'Rhea

I SLOWLY FOLDED the letter back up, then closed my eyes and leaned my head back against the lounge chair. The irony of this situation washed over me in thick waves, and I groaned aloud, wondering what the hell to do with this. Did Isana, who was probably barely eighteen, have any inkling how closely related we were, and how much her family stood to lose if the truth became public? If *she* had guessed at our connection, it would not take long until others did so as well.

Should I ignore this letter from my half-sister, and spurn the opportunity to meet a close relative? Or did I write back, and in doing so, risk drawing my father's attention, and possibly endanger my marriage to Iannis?

The air above the table shimmered, and the ether parrot appeared, lighting the space with his blue glow. He perched on the edge of the table and squinted at me and the letter I was still holding, wicked intelligence gleaming in his eyes. His beak opened.

"Go ahead, say it," I told the bird. His phrase certainly fit the situation, though I should probably teach him some other expressions, especially if he was going to keep on popping in unexpectedly like this. It would be hilarious, but awful, if he manifested during an interview or public event and began spouting curses.

"Ha-ha-ha," he squawked, mocking me.

"Oh, fuck off." I tossed a pillow at the parrot, but he winked out of existence before it could hit. It bounced off the balcony railing instead.

"What next?" I asked the open air, half hoping someone might answer.

But of course, no one did. There would be no deity coming to my rescue, whispering words of advice in my ear, not this time.

Whatever happened next was up to me.

To be continued...

Sunaya Baine's adventure will continue in **Deceived by Magic**, Book 6 of the Baine Chronicles! Make sure to join her mailing list so you can be notified of future release dates, and to receive special updates, freebies and giveaways!

Join at www.jasminewalt.com/newsletter-signup

If you want to keep up with Jasmine Walt in the meantime, you can like her Facebook page, and follow her on Twitter, Goodreads, and Amazon.

DID YOU ENJOY THIS BOOK? Please consider leaving a review. Reviews help us authors sell books so we can afford to write more of them. Writing a review is the best way to ensure that the author writes the next one as it lets them know readers are enjoying their work and want more. Thank you very much for taking the time to read, and we hope you enjoyed the book!

GLOSSARY

Annia: see under Melcott, Annia.

Ancestral Spirits: according to Shifter belief, once a being is done with reincarnation, they may become an ancestral spirit.

ar': suffix in mages' family names that denotes they are of noble birth, and can trace their descent to one of Resinah's twelve disciples.

Baine, Sunaya: a half-panther shifter, half-mage who used to hate mages and has a passion for justice. Because magic is forbidden to all but the mage families, Sunaya was forced to keep her abilities a secret until she accidentally used them to defend herself in front of witnesses. Rather than condemn her to death, the Chief Mage, Iannis ar'Sannin, chose to take her on as his apprentice, and eventually his fiancée. She struggles to balance her shifter and mage heritage.

Baine, Melantha: Sunaya's cousin, and daughter to the Jaguar Clan's Chieftain.

Baine, Mafiela: Chieftain of the Jaguar Clan and Sunaya's aunt.

Baine, Mika: a young jaguar shifter, daughter of Melantha Baine.

Baine, Rylan: one of Chieftain Baine's least favored children, and Sunaya's cousin. An active member of the Resistance, with the rank of Captain, he was captured and imprisoned during the uprising in Solantha.

Ballos, Jonias: an elderly reclusive mage in Solantha.

Benefactor: the name the Resistance called their anonymous, principal source of financial support, before Sunaya unmasked the master criminal.

The Black Curtain: shop owned by Elania Tarrignal in Witches' End, where under-the-table hexes can be discreetly obtained.

Black Lion Inn: an inn located in Nika, Osero.

Bosal ar'Nuris: mage, Secretary of Education and Culture of Canalo, member of the Canalo Delegation to the Convention.

Boran, Resa: mage, Financial Secretary of Osero.

Canalo: one of the fifty states making up the Northia Federation, located on the West Coast of the Northia Continent.

Canalo Council, usually just the **Council:** a governmental body composed of eight senior mages, supposed to advise the Chief Mage and substitute for him in case of sudden death or incapacity.

Capitol: building in the capital Dara, where the Convention of Chief Mages meets every other year to conduct government business.

Carsid: Legal Secretary of Osero.

Chen, Lalia: the current Director of the Canalo Mages Guild in Solantha. She serves as deputy to Iannis ar'Sannin, the Chief Mage.

Chartis, Argon: former Director of the Canalo Mages Guild, dismissed by the Chief Mage for insubordination and attempts to undermine the Chief Mage's authority. He subsequently joined forces with the Benefactor to avenge his dismissal.

Chieftain: a title used to distinguish the head of a shifter clan.

Calmias, Father Monor: a charismatic preacher in Ur-God temples, with many followers all over Northia.

Castalis: a country and peninsula at the southwestern edge of the Central Continent, ruled by a High Mage.

Cedris ar'Tarea: Chief Mage of Rhodea, a small island state on the east coast of Northia.

Central Continent: the largest of the continents on Recca, spanning from Garai in the east to Castalis in the west.

Coazi: a group of related tribes controlling large parts of Mexia and adjoining states.

Chanie, Gena: journalist working for the celebrity magazine *Now*.

Coman ar'Daghir: Member of the delegation of Rhodea to the Convention, Legal Secretary of that state.

Comenius Genhard: a hedgewitch from Pernia, owner of the shop Over the Hedge at Witches' End. Close friend of Sunaya Baine, employer of Noria Melcott, and lover of the witch Elania.

Creator: the ultimate deity, worshipped by all three races under different names.

Crystal Hotel: a hotel in Dara, favored by delegations attending the Convention.

Dira: mage, one of the secretaries at the Mages Guild.

Dara: capital of the Northia Federation, located on the east coast of the Northia Continent.

Darca: a human formerly employed as accountant by the Financial Secretary in Solantha.

The Dromach: a sect of powerful mages in Manuc who are specially trained to deal with the Tua, and charged with maintaining the walls that separate Recca from their realm.

Elania Tarrignal: girlfriend of Comenius; a witch specializing in potions, with a shop in Witches' End called The Black Curtain.

Elnos: see under Ragga, Elnos.

Enforcer: a bounty hunter employed by the government to seek out and capture wanted criminals. They operate under strict rules and are paid bounties for each head. While the majority of them are human, there is a strong minority of shifters, and even the occasional mage.

Enforcers' Guild: the administrative organization in charge of the enforcers. Also, the building from which the various enforcer crews work under their respective foremen.

Faonus: one of the three founding mages of the Federation.

Fenris: a clanless wolf shifter of unusual antecedents, close friend and confidant of Chief Mage Iannis ar'Sannin. No known last name.

Firegate Bridge: Solantha's best-known structure, a large red bridge spanning the length of Solantha Bay. It is accessible via Firegate Road.

Gallie: server at the Black Lion Inn in Nika, Osero.

Captain Galling: the human captain of the Enforcer's Guild in Solantha City, appointed by the former Chief Mage and Council.

Garai: the largest and most populated country on the Eastern Central Continent. Garaians are known for slanted eyes and ivory skin as well as their complicated, rune-like alphabet.

Garidano, Cirin: Finance Secretary of the State of Canalo.

Gaston: a city on the eastern coast of Northia.

Gor, Faron: shifter, Chief Editor of the Shifter Courier, the Solantha newspaper for the shifter population. He provided important information to Sunaya during the investigation into the Shifter Royale.

Graning, Zavian: mage, currently Minister of the Northia Federation. Elected by the Convention for an indefinite term, he is charged with coordination of governmental business and particularly foreign affairs, between the biannual Convention sessions that he prepares and presides.

Great Accord: a treaty struck by the ruling mages centuries ago, which brought an end to a devastating war known as the Conflict. It is still the basis upon which mages rule their countries and territories. All new laws passed must be in accordance with the provisions of the Great Accord.

Gulaya: a star-shaped charm, usually made of metal, that is anchored to a specific location and can take its wearer back there at need. They are rare and difficult to recharge.

Haman ar'Rhea: High Mage of Castalis, a country in the southwest of the Central Continent.

Hennis: a jaguar shifter, butler in the home of Mafiela Baine, the Chieftain of the Jaguar Clan.

Herald, The: the main newspaper in Solantha City, which used to belong to Mills Media and Entertainment; it is geared towards the human majority population.

Iannis ar'Sannin: Chief Mage of Canalo. He resides in the capital city of Solantha, from which he runs Canalo as well as the Mages Guild with the help of his Deputy and Secretaries. Originally a native of Manuc, a country located across the Eastern Sea.

Isana ar'Rhea: daughter of the High Mage of Castalis.

Janta Urama: mage and scholar, head librarian in the Solantha Mages Guild.

Jeremidah: one of the three founding mages of the Northia Federation ("The Founding Trio") together with Faonus and Micara.

Lakin, Boon: a jaguar shifter from Parabas, appointed as Solantha's new Shiftertown Inspector following Roanas's death. Sunaya and he are friends and occasional allies. It was a case he investigated and discussed with Sunaya that led to the eventual exposure of the Shifter Royale.

Lanyr Goldrin: supposedly a tiger shifter engaged as guard in Solantha Palace; pseudonym of Rylan Baine.

Leniang Port: a lawless port city on the south coast of Garai.

Logar ar'Dronach: Chief Mage of Osero.

Loranian: the difficult, secret language of magic that all mages are required to master.

Loris ar'Mengis: one of Minister Graning's aides at the Capitol building in Dara.

Mages Guild: the governmental organization that rules the mages in Canalo, and supervises the other races. The headquarters are in Solantha Palace. They are subordinate to the Chief Mage. (Each of the states in the Federation has a Mages Guild.)

Magi-tech: devices that are powered by both magic and technology.

Main Crew: the largest group of Enforcers in the Guild. They are generally favored over the other crews and get the most lucrative dockets.

Manuc: an island country off the west coast of the Central Continent.

Magorah: the god of the shifters, associated with the moon.

Melcott, Annia: a human enforcer. She is a close friend of Sunaya, and Noria's older sister.

Melcott, Noria: Annia Melcott's younger sister. A gifted inventor, who used to work part-time in the shop Over the Hedge, belonging to Comenius Genhard, and has a mage boyfriend, Elnos. She passionately believes in equality between all races and supports the Resistance, which she eventually joined.

Mexia: one of the fifty states making up the Northia Federation.

Micara: one of the mages who made up the Founding Trio of the Federation, together with Faonus and Jeremidah.

Millawette River: river in Parabas, the capital of Osero.

Mills, Thorgana: human socialite, married to Curian Vanderheim, and former owner of a news media conglomerate as well as numerous other companies. After being exposed as the Benefactor by Sunaya, she was imprisoned. Her companies were seized and auctioned off.

Minister: the mage who presides the Convention of Chief

Mages, and coordinates the affairs of the Northia Federation between sessions, particularly foreign relations. The office is currently held by Zavian Graning.

Mitas, Dr. Elan: a general practitioner of medicine in Dara, member of the Resistance.

Miyanta: daughter and disciple of the First Mage Resinah, from whom the ar'Rhea family traces its descent.

Motoac River: a river in the Federation capital Dara.

Nayra: one of the fifty states of the Northian Federation.

Narina Sernan: a pseudonym used by Sunaya in Dara.

Nebara: one of the fifty states making up the Northia Federation.

Nika: a small town in Osero.

Noria: see under Melcott, Noria.

Northia Federation: a federation consisting of fifty states that covers the entire northern half and middle of the Western Continent. Canalo is part of this federation.

Omonas ar'Candar: mage, senior member of the Canalo Council. Not a fan of Sunaya.

Lord Ortho: Chief Mage of Suluris, a state in the southeast of the Federation.

Osero: one of the fifty states of the Northia Federation, located north of Canalo on the continent's west coast.

Over the Hedge: a shop at Witches' End selling magical charms and herbal remedies, belonging to Comenius Genhard.

Pandanum: a base metal used, inter alia, for less valuable coins.

Parabas: a city north of Solantha, capital of the state of Osero.

Pamina: receptionist at the Capitol in Dara.

Pernia: a country on the Central Continent, from which Sunaya's friend Comenius Genhard hails.

Polar ar'Tollis: former Chief Mage of Nebara, who vanished after being condemned to death by the Convention.

Prison Isle: an island in the middle of Solantha Bay that serves as a prison for Canalo's worst criminals.

Privacy Guard: a company that used to lease uniformed guards to governments and other institutions all over the Federation.

Ragga, Elnos: Noria Melcott's boyfriend. He is a student at Solantha academy and one of the few mages who believes in equality amongst the races. He and Noria worked together to develop new magi-tech devices.

Ragir, Lady Aria: wife to the High Mage of Castalis and First Lady of that country (since her marriage styled Lady Aria Ragir ar'Rhea).

Recca: the world of humans, mages, and shifters.

Residah: the mages' book of scripture that holds Resinah's teachings.

Resinah: the first mage, whose teachings are of paramount spiritual importance for the mages. Her statue can be found in the mage temples, which are off-limits to non-mages and magically hidden from outsiders.

Resistance: a movement of revolutionaries planning to overthrow the mages and take control of the Northia Federation, financially backed by the Benefactor. Over time, they became bolder and more aggressive, using terrorist attacks with civilian casualties, as well as assassination. They even tried to take over Solantha, when the government was in disarray after they had engineered the Chief Mage's disappearance. Sunaya's discovery that the Benefactor and the human leaders of the Resistance were planning to turn on the shifters once the mages were defeated dealt a blow to the unity of the movement, but its human component is far from completely defeated, and is working on "secret weapons."

ar'Rhea: family name of a noble Castalian family of mages, who trace their descent to the first mage Resinah through her daughter Miyanta.

Rhodea: smallest of the fifty states that make up the Northia Federation, on the east coast of the continent.

Rowanville: the only neighborhood of Solantha where all three races mix.

Sandia: a large country (and subcontinent) of the Central Continent, populated by many different peoples.

Sandin Federal Bank: a bank with branches in all fifty states of the Federation; its Canalo manager was Danrian Warin. It was shut down after Sunaya brought a scheme of "interest-free loans," financed with illegally mined gold, to the Chief Mage's notice.

Serapha charms: paired amulets that allow two people, usually a couple, to find each other via twinned stones imbued with a small part of their essence. Normally, only the wearer can take a serapha charm off.

Shifter: a human who can change into animal form and back by magic; they originally resulted from illegal experiments by mages on ordinary humans.

Shifter Courier: Solantha newspaper specifically geared towards the shifter population.

Shifter Royale: an illegal underground betting concourse where kidnapped and drugged shifters were forced to fight against each other, sometimes to the death. Discovered and exposed by Sunaya, with help from Boon Lakin and Annia Melcott, after her cousin Mika had been kidnapped by the organizers.

Shiftertown: the part of Solantha where the official shifter clans live.

Shiftertown Inspector: a shifter chosen by the Shiftertown Council to police shifter-related crime. The position is currently held by Boon Lakin, a jaguar shifter, appointed after the murder of his predecessor Roanas Tillmore.

Solantha: the capital of Canalo State, a port city on the west coast of the Northia continent, home of Sunaya Baine.

Solantha Palace: the seat of power in Canalo, where both the Chief Mage and the Mages Guild reside. It is located near the coast of Solantha Bay.

Taili the Wolf: in shifter legend, the very first shifter (a female).

Lady Talari ar'Dronach: mage, wife to the Chief Mage of Osero.

Mrs. Tandry: human, head chef in the kitchens of Solantha Palace.

Tanzarite: a rare semi-precious stone.

The Twilight: a bar in Rowanville where Sunaya used to bartend.

Thrase, Nelia: a young human, Sunaya's social secretary.

Timbran's Gourmet Food: a meat-canning company, with a factory north of Turain.

Tillmore, Roanas: the former Shiftertown Inspector and father figure/mentor to Sunaya. He was poisoned while digging into the silver murders, prompting Sunaya to take over the investigation.

Tua: a legendary and highly dangerous race of very long-lived beings with powerful magic, who sometimes cross from their own world into Recca, most frequently in Manuc.

Tular, Jolen: Director of the Osero Mages Guild.

Turain: a small town north of Solantha, where the Shifter Royale took place.

Ur-God: the name the humans call the Creator by.

Vanderheim, Curian: human millionaire and businessman, husband to Thorgana Mills.

Wacoma: an area in the Northwest of the Federation, part of Osero.

Willis: a human member of the Resistance, rank of Private.

Witches' End: a pier in Solantha City, part of the Port, where immigrant magic users sell their wares and services.

Witley, Captain: night watch captain of the Resistance lab facility in Osero; impersonated by Rylan Baine.

Word(s): magically imbued phrases, ranging in length from a single word to a long sentence, typically in Loranian. Mages use them to practice and focus their magic. Without Words, 'instinctive' magic requires far more energy, and is less predictable in its effects.

Yantz, Petros: the former Chief Editor of the *Herald*, implicated in the silver murders. A close collaborator of the Benefactor, he found refuge in her Solantha mansion as a fugitive.

Zavian Graning: see under Graning, Zavian.

Zuric, Harun: human, employed as handyman in Solantha Palace.

ACKNOWLEDGMENTS

I'd like to give a BIG thank you to my beta readers, for providing great feedback despite the tight deadline they had to work with. Special thanks again to Victoria Newman, who as always is very thorough. You guys are invaluable to my writing process. <3

Thank you to Mary Burnett, for getting to the finish line with me on Book 5! I am very lucky to have found someone I work so well with, and have come to realize you are truly one of a kind.

I'd also like to thank Michael Anderle, for being a true champion for indie authors, and a defender against trolls. You rock! ;)

And thank you to my illustrator, Judah Dobin, for providing such awesome cover art. I know this one was a little rocky, but I really love the way it turned out. And I love you. <3

ABOUT THE AUTHOR

Jasmine Walt is obsessed with books, chocolate, and sharp objects. Somehow, those three things melded together in her head and transformed into a desire to write, usually fantastical stuff with a healthy dose of action and romance. Her characters are a little (okay, a lot) on the snarky side, and they swear, but they mean well. Even the villains sometimes.

When Jasmine isn't chained to her keyboard, you can find her practicing her triangle choke on the jujitsu mat, spending time with her family, or binge-watching superhero shows on Netflix.

Want to connect with Jasmine? You can find her on Twitter at @jasmine_writes, on Facebook, or at www.jasminewalt.com.

ALSO BY JASMINE WALT

The Baine Chronicles Series:

Burned by Magic

Bound by Magic

Hunted by Magic

Marked by Magic

Betrayed by Magic

Deceived by Magic

Scorched by Magic

Tested by Magic (Novella)

Forsaken by Magic (Novella)

The Nia Rivers Adventures

Dragon Bones

Demeter's Tablet

Templar Scrolls

Serpent Mound

Eden's Garden

The Gatekeeper Chronicles

Marked by Sin

Hunted by Sin

Claimed by Sin

The Dragon's Gift Trilogy

Dragon's Gift

Dragon's Blood

Dragon's Curse

The Legend of Tariel

Kingdom of Storms

Den of Thieves

Empire of Magic

Printed in Great Britain
by Amazon